William Alfred Cotton

Bromsgrove Church

its history & antiquities - with an account of the Sunday schools, churchyard, and

cemetery

William Alfred Cotton

Bromsgrove Church
its history & antiquities - with an account of the Sunday schools, churchyard, and cemetery

ISBN/EAN: 9783337406790

Printed in Europe, USA, Canada, Australia, Japan

Cover: Foto ©Andreas Hilbeck / pixelio.de

More available books at **www.hansebooks.com**

Bromsgrove Church.

NORTH-WEST VIEW.

Bromsgrove Church:

ITS HISTORY & ANTIQUITIES:

WITH AN ACCOUNT OF THE

Sunday ÷ Schools, ÷ Churchyard, ÷ and ÷ Cemetery,

COMPILED FROM THE

PARISH BOOKS, REGISTERS, AND OTHER AUTHENTIC SOURCES,

BY

WILLIAM H. COTTON.

"Out of Monuments, Names, Words, Proverbs, Traditions, Private Records and Evidences, Fragments of Stories, Passages of Books, and the like, we do save and recover somewhat from the deluge of Time." —BACON'S ADVANCEMENT OF LEARNING.

London:
SIMPKIN, MARSHALL, AND CO., STATIONERS' HALL COURT.

Bromsgrove:
"MESSENGER" PUBLISHING COMPANY, HIGH STREET.

———

Price 7s. 6d.

PREFACE.

———o———

The Author was tempted to undertake the task of compiling a History of Bromsgrove Church by the repeated solicitation of many friends, and by having observed that no complete work on the subject, giving full particulars from the earliest period to the present time, not only of the structure, but also of all those who have been, or are, connected or associated with it, has yet been published. The task completed, he submits the result to the judgment of his readers, not without considerable diffidence, and yet with the hope that his labours have not been altogether unsuccessful, and that some, at least, of the incidents and facts which he has collected may be found to be original and interesting. That the facts contained in the work may be relied upon, the Author has no reason to doubt. His enquiries for information have met with such a ready response from the clergy, gentlemen, and others in possession of records, that he has been enabled to compare dates and figures with the originals, and to test fully the accuracy of nearly every statement made. For the assistance thus rendered, and for which he is so deeply indebted, he tenders grateful acknowledgments and thanks.

All the old deeds and documents contained in this history have been carefully translated where necessary, and this the Author hopes will add to the general interest of the work. The plates are copied from original drawings, and the woodcuts are engraved from photographs of the objects depicted, except where otherwise mentioned.

The Author gladly avails himself of this opportunity of thanking the noblemen, clergymen, ladies and gentlemen who have become subscribers for copies of the work, and have thus encouraged him in his endeavour to make it as complete as possible.

Bromsgrove, March, 1881.

SUBSCRIBERS.

Abell, Mr. George E., Worcester.
Albright, Mr. Arthur, Finstall.   (2 copies.)
Albutt, Mr. Henry, Bromsgrove.
Amess, Mr. James, Bromsgrove.
Andrews, Mr. Richard, Bromsgrove.
Asinelli, Miss D., Westbourne House, Bromsgrove.

Bainbrigge, Rev. J. H., B.A., The Vicarage, Finstall.
Badley, Mr. Henry P., Insiton, Belbroughton.
Baldwin, Mr. Alfred, Wilden House. Stourport.
Barnett, Miss A. M., Finstall Vale, Bromsgrove.
Barrett, Mr. Henry, The Lilies, Bromsgrove.
Barham, Mr. F. F., The Clock House, Fockbury, Bromsgrove.
Bayley, Mr. Charles H., West Bromwich.
Baylis, Mr. Alfred M., Worcester.
Baylis, Mr. W. T., Bromsgrove.
Bate, Mr. J., Belbroughton.
Beauchamp, Right Hon. the Earl of, Madresfield Court.
Bennett, Mr. Alfred, Bromsgrove.
Bigwood, Mr. Ernest J., The Linthurst.
Billingham, Mr. T., Bromsgrove.
Bindley, Mr. T. Herbert, Merton College, Oxford.
Birbeck, Mr. C. H., 23, Foregate Street, Worcester.   (2 copies.)
Blick, Mr. John, Hill Court, Dodderhill.
Blore, Rev. George, D.D., King's School, Cambridge.
Bolam, Mr. H. G., Ingestre, Stafford.
Bourne, Mr. Robert, J.P., Grafton Manor, Bromsgrove.
Bourne, Rev. Joseph G., M.A., Broome Rectory, Stourbridge.
Bown, Mr. George, The Crescent, Bromsgrove.
Brazier, Mr. Jonathan, Bromsgrove.
Brazier, Mr. David, Stirchley Street, Birmingham.
Brewster, Mrs. S., Westbourne House, Bromsgrove.   (2 copies.)

Brooke, Mr. F. S., Raglan House, Bromsgrove. (2 copies.)
Brown, Mr. J. F., Faulkner Street, Gloucester.
Brown, Mr. W., Bromsgrove.
Brydone, Mr. John, Field View, Stoke Prior.
Burford, Mr. John, Bromsgrove.
Burrows, Mr. George, Bromsgrove.

Caddick, Mr. Edward, Wellington Road, Edgbaston.
Carey, Mr. Charles, Bromsgrove.
Cashmore, Mr. W. W., Handsworth Road, Birmingham.
Clough, Mr. H., Stoney Hill, Bromsgrove.
Coleman, Rev. Ernest E., Bromsgrove.
Colmore, Rev. W. H., M.A., The Vicarage, Moseley.
Comber, Mr. W. C. A., Bromsgrove.
Cooke, Miss Jane, Bromsgrove.
Cook, Mr. Richard, Bromsgrove.
Coombs, Mr. James, High Street, Worcester. (2 copies.)
Corbett, Mr. John, M.P., Impney, Droitwich.
Corbett, Mr. F., The Crescent, Worcester.
Corbett, Mr. H., Fort Royal, Worcester.
Corbett, Mr. W., The Crescent, Bromsgrove.
Corbett, Mr. E., Chaddesley Corbett.
Cordell, Mr. R., Bromsgrove.
Cordell, Mr. J., Bromsgrove.
Cossins, Mr. Jethro A., Unity Buildings, Temple Street, Birmingham.
Cotton, Mrs. A., Westbourne House, Bromsgrove. (5 copies.)
Cotton, Mr. John, Temple Row, Birmingham. (2 copies.)
Cotton, Mr. E. B., Darlaston.
Crawford, Mr. Oliver, Fitzroy, Melbourne, Australia.
Creswell, Mr. J. Nash, Bromsgrove.
Curtler, Rev. Thomas G., M.A., Bevere Knoll, Worcester.
Curtler, Mr. Martin, Lansdowne, Worcester.

Davenport, Rev. James, B.A., Alcester.
Day, Mrs., Davenal House, Bromsgrove.
Day, Mr. Ernest A., The Lilacs, St. George's Square, Worcester.
Deakin, Mrs. S., Woodcote Manor, Bromsgrove.
Dipple, Miss, Bromsgrove.
Dipple, Mr. Alfred, Bromsgrove.

Dixon, Miss, Stoke Prior Grange, Bromsgrove.
Dixon, Mr. Thomas, Stoney Lane, Tardebigge.
Dodd, Mr. W., Bromsgrove.
Douglas, Rev. W. W., M.A., Salwarpe Rectory, Droitwich.
Downing, Mr. William, 74, New Street, Birmingham.   (3 copies.)
Drury, Mrs. M. A., Bromsgrove.
Dunn, Mrs., Fairfield House, Bedminster, Bristol.
Dunn, Rev. Oliver J., LL.B., Darlington Street, Wolverhampton.

Eaton, Rev. Canon, M.A., The Rectory, Alvechurch.
Eaton, Mr. W. H., Stoney Hill, Bromsgrove.   (2 copies.)
Edwards, Mr. Thomas, Chapel Street, Bromsgrove.
Ellingworth, Mr. Charles, Bromsgrove.
Emmott, Miss A. S., Badsey Vicarage, near Evesham.
Evans, Mr. C., Bromsgrove.
Everitt, Mr. W. E., J.P., Finstall House, Bromsgrove.
Everitt, Mr. Allen E., City Chambers, Birmingham.

Fawke, Mr. Walter, Bromsgrove.
Field, Mr. Charles, Bristol.
Fitch, Mr. J. W., Bromsgrove.
Fowler, Mr. Edward, Abberley, Edgbaston.

Gardner, Mr. John, Finstall, Bromsgrove.
Gibson, Mr. G. W., Bromsgrove.
Godsall, Mr. A. H., Bromsgrove.
Goodwin, Rev. John, M.A., The Parsonage, Bromsgrove Lickey.
Gosling, Mr. F. N., Worcester.
Green, Mr. John, Whitford Hall, Bromsgrove.
Gray, Mr. George, Bromsgrove.
Grey, Mr. Thomas, Bromsgrove.
Guest, Mr. T., Rock Hill, Bromsgrove.

Hadley, Mr. Enoch, Barnsley Hall, Bromsgrove.   (3 copies.)
Haines, Mr. J. J., Bromsgrove.
Haines, Mr. T., Bromsgrove.
Halliday, Mrs. A., West View, Torquay.

Harper, Mrs. E., The Crescent, Bromsgrove.
Harris, Mr. Thomas, Stoney Lane, Tardebigge. (2 copies.)
Harriss, Mr. John, Hill End, Droitwich.
Harrison, Rev. C. F., The Vicarage, Llangynllo
Harrison, Rev. A. R., M.A., The College, Stratford-on-Avon.
Harrison, Mr. W., Worcester Road, Bromsgrove.
Hartle, Mr. H., Bromsgrove.
Harvey, Mrs. J., Charford, Bromsgrove.
Harvey, Mr. Samuel, The Shrubbery, Walsall.
Henderson, Mr. J. A., Alvechurch.
Hitchman, Mr. John, 2, Cherry Street, Birmingham. (2 copies.)
Hill, Mr. T. Rowley, M.P., Worcester.
Hill, Mr. Jos., Birmingham.
Hill, Mr. W., Bromsgrove.
Hobbiss, Mr. W. H., Masbro' Road, London, W.
Hobbiss, Mr. T. P., Bromsgrove.
Hobbiss, Mr. H. L., Saltley College, Birmingham.
Hobbiss, Mr. A. J., Bromsgrove.
Holl, Dr. Harvey B., F.G.S., Worcester.
Holland, Mr. Walter, Rose Hill, Worcester.
Holt, Mr. James, Bromsgrove.
Holyoake, Mr. John, Droitwich.
Holyoake, Mr. W., Bromsgrove.
Horniblow, Mr. C. S., Catshill.
Horton, Mr. J. R., The Oaklands, Upton Warren, Bromsgrove.
Hoult, Mr. C. F., Stourport.
Humphreys, Mr. John, Bromsgrove.
Humphreys, Mr. E. H., Bromsgrove. (2 copies.)
Humphreys, Mr. E. G., Stratford-on-Avon.
Humphreys, Mr. C., Bromsgrove.
Hunt, Mr. George, Stoke Prior.

Ince, Mr. T. E., Bromsgrove.

Jefferies, Mr. William, Bromsgrove.
Jeffrey, Mr. William, Bromsgrove.
Johnson, Miss E., Fernleigh, Bromsgrove.
Jones, Mr. Joseph, Park Hall, Bromsgrove.

Keep, Mr. Kenaz, Bromsgrove.
Kidd, Rev. J., The Vicarage, Catshill.
King, Mr. J., Glenthorne Villa, Bromsgrove.

Lacy, Mr. George, Warwick.
Langford, Dr. J. A., Gladstone Road, Sparkbrook, Birmingham.
Laughton, Mr. James, Bromsgrove.
Lawrence, Rev. J. R., B.A., Offord Cluny Rectory, Huntingdon.
Lea, Miss M. E., The Rookery, Feckenham.
Lea, Mr. James, Bromsgrove. (2 copies.)
Ledbury, Mr. W., Bromsgrove.
Ledbury, Mr. W. R., Bromsgrove.
Lee, Mr. Samuel, Small Heath, Birmingham.
Leigh, Hon. and Rev. Canon, M.A., The Vicarage, Leamington.
Levens, Mr. P., Bromsgrove.
Lewis, Mr. H. W., Rock Hill, Bromsgrove.
Llewellin, Mr. W., Bromsgrove.
Lloyd, Mr. James W., Kington, Herefordshire.
Lowe, Mr. C., Broad Street Corner, Birmingham.
Lowe, Mr. Henry, Cannon Street, Birmingham. (3 copies.)
Lucas, Mr. Joseph, Bromsgrove.
Lyttelton, Right Hon. Lord, Hagley Hall.

Marcus, Mr. E., Albany House, Worcester.
Massey, Hon. and Rev. A. H. T., M.A., The Vicarage, All Saints, Bromsgrove.
Mason, Mr. R. C., Bromsgrove.
Milman, Mr. C. B., Lower Mitton, Stourport.
Milton, Miss M., Primrose Cottage, Grimley, Worcester.
Milton, Mr. Joseph, Bromsgrove.
Milton, Mr. W. B., Small Heath, Birmingham.
Milton, Mr. C. J., Bromsgrove.
Milward, Mr. R. H., J.P., Highfield House, The Linthurst.
More-Molyneux, Mrs. A. S., Bishop's Lodge, Compton, Guildford. (2 copies.)
Murray, Rev. Canon, M.A., The Vicarage, Bromsgrove.

Neale, Mr. J. W., Monsieur's Hall, Bromsgrove.
Newbold, Mr. T., Worcester Road, Bromsgrove. (2 copies.)

Nicholls, Mr. G., Willow Terrace, Bromsgrove.
Nock, Mrs. E., Lickey End, Bromsgrove.
Nowell, Mr. R. H., Bromsgrove.

Parry, Mr. T. A., The Woodrow, Bromsgrove.
Parry, Mr. J. S., The Laurels, Catshill, Bromsgrove.
Parry, Mr. Walter, The Crescent, Bromsgrove.
Parsonage, Mr. Joseph, Bromsgrove.
Partridge, Mr. W., The Grammar School, Alvechurch.
Partridge, Mr. John, High House, Burcot.
Penn, Mr. Thomas, Bromsgrove.
Perks, Mr. Edwin, Bromsgrove.
Pike, Mr. W. G., 3, Britannia Square, Worcester.
Popplewell, Mr. F., The Elms, Wychbold, Droitwich.
Porter, Mr. Paxton, Midland Institute, Birmingham.
Prosser, Mr. Roger, Bromsgrove.
Price, Miss S., Ardwick, Manchester.

Rhoades, Mr. W., Charford Lodge, Bromsgrove.
Richardson, Mr. A. H., Rose Villas, Bromsgrove.
Roper, Mr. Dan, Bromsgrove. (2 copies.)
Rose, Mr. J. W., The Cemetery Lodge, Bromsgrove.
Rowland, Mr. Edward, Bryan Offa, Wrexham.

Sanders, Mr. Thomas Tudor, Bromsgrove.
Sanders, Mr. Thomas, Promenade, Cheltenham. (3 copies.)
Sanders, Mr. B. H., The Steps, Bromsgrove. (2 copies.)
Sanders, Mr. James, Street Court, Kingsland, Herefordshire.
Saunders, Mr. W. L., Wakefield.
Saywell, Mr. S., M.A., The College School, Bromsgrove. (2 copies.)
Scott, Mr. T., The Shrubbery, Bromsgrove.
Scroxton, Mrs. J. H., Raleigh Villa, Bromsgrove.
Seymour, Miss M. A., Bromsgrove.
Shaw, Mr. David, St. John's House, Worcester.
Silvester, Mr. T. B., West Bromwich.
Simmons, Mr. W. R., Bromsgrove.
Simms, Mr. John, Bromsgrove.
Smallwood, Mr. Robert, J.P., Rigby Hall, Bromsgrove.

Smith, Rev. Prebendary I. Gregory, M.A., Malvern House, Great Malvern.
Smith, Mr. Edwin, Elvetham Road, Birmingham.
Smith, Mr. Edward, Bromsgrove.
Smith, Mr. J. A., Bromsgrove.
Snell, Mr. T., Bromsgrove.
Spencer, Mr. H., The Weights, Redditch.
Stanley, Mr. Moses, Addison Street, Nottingham.
Stanton, Mr. G. K., Windsor Place, Bromsgrove.
Steedman, Mr. C. B., Bromsgrove.
Stone, Mr. George, Bromsgrove.

Talbot, Right Hon. Lord Edmund, 10, Eaton Terrace, London, S.W.
Taylor, Mr. Henry, Blackwell.
Taylor, Mr. W. G., Charford, Bromsgrove.
Taylor, Mr. G. E., Finstall, Bromsgrove.
Temple, Sir Richard, The Nash, Kempsey, Worcester.
Thomas, Mr. T. D., Stourbridge. (2 copies.)
Thorn, Rev. W., Ivy Gate, Worcester.
Timmins, Mr. Samuel, Elvetham Lodge, Birmingham.
Tomson, Mr. James John, Barnt Green House, Lickey.
Townsend, Mr. E. J., Bromsgrove.
Tirbutt, Mr. J. B., Albert Cottage, Bromsgrove.
Turton, Mr. F. W., Bromsgrove.
Turton, Mr. A. M., Bromsgrove.
Twemlow, Mrs. R., Alvechurch.

Udall, Mr. R. J., B.A., The College School, Bromsgrove.
Unite, Mr. G. R., Blackwell Court.

Veal, Mr. John, Fockbury, Bromsgrove.
Vernon, Mr. H. F., J.P., Hanbury Hall, Droitwich.
Verrinder, Miss F. M., St. John's, Worcester.
Verrinder, Mr. H. D., Wolverhampton.

Wall, Mr. H. G., Bromsgrove.
Ward, Mr. Edwin, Aston, Birmingham.
Ward, Mr. W., Bromsgrove.
Watson, Rev. George William, B.A., Bromsgrove. (3 copies.)

Watt, Mr. Francis, J.P., Penally, Tenby.

Watton, Mr. Josiah, Bromsgrove.

Weaver, Mr. William, Bromsgrove.

White, Mr. Thomas, The Newlands, Bromsgrove.

Whitfield, Mr. H. S., Bromsgrove.

Wilden, Mr. C., Stoney Hill, Bromsgrove.

Williams, Rev. Arthur Garnons-, B.A., Bromsgrove.

Williams, Mr. Charles, Moseley Lodge. Moseley.

Willis, Mr. S., Kidderminster Road, Bromsgrove.

Willis, Mr. Jabez, Kidderminster Road, Bromsgrove.

Wilson, Mr. J. B., Bromsgrove.

Wilson, Mr. J. T., Bromsgrove.

Wilson, Mr. James, 35, Bull Street, Birmingham.   (2 copies.)

Witheford. Mr. Benjamin, Hanover House, Bromsgrove.

Worcester, Right Rev. The Lord Bishop of, Hartlebury Castle.

Worthington, Mr. Thomas, Broomfield Gables, Alderley Edge, Cheshire.

Wood, Mr. Richard, Bromsgrove.

Wright, Mr. Charles, Bromsgrove.

Wright. Mr. Henry, Bromsgrove.

INDEX.

INDEX TO PLATES.

INDEX TO WOODCUTS.

BROMSGROVE CHURCH:

ITS HISTORY AND ANTIQUITIES.

> " The pile
> Was large and massy, for duration built ;
> With pillars crowded, and the roof upheld
> By naked rafters intricately cross'd,
> Like leafless underboughs in some thick grove,
> All wither'd by the depth of shade above.
> . . . . The floor
> Of nave and aisle, in unpretending guise,
> Was occupied by oaken benches ranged
> In seemly rows ; the chancel only show'd
> Some inoffensive marks of earthly state
> And vain distinction. . . . .
> And marble monuments were here display'd
> Upon the walls ; and on the floor beneath
> Sepulchral stones appear'd, with emblems graven,
> And foot-worn epitaphs, and some with small
> And shining effigies of brass inlaid."
>
> *Wordsworth.*

HE Parish Church of Bromsgrove is a noble structure, of very graceful and dignified proportions, built of local sandstone, and situated on a beautiful and commanding eminence on the western side of the town : it consists of a chancel, vestry on the north side, nave with clerestory, aisles, and western tower and spire. It is dedicated to St. John the Baptist,* whose statue, between those of St. Peter and St. Paul, is placed in a recess on the western face of the tower. Mr. Noake, in his "Notes and Queries for Worcestershire," says : "Above the western window of St. John's Church, Bromsgrove, are three figures of the full size of life, said to represent St. Peter, St. Paul, and the Blessed Virgin. They are in a good state of preservation, although they have, no doubt, been there 450 years.

---

* This day commemorates the *birth* of the Baptist, as Christmas does that of Christ. Both events are veiled in equal uncertainty ; but the former is known to have preceded the latter by six months, and is accordingly held June 24th. In the year 506 this day was received among the great feasts of the Church, like Easter, Christmas, and other festivals ; and was celebrated with equal solemnity and in much the same manner.

A

and very likely escaped mutilation at the Reformation from the great height they are from the ground ; for the window is one of the highest, if not *the* highest, of all the western church windows in the county." Dr. Nash, the historian of Worcestershire, who saw the figures when in a much more perfect state than they now are, deems the central figure to represent St. John the Baptist, with SS. Peter and Paul on either side. A spectator carefully observing the figures, will perceive that the one on his left hand (or in the north niche) is intended for St. Peter, the figure holding in the right hand the remains of what are evidently intended for two keys, and in the left hand an open book. The face has something of a feminine aspect, unlike the bearded representations of the apostle usually met with, and the sculptured keys held in the hand may have been mistaken by a cursory observer for lilies, thus inducing a supposition that the figure represented the Virgin. The figure on the observer's right hand (or in the south niche) is that of a man holding a long straight sword in his right hand, and in his left what seems an open book, and it is certainly intended for St. Paul. The centre figure is bearded, like the former one, clothed in a scanty manner, with a girdle round his waist, and bearing on his left arm the remains of what appears to have been the image of a lamb, thereby betokening, according to ancient symbolism, St. John the Baptist, clothed in camel's skin, and placed as patron saint in the post of honor between St. Peter and St. Paul, the great bulwarks of the Church. The festival of St. John the Baptist, the 24th of June, is still associated with the Midsummer fair day,* and a fair was also formerly held on August 29th, being the decollation of the Baptist. A writer in the Bromsgrove *Messenger*, observes of these statues, that "although weather-worn, grey, and lichen-grown, they bear evident traces of the old Gothic carver's skill ; the artistic arrangement of the drapery on the figures, their good proportion and gracefully effective attitudes, so well adapted to the height at which they are placed, attest the proficiency of the sculptor who hewed them."

It is impossible, after the lapse of so many years, to say with any degree of certainty from whence the stone was quarried with which the church was built, but, as stone of the same description abounds in the immediate neighbourhood, it would be unreasonable to suppose that it was conveyed from any great distance. There is, however, some ground for believing, that as great difficulty was experienced in obtaining good foundations upon which to build the National Schools (the site

---

* Among the mediæval Christians, upon any extraordinary solemnity, particularly the anniversary dedication of a church, tradesmen were wont to bring and sell their wares even in the churchyards, which practice continued especially upon the festivals of the dedication. The custom was kept up till the reign of Henry VI. A great many fairs were kept at these festivals of dedication, but the great gatherings of people being often the occasion of riots and disturbances, the privilege of holding a fair was restricted to those granted by Royal charter. King John granted a market to Bromsgrove and fairs on Midsummer day and the first of October.

being what is generally termed "made ground"), some of the stone may have been quarried on the spot where the schools stand.

The church is approached at the west end, from the Kidderminster Road, by Adams' Hill (so called because Captain Adams lived at Perry Hall, which is situated at the foot of the hill); at the east end from Church Street, through Crown Close : on the north side from Sidemoor and the Cemetery ; and on the south-east side from the street bearing the name of its patron saint, by a flight of 48 stone steps, at the top of which are the remains of an old lich gate,* with the date of its erection—1656—

inscribed on the cross beam. The steps were repaired August, 1839 ; and on October 7th, 1861, at a meeting of the Bromsgrove Local Board, Mr. Henry Hill's contract of £102 "for the making of the church steps," was accepted. On the 6th of January following, Mr. William Cotton, the surveyor employed, reported to the Board that Hill had performed the "church steps" contract satisfactorily, and that the contractor was entitled to receive £128, including extras, the amount due to him. It was decided that payment should be made out of the owners' rate. The old worn steps were carted to the New Buildings. It was at this time that the steps were reduced in number from 63 to 48, and that the double gates which were at the top were removed.

The tower and spire are 198 feet high, and standing on a majestic position, become "a landmark for all the country round." The length of the edifice is 138 feet, and the breadth 77 feet, the whole forming, as Nash says, "one of the completest buildings in this county."

---

* This gate is mentioned in "Stones of the Temple" as being amongst the most interesting of the ancient lich gates still remaining.

Architectural Details.

IN Domesday Book mention is made of a church and a priest at Bromsgrove, but if any portion of the foundation or walling of the present church formed part of that referred to, it is now impossible to identify it. The architectural details of the building, however, indicate sufficiently the periods at which the various recognized parts of the church were erected, and illustrate the changes that have from time to time taken place in its structural history. The most ancient portions of the church now distinguishable are the north and south doorways; these are of the late Norman period, and were probably built early in the latter half of the 12th century. They are, however, very poor specimens, as the Norman builders usually bestowed much pains and artistic skill in ornamenting with elaborate sculpture and mouldings the entrances to churches erected by them.

The arch on the north side nearest the chancel is apparently of later date than the doorways, " although (if, as is asserted, it has been accurately restored), from the Norman character of its impost or abacus mouldings, and peculiar features in portions of the carving of the corbels, it would appear to have been executed before the chancel arch, and before the other portions of the north arcade were executed."—*Vide* letter in the Bromsgrove *Messenger* before quoted from. It is of Transitional character, merging into the Early English style, and dates towards the close of the 12th century.

To the *Lancet, First Pointed*, or *Early English* style, roundly termed *13th Century Gothic*, may be ascribed :—

The chancel arch.

The three western arches on the north side of the nave, "which are amongst the most attractive features of the church, the capitals of the piers exhibiting great depth of moulding, beauty of profile, and consequent grace of light and shade."

(The narrow arch adjoining is modern, being erected at the restoration of the church, in place of two semicircular openings of a very nondescript character.)

The small arch on the south side beside the great chancel arch.

The west doorway, which appears to have been preserved and inserted in the later work of the tower.

The east window of the south aisle.

The great east window of the chancel, with five lancets under one arch, the spandrils being pierced so as to let the light be seen through them. This marks the origin of *tracery* in window heads.

The three side windows in the chancel which were opened at the restoration of the church. These appear of rather later date, exhibiting some of the characteristics of the Decorated style, which followed.

The south wall and buttresses (and probably the north wall), though the masonry has been much disturbed by the subsequent insertion of windows of the 15th century date, and the addition of a parapet in the then prevailing style.

The beautiful trefoil-headed piscina, with shelf, in the south aisle. The position of this piscina would indicate the existence of a chapel and altar here in early times. Some years ago the piscina was moved a short distance from its former position to admit of the lowering of the window-sill; after its removal a pair of folding doors and a hasp were put to it by Joseph Rose, sexton at that time, but these have been taken away.

Other parts of the church may have been of Early English character; but the indications of it that have survived successive changes and the waste of age are but few. It is probable that the nave was, at this period, covered by a high pitched roof, traces of the drip stone being still plainly visible on the tympanum, or flat wall, over the chancel arch, and likewise on the corresponding part of the east wall of the tower.

To the *Decorated* or *Second Pointed* style, prevailing during the 14th century—

The windows on each side of the north door; that on the west is original; that on the east was restored so as to correspond with it, the base, the mullions, and the mouldings of the jambs, where not mutilated, showing clearly that the two had at one time been exactly the same.

The tracery of the north and south windows of the tower, which appear to have been preserved and inserted into the later work, in the same way as was the western doorway. There is a window at Dorchester church, Oxfordshire, with tracery extremely similar, stated to have been executed as early as 1275.

The vestry is also ascribed to the commencement of this style, although Dr. Collis notes it as belonging to the Perpendicular period.

Generally speaking there is comparatively little work of this style in the church.

To the *Perpendicular* or *Third Pointed* style, called also *15th Century Gothic*—

The south arcade.

The ten windows of the clerestory and the oak roof of the nave.

The east and west windows of the north aisle; the latter being an excellent specimen of this style.

The windows of the south aisle (except that at the east end), and square-headed windows in north aisle.

The south porch.

"The manner in which the south side is broken up by the projecting porch, and elegant and somewhat singular bay window, with the exquisite long-mullioned and transomed tracery of the square-headed adjoining windows, is picturesque and beautiful in the extreme."—*Vide* letter in *Messenger* before referred to. (Plate 1.)

The tower, with its fine west window and majestic octagonal spire. The tower is of three stages, with an embattled parapet, and is relieved on the belfry stage with panelling and niches, the spire above springing from within the parapet that crowns the tower.

The four-centered arch near the organ, with its ribbed roof and bosses at the intersections, is of debased Perpendicular or Tudor character, and dates towards the close of the 15th or the commencement of the 16th century.

A splendid rich oak roof of this style, with moulded beams, eighteen inches in thickness, resting on brackets of carved angels, was condemned in 1814, taken down, and sold for firewood! Had it been repaired instead of being destroyed, it might have served for a model for the ceiling of the south aisle. A flat lath-and-plaster ceiling of the meanest description was put up instead.

The architectural particulars are chiefly gleaned from a pamphlet published by the late Rev. J. D. Collis, D.D., when the church was re-opened after restoration, and from consultation with the author's brother, Mr. John Cotton, architect, of Birmingham.

No additions have been made to the stone work of the church, probably, since the Reformation.

There was a south gallery in existence at the time of the restoration, but the exact date of erection cannot be ascertained. It was enlarged and re-arranged in 1824, and the church ordered to be "whitewashed." It was also "resolved that the workmen in the church have 10s. to spend."

On December 6th, 1765, at a vestry meeting, it was "Agreed upon as under that whereas William Green with is Servants and Workman have Clandestinatly began to Erect a Loft in the North Isle of Bromsgrove Church without the Consent of the parishoners and which will be very prejudiciall to some of the Inhabitants of the said Parish. And whereas the Present Churchwardens have commenced a prosecution against them in the Ecclesiastical Court of the Bishop of Worcester in order to prevent their proceedings and erecting the said Gallery Now we Do hereby agree that John Willson John Chellingworth Thos. Suffield and John Brace the present

SOUTH SIDE OF BROMSGROVE CHURCH

Plate 1

church Wardens shall be paid and Reimbursed all the charge trouble and expense that they shall be put unto in the aforesaid prosecution against the said William Green and others."

There is this note at the foot of the resolution in another handwriting : *"False Grammar." "Signed by nobody."*

A north gallery was erected in 1768, at which time the heads of three of the windows in the north wall were cut out, all the tracery destroyed, and iron rods, in continuation of the mullions, run up nearly to the wall plate, in order to throw "more light into the new gallery."

The bellringers' floor was formerly much lower, being so placed as to bisect the west window, the upper part of which lit the belfry and the lower part lit the children's gallery, situated in the basement of the tower.

The organ loft, erected in 1756, occupied one bay of the nave arcading, completely excluding the tower from the interior. There was an entrance to this gallery from the south front, under the window west of the porch, by a doorway of the most execrable description. The lowering of the window to its present level has happily destroyed all vestige of this extraordinary arrangement.

In 1684. It is agreed to give Thos. Britton £2 10s. per year to keep the lead on the church in good repair during his life, and to new cast two sheets every year to the same weight as the old ones.

In 1769. The south aisle was "repaired and new leaded."

Attached to one of the sheets of lead on the roof of the north aisle of the church is a brass plate, bearing the following inscription :—

Bromsgrove

This sheet of lead was used as a pan
under an ox which was roasted near
the Market Hall in this Place on the
10th day of June, 1814, in commemoration
of peace.

Churchwardens

John Bell	William Palmer
William Ward	Thomas Wright

This north side of the church was
new timbered, leaded and repaired
Anno Domini 1814

By Thomas Edwards, Builder
Richard Brown, Plumber
Thomas Bateman, Architect, Birmingham.

Restoration of the Church.

UCH of the following history of the restoration is taken from the pamphlet published by the Rev. Dr. Collis, shortly after the re-opening of the church, which took place on Thursday, January 27th, 1859.

"A meeting was held in January, 1843, the then vicar, the Lord Bishop of Rochester, being in the chair, to take into consideration how increased accommodation for the poor could be obtained. A committee was formed, and a plan was submitted by Mr. Henry Day, of Worcester, for re-pewing a great part of the floor, with seats of deal upon a uniform plan. It was not then proposed to do anything for the restoration of the building, or to alter the galleries. The entire expense was estimated at £800, towards which the Diocesan Church Building Society voted £180, and the Incorporated Society £100. The issue of a faculty for these changes was successfully opposed ; and the project, happily, fell to the ground. The whole arrangement was, at best, a compromise, and a palliation of existing deficiencies ; I have no hesitation in saying that had it been carried out, it would have spoiled the church, and for many years delayed its proper restoration. It was not, of course, the architect's fault, that the cost was limited to so small a sum.

" When the present vicar, the Rev. William Villers, came to the parish, to which he was appointed in 1846, one of the very first projects that he set on foot was the restoration of the church.

" In 1848, a second committee was formed—and plans, on a much more enlarged scale than those of 1844, were prepared by Mr. Henry Day. It was then proposed to re-pew the entire floor, to lengthen the north gallery ; to re-construct, in one large arch, the semi-Norman arch on the north side, and the two semi-circular openings next to it ; and likewise to continue the south aisle nearly as far as the east wall of the chancel, so as to provide 100 sittings for the pupils and others connected with the Grammar School, to be called ' King Edward's Chapel,' for the erection of which I undertook to raise or contribute £500. To this plan it was objected that it would make the church, already a difficult one for clergymen to read and preach in, far too large ; it was also thought, by some persons, unadvisable (to say the least of it) that any particular portion should be assigned to the Grammar School. Whatever the motive of the opposition, it was effectual ; the faculty was never applied for, and the church remained as it was, till a better feeling arose towards the close of 1856.

"In May, 1850, despairing of any immediate prospect of improvement in the church, I commenced collecting funds for building a chapel for the Grammar School, the first stone of which was laid on the 19th of June, and the building opened for Divine service, under license from the Bishop of Worcester, on the 22nd of November, 1850. It has cost, from first to last, £1100, including the stained-glass windows, which are all gifts presented since 1853.

"Finding that the vicar and churchwardens were, about September, 1856, seriously beginning to moot the question of the restoration of the church, I ventured to write a letter to them, touching upon the various points which seemed to require alteration and amendment in the church, and suggesting the desirableness of getting the opinion of some eminent London architect (I named Mr. George Gilbert Scott, as the person at the head of his profession), whose large experience might point out the best method of accomplishing the object so much desired by all.

"Shortly after, it was determined to lay the matter before the parishioners—and a meeting was accordingly held in the Town Hall, on December 4th, 1856, at which a committee was nominated.

"Mr. G. G. Scott examined the church on the 17th of December, and sent in a report on its then state, and on the best method of restoring it.

"Mr. Scott's plan was sanctioned at a parish meeting, held on April 15th, 1857.

"In August, 1857, Mr. W. M. Cooper, of Normanton Works, Derby, obtained the contract for carrying the restoration into effect.

"He took possession of the church on January 4th, 1858, and the west and north galleries were at once taken down. The improvement in the building was so manifest, that in a very short time another parish meeting was held (February 4th), at which it was determined that the south gallery also should be taken down ; a point which had been often urged by Mr. Scott. As that gallery was to be given up entirely for free sittings, it was decided that, as a compensation for the loss of these, the entire of the north aisle should be free and unappropriated for ever."

The following description of the progress of the restoration is based principally upon detailed notes, furnished by Mr. W. Prosser, the able and intelligent clerk of the works, appointed by Mr. Scott :—

Shortly after Mr. Cooper took possession of the church, the whole of the old seating and the galleries were removed.

The nave roof was concealed by a lath-and-plaster ceiling (drawn under the open timber roof in 1758 or 1768), under the tie beams, the spandrils and corbels of which were destroyed, and consoles of a quasi-Italian character substituted, and the whole surmounted by a deep plaster cornice. (At this time the roof was leaded.) The whole of this was cleared away, and the effect exceeded the most sanguine expectations. It at once appeared that the mutilations and defects concealed by the seating and

B

plastering, were of a more serious description than was at first anticipated. Incredible as it may now appear, the beams of the north gallery were let into the caps of the pillars of the arcading, destroying the cap, and periling the safety of the fabric by diminishing the points of bearing—a most dangerous arrangement. The ashlar surface of the south wall was in a most dilapidated state, and the foundations of the whole building, excepting the tower, were found to be seriously defective, so that it was necessary to under-pin the walls to an average depth of 18 inches. The nave roof was found to be in good preservation : new moulded ridge pieces and purloins, and some new rafters, which were required, were added, and the whole thoroughly repaired. The spandrils under the end of the tie beams were restored, and also the stone corbels, copied from a fragment of the original which was found. The roof was felted and plastered between the rafters, the plastering being coloured blue. The carved bosses were restored at considerable expense. On the easternmost bay some old decoration* was found, and as it was an interesting example and worthy of preservation, Mr. Scott directed its restoration ; this was done strictly after the original, excepting the ornamentation in the spandrils. On the tie beam nearest the chancel is a Latin text, " 𝔙𝔢𝔫𝔦𝔱𝔢 𝔟𝔢𝔫𝔢𝔡𝔦𝔠𝔱𝔦 𝔓𝔞𝔱𝔯𝔦𝔰 𝔪𝔢𝔦, 𝔡𝔦𝔰𝔠𝔢𝔡𝔦𝔱𝔢 𝔞 𝔪𝔢 𝔪𝔞𝔩𝔢𝔡𝔦𝔠𝔱𝔦 "— Come ye blessed of my Father, depart from me ye cursed—having reference to an old painting in distemper over the chancel arch, representing the Last Judgment, the remains of which were found, but so much mutilated and defaced that none of it could be preserved. On the second tie beam are the words : " 𝔚𝔬𝔯𝔰𝔥𝔦𝔭 𝔱𝔥𝔢 𝔏𝔬𝔯𝔡 𝔦𝔫 𝔱𝔥𝔢 𝔟𝔢𝔞𝔲𝔱𝔶 𝔬𝔣 𝔥𝔬𝔩𝔦𝔫𝔢𝔰𝔰."†

The stone-work throughout the interior was thoroughly restored, the walls scraped clean from whitewash, and the natural surface of the stone brought to view and re-pointed. The caps of the pillars in the north arcading were all carefully restored, and also the bases. The easternmost pillars in this arcade were entirely restored, and also the respond against the wall. The restoring of this was a difficult undertaking, as the easternmost arch had been so mutilated and cut away as to render it positively unsafe ; proper precautions were taken to secure it and the superincumbent weight during the operation, and the work was successfully performed. The first order of this arch had been cut away, together with the corbels from which it sprung ; it was restored according to the evidence which was found, the corbels having the same outline and form as the originals.

---

* It is probable that the interior of almost every old church in the country has at some time been decorated with wall-paintings—very many of them have been brought to light in recent works on church restoration. The favourite subjects were representations of Heaven and Hell, and of the Day of Judgment. In many cathedrals and some parish churches the *Dance of Death* was painted on the walls. This was one of the most popular religious plays about four centuries ago.—" Stones of the Temple."

† Some old tiles were also found, forming part of an earlier floor, in the chancel. Dr. Collis had several of them, and the writer has two in his possession.

All the label mouldings surrounding these arches and the chancel arch were cut away. They were all restored, the terminals having heads of the apostles, &c., carved in a very effective manner by Mr. Irving, of Leicester, who executed all the new carving in the church.

The cusping to the tracery of the ten clerestory windows was all restored. This had all been cut away at some time, perhaps to save the glazier a little trouble and labour. The windows in the south aisle were all restored, some with cuspings, mullions, tracery, and new jambs, and restored to their original level. The west window in this aisle was entirely restored, after the old design. The windows in the north aisle, from which the tracery and heads had been removed, and the jambs continued up to the parapet to give light to the galleries, were restored to their original position and design, with new tracery, mullions, and heads, with carved angels at the terminals of the label. The large orifice which was over the north door, and dignified by the name of a window, made to light the gallery, was walled up. A board, requesting females to take off their pattens before entering the church, which was nailed to the wall between the window and the door, was also removed. The tracery in the east window in this aisle was also restored to its original design. The two windows in the south wall of the chancel, and one on the north side, were re-opened ; Bishop Hall's monument, which blocked up one of the windows, being fixed on the north-eastern wall, and the other tablets in the north aisle. The two windows in the porch were also re-opened and restored.

The area of the church was concreted, forming a hard basement for the sleeper walls of the seat flooring. The passages and porch were laid with blue and red Staffordshire tiles, the chancel being paved with Minton tiles. The old octagonal paving was used again in the centre of the chancel.

A new doorway was made from the chancel to the vestry, with moulded jambs and heads ; also a priests' doorway to the chancel, of appropriate design, with octagonal shafts and bases attached to the jambs.

The exterior of the chancel and vestry was denuded of the ugly and incongruous battlements and embrasures running up the gables ; the eaves were brought down to their original level, with stone cornice and iron gutterings ; new coping and crosses were added to the gables and ornamental ridging to the roofs, and chimneys were put to the vestry and heating apparatus.

(The battlements and embrasures were put round the chancel as recently as 1830, at the expense of the Dean and Chapter of Worcester, and round the vestry at a cost of £72 to the parish.)

The whole exterior of the church was re-pointed in Portland cement, and the gurgoyles or water spouts and parapets restored. Two new gurgoyles were added to the south side of the tower, the old ones having at some period been destroyed.

"The gurgoyles on the tower exhibit more of the ludicrous and imaginative conception of mediæval builders than of their sense of purity and propriety," says Mr. Noake, in the "Rambler."

New pinnacles were placed on the parapets from a design by Mr. Scott, having carved crockets at the angles, and crowned with a finial ; there is a gablet to each face ; at the springing are some very spirited carvings of heads, animals, foliage, &c.

The old zinc rain pipes were removed and new ones of cast iron, of appropriate design, substituted. New wrought-iron gates of ornamental design were also put to the porch.

New oak doors, framed and panelled on the back, and hung with wrought-iron ornamental hinges, were fixed to *all* the doorways, except the one on the north side.

During the time occupied by the work of restoration the services were held in the National School.

The church was re-opened for Divine service on Thursday, the 27th of January, 1859, on which occasion several of the leading nobility and gentry of the neighbourhood attended. There was a procession of 68 of the clergy in their surplices and hoods. The sermons were preached on

Thursday. January 27th, a.m.—by the Lord Bishop of Worcester,
      ,,   ,,   p.m.—by the Rev. P. C. Claughton, M.A., Bishop Designate of St. Helena,
Friday,   January 28th, a.m.—by the Ven. Archdeacon Hone, M.A.,
    ,,   ,,   p.m.—by the Rev. Canon Wood, M.A.,
Sunday,   January 30th, a.m.—by the Rev. J. D. Collis, M.A.,
    ,,   ,,   afternoon—by the Rev. John Goodwin, M.A.,
    ,,   ,,   evening —by the Rev. William Villers, M.A.,
And on Sunday, February 6th—by the Rev. T. L. Claughton, M.A.

The collections after these services amounted to nearly £300.

The restoration committee consisted of the following persons :—

Rev. William Villers, Vicar of Bromsgrove, chairman.

Rev. John Day Collis, M.A., } Hon. Secretaries.
Mr. Thomas Scott,

Mr. George Dipple, } Churchwardens.
Mr. Richard Dunn,
Mr. Alfred Palmer,
Mr. T. D. Thomas,

Mr. Walter Brooke,	Rev. Thomas Housman,
Mr. John Cordell,	Mr. B. Maund,
Mr. Henry Curtler,	Mr. B. H. Sanders,
Mr. Thomas Day,	Mr. James Tomson.
Mr. George Horton.	

The entire cost of the restoration, from first to last, amounted to £5,414 5s. 7d., as per the following audit-sheet :—

AUDIT SHEET.

EXPENSES.	£	s.	d.			ASSETS.	£	s.	d.
I. Building and Fittings	4106	2	0		I.	Subscriptions	4400	0	5
II. Architect and Clerk of Works	383	13	9		II.	Collected after Sermons	295	9	6
					III.	Materials Sold, Interest at Bank, &c	61	8	2
III. Heating Apparatus 160 0 0					IV.	Drawback of Duty on Timber	61	0	0
Clock, Chimes, and Belfry 100 0 0						Deficit	596	7	6
Gas Fittings, Standards, and Meter 148 18 0									
Organ 335 0 0									
Printing and Stationery 42 15 4									
Postage and Incidentals 26 16 9									
Hassocks, Curtains, &c 22 11 6									
Gas, Coke, &c 31 10 4									
Cleaning 10 0 0	877	11	11						
IV. Expenses for Faculty, Commission for Allotment of Pews, &c	31	10	1						
V. Lay Clerks' and Choristers' Expenses at Opening	15	7	10						
	£5414	5	7				£5414	5	7

March 16th, 1859.

W. VILLERS, Chair.

J. D. COLLIS,
WALTER BROOKE,
THOMAS DAY,
GEORGE DIPPLE,
} Auditors.

To the deficit had to be added the Bank Interest, making in all £650, which by June 17th, the same year, was reduced less than one half, and by subsequent exertions was entirely removed.

In the annual report for 1859, of the "Worcester Architectural Society," the following reference is made to the restoration of this church :—

"Several restorations of consequence had taken place during the year, the most interesting of which was that of Bromsgrove church, by Mr. Scott. Previous to that restoration, the church of Bromsgrove had presented combinations of almost every kind of disfigurement ; and with regard to the new work, which was in general highly approved of in the report, it was stated that the reredos was not effective, and that more stained glass and additional polychromatic decorations were much wanted to relieve the somewhat cold and cheerless aspect of the interior, notwithstanding the solidity and beauty of the fittings ; also the 17th century monument, which still encumbered the south side of the sanctuary, should have been removed."

In the *Civil Engineer and Architects' Journal*, for 1858, the following allusion is made to Bromsgrove church : "A restoration of this church has made considerable progress, under the direction of Mr. Scott. The old north and west galleries were first taken down, and subsequently the south gallery also. When the flat ceiling was removed, a fine ancient oak roof was disclosed, and found to be in excellent preservation. Among other improvements may be enumerated the clearing of the whitewash from all the stonework, the rebuilding of some of the piers, the opening out of several windows which had been blocked up, with the repairing of no less than 30 others which were more or less mutilated, and the removing of the late belfry floor, which divided into two the great western window, and has necessitated the transferring to a higher floor the clock and chimes, opportunity being taken for their refitting and improvement. New and substantial ceilings have likewise been added in the chancel, aisles, and belfry ; some ancient colouring upon one bay of the roof of the nave has been restored, with admirable effect to the general appearance of the church ; and the entire reglazing of the windows has been undertaken. Two of the latter are to be memorial, and a subscription is commenced for filling the east window also with stained glass. *   *   * The amount of labour and expense involved by these alterations is about equivalent to the entire rebuilding of one-third of the interior of the church."

There are other parts of the church, not already noticed, and objects of interest therein, worthy of description.

The chancel ceiling is of oak, divided into panels, with carved bosses at the intersections of the ribs, which spring from a rich cornice, having carved pateras in the hollow.

The ceilings of the aisles are of red fir, stained and varnished, and divided into panels, having carved bosses at the intersections, with monograms, arms, crosses, crests, initials, date of restoration, and other carved devices. The tower floor is divided into panels of a bold description, with carved bosses, and an octagonal opening formed in the centre, in case of a necessity arising to lower or repair the bells, &c.

On the ridge of the roof outside the church, at the junction of the nave and chancel, is the place where formerly hung the sanctus bell, used in the services of the Roman Catholic Church to call attention to the more solemn parts of the mass. It was always rung at the words, "*Sancte, Sancte, Sancte, Deus Sabaoth,*"—"Holy, Holy, Holy, Lord God of Sabaoth;" and whoever heard it was expected to prostrate himself.

On the north side of the exterior of the church are two bosses to one of the windows, representing persons with distorted faces, caused by the one having a violent ear ache, and the other a gnawing tooth ache, but exposure to the action of the weather has nearly destroyed the identity of them.

In the south porch,* we may observe still remaining the stoup, or small niche or basin which used to contain the holy water, into which each person dipped his finger and crossed himself in sign of purification when passing the threshold of the sacred edifice.

The chancel was formerly separated from the nave by a beautiful and highly decorated screen of open work; above this was a cross beam, richly carved, supporting a gallery, the passage to which was up a flight of stone steps in the north wall, immediately adjoining. This gallery was called the rood loft, where the crucifix or rood, together with images of John the Baptist and other saints most esteemed by the parishioners, were placed. Rood lofts were ordered to be removed at the Reformation, and at the same time the Royal arms were substituted. At the restoration of the church the rood loft doorway and stairs were re-opened, but the defective state of the wall necessitated the making of this pier solid, to resist the pressure of the chancel arch. The doorway was preserved and restored, and now forms a repository for music, &c.; the upper part of the stairs, with the stone ceiling and centre panel, were thrown open to view.

In the south wall of the vestry is a squint, or opening in an oblique direction, used in Roman Catholic times for the purpose of enabling persons to see the elevation of the host at the high altar.

In the south wall of the chancel is a trefoil headed piscina, or shallow stone basin, having a hole in the bottom, with shelf over, formerly placed near the altar in Roman Catholic churches, and fixed at a convenient height above the floor, to hold the water in which the priest washed his hands; also for rinsing the chalice at

---

* The porch was a very ancient appendage to a church, and was made use of for a variety of purposes, both civil and religious; it was here the parishioners met to settle disputes, and here also portions of the marriage service were performed.

the time of the celebration of the mass. It was usually, as in this case, on the right-hand side, on the approach to the altar.

The church has, from time to time, suffered considerably from the effects of lightning. On February 3rd, 1843, the church was struck by lightning, which partially destroyed some of the figures on the clock face. On June 23rd, 1846, the lightning ran down the wire belonging to the "tolling hammer" and set fire to some old mats in the coal hole. On June 19th, 1852 (Sunday), just before the close of the afternoon service, a most tremendous shock was felt in the church, caused by the lightning striking the spire and running down the "weight hole" and bursting open a door in the tower gallery, which was at that time filled with boys; fortunately none of them were hurt. A great cry was raised, and a rush to get out was made by the congregation. In the evening a thanksgiving service was held, and allusion made to the almost providential escape of the children and others. Shortly after this event the lightning conductor was put up by Messrs. Brown, of Sheffield.

On February 1st, 1868, considerable damage was done to the church by a severe gale, which displaced the two topmost stones of the pinnacle at the south-west corner of the tower. These stones weighed together about two hundredweight, and, as they fell a distance of between 30 and 40 feet, came down with sufficient force to make a hole in the leaden covering of the nave roof, the timbers of which were splintered by the blow they received. Happily, no injury was done to the interior of the church. The cost of reparation, and securing of one of the other pinnacles, &c., was about £120. On a stone near the north-west pinnacle is the following :—

THIS AND NORTH EAST,
PINNACLES,
REBUILT, A. D. 1868.

E. HOUSMAN.
W. HOLYOAKE. } CHURCHWARDENS.
G. KINGS.
A. BENNETT.

H. W. LEWIS.   BUILDER.

On the south-west pinnacle is a date—166-, and on various parts of the battlements and the lower part of the spire, persons have exhibited much patience by carving their names, &c., on the stonework. Amongst them may be noticed :—

"Robert Francis Mumford
Senior Curate of
Bromsgrove 1863."

"William Llewellin 1849"

both of which were carved by an experienced workman, and not with a penknife, as the greater part of the remainder appear to have been.

In 1825 the steeple was repaired by Mr. Joseph Johnson, of Redditch, at a cost of £65; but the work was done badly, and in September, 1836, it was again repaired by Mr. Robinson, of Redditch, at a cost of £106 1s. 5½d. Further repairs were executed by Mr. Brown, of Sheffield, in July, 1859.

At the east and west corners of the church are echoes: also in the Crown Close, and other parts of the town.

At the vestry meeting on Easter Monday, 1869, the fire insurance on the church was increased from £2500 to £4000, at which sum it still remains.

The above engraving, from a photograph, represents the present aspect of the church, as seen from within the west door, looking south-east.

The Pews and Seats.

 IT was ordered on September 28th, 1720, "that the seats in the church shall be rebuilt at the expense of the parish, and the parishioners shall have their seats as near as possible to the old ones;" and at a vestry meeting held July 9th, 1758, "there was granted to George Draper Rich⁴ Brookes Thos. Rose and Thos. Smith ten single Lones to defray part of the charge of their said office and we do hereby further agree to have the Church Ceated and other Repaires that are wanting to be done to the church has soon has possible in the Best way and manner that they can and that they shall have more lones Granted at other proper times has the Churchwardens shall want for their use and to account for the money that they have now granted being a mejoryty of the parshones of this meeting."

On November 6th, 1771, it was agreed to "Indemnify the churchwardens in any action that Mr. Normeyeuth (?) shall Bring on account of a seat in the Church."

On March 30th, 1807, two new seats were erected, at a cost to the parish of £7 8s. 6d., "in that part of the Church where the Font used to be, and Let one of them to Mrs. Best for one year at one guinea, the other set to Mr. John Duffill at Fifteen shillings pr. year." On the same date was "Purchased one half of a seat belonging to the late Mr. John Saunders near the pulpit in Bromsgrove Church of Mr. Isaac Parkes trustee Mrs. Mary Saunders and Mr. Thos. Saunders the other half belonged to the parish before and it cost £6 6s. and the parties agreed to make a title to the seat at any time when demanded and a receipt was given by the parties."

These pews were of oak, very high, with doors and fastenings ; as before stated, they were cleared away at the church restoration.

The south gallery, prior to 1824, contained 31 pews, which were owned as follows :—

No. 1.	Benjamin Johnson.	No. 2.	Thomas Sanders.
3.	Thomas Sanders.	4.	Late Benjamin Haines, sen.
5.	Mrs. Powell.	6.	William Ward.
7.	Thomas Kings.	8.	James White.
9.	John Lacy.	10.	John Cromwell.
11.	Benjamin Witheford.	12.	Thomas Juggins.
13.	Benjamin Taylor.	14.	Joseph Brooke.
15.	Mrs. Clements.	16.	William Wilson.
17.	Sarah Hartle.	18.	John Palmer.
19.	John Palmer.	20.	Mrs. Milward.
21.	Thomas Barratt.	22.	Mrs. Smith.
23.	Benjamin Taylor.	24.	—- Dunn (Coventry).
25.	William Bradley.	26.	Miss Molesworth.
27.	Joseph Banner.	28.	Thomas Penn.
29.	William Ward.	30.	Joseph Woolmore and Joseph Jew.
31.	John Lacy.		

At a vestry meeting, held January 5th, 1824, it was resolved, "That as the accommodation in the church is insufficient for the increased population, some alteration appears desirable."

"That the plans and specifications for alterations in the north and south galleries and tower, drawn and proposed by Messrs. Rickman and Hutchinson, appear most desirable and advantageous, and that they be carried out."

Messrs. Hepworth and Davis's tender, amounting to £349 19s. 7d., was accepted. It was further decided that the extra pews obtained by the alteration should be sold by auction, in order to defray the cost.

At a meeting of the committee, held February 6th, 1824, it was "Resolved that the occupiers of the Front Pews in the North Gallery shall have the new front pews, and that the occupiers of the other Pews shall be brought forward in Rotation, so that the back pews may be sold."

"That the first and Second Row of pews (ten in number) to the front of the South Gallery to be erected, be allotted to the proprietors of the ten front pews of the present gallery."

"That Mr. Thomas Sanders be allowed, in lieu of his two pews in the present Gallery, the two pews No. 7 and No. 12 in the New Gallery."

"That Mr. Benjamin Taylor and Mr. Juggins be allowed a pew and a half each, in consequence of their pews in the present gallery being larger than usual."

At a meeting on February 11th, 1824, it was "Agreed that Mr. Jos. Brooke and Mr. Benj. Taylor shall *draw cuts* which shall have the front pew No. 36, the other to have the choice of having the pew No. 38 or the pew No. 39, Instead of the pew No. 37."

"That Notice be given in the Church on Sunday next, calling a Meeting of the proprietors of the whole of the Pews in the South Gallery, on Wednesday the 25th inst., in the vestry, at two o'clock in the afternoon, to produce their respective titles or claims before the Committee."

At this meeting all the claims were allowed, except to pews Nos. 4, 8, and 28.

On June 15th, 1824, "It was ordered that pew No. 4 in the old South Gallery be allotted to the Descendant of the late Mr. Benj. Haines, formerly of the Saracen's Head Inn, Bromsgrove, in lieu of which they are to have the pew No. 5 in the new South Gallery."

Thomas Penn's claim to pew No. 28 was allowed.

"That the pews at the end of the Organ Gallery be raised so as to be upon a Level with the pews in the South Gallery; the work to be done by Mr. Joseph Brooke."

"That the windows under the South Gallery be enlarged; Mr. Davis to give in his estimate."

"That the pews in the South Gallery be Numbered, and that Notice be Given in the Church on Sunday next and the following Sunday (and by hand bills) that nine pews and half a pew in the South Gallery, viz., Nos. 2, 10, 11, 18, 19, 24, 25, 32, and 39, and the half of No. 33, will be sold by auction in the Town Hall on Wednesday, the 30th of June inst."

A further meeting was held on June 29th, and conditions of sale drawn up. Mr. Thomas Ward was auctioneer, and the amount realised by the sale was £279 10s.

The purchases and sittings were then as follows:—

No.		No.	
1.	Joseph Woolmore and Joseph Jew.	3.	William Ward.
2.	Bought by William Penn for £10 10s.	5.	Late Benjamin Haines.
4.	John Lacy.	7.	Thomas Sanders.
6.	Benjamin Johnson.	9.	Mrs. Powell.
8.	William Ward.	11.	Bought by Benjamin Maund, £34.
10.	Bought for William Ward for £30.	13.	Thomas Penn.
	(This pew was first purchased by Mr. G. C. Vernon.)	15.	Miss Molesworth.
12.	Thomas Sanders.	17.	William Bradley.
14.	Joseph Banner.	19.	Bought by Mr. W. Partridge, £34 10s.
16.	— Dunn.		(Transferred to Mr. G. C. Vernon.)
18.	Bought by Mary Gale, £32.	21.	James White.
20.	Thomas Kings.	23.	Thomas Lacy.
22.	John Cromwell.	25.	Bought by George Stonehall, £24.
24.	Bought by William Higgs, £34.	27.	Mrs. Millward.
26.	Mrs. Smith.	29.	William Wilson.
28.	Benjamin Taylor.	31.	John Palmer.
30.	Sarah Hartle.	33.	Thomas Juggins.—Half of this pew
32.	Bought by James Green, £32.		sold to James Juggins for £13.
34.	Thomas Juggins.	35.	Benjamin Witheford.
36.	Joseph Brooke.	37.	Benjamin Taylor.
39.	Bought by James Blew, £27 10s.	38.	Benjamin Taylor.
41.	Thomas Barrett.	40.	Mrs. Clements.
		42.	John Palmer.

By the alterations in the north gallery eight additional pews were gained. These were disposed of by auction, at the Town Hall, on October 25th, 1824, to the following purchasers:—

No. 5.	To Mr. William Drury		£18	10	0
6.	William Ward	...	20	10	0
12.	John Sheppy	...	7	0	0
13.	John Bell Crane	...	10	0	0
18.	John Dipple		9	10	0
19.	do.		10	0	0
29.	do.		10	10	0
33.	do.		17	0	0
		Total ...	£103	0	0

On October 11th, 1824, " It was Resolved that Mr. John Ashmore and Mr. Thomas Greening's seats appearing to be benefited in a greater proportion than others by the alterations in the North Gallery, they should pay in consideration of the advantage respectively derived—

Mr. John Ashmore   £3   0   0

Mr. Thomas Greening   4   0   0 "

Formerly a seat was allotted to the bailiffs and aldermen of the town, and another to the wives of the latter. In 1703 (March 29th), at a parish meeting, "It is ordered that notice be given in the Church on Sunday next, that no person shall sit in the Bailiff's and Alderman's seat, but such substantial house-dwellers that the church-wardens shall order, and that no servants shall sit in the Alderman's wives' seat."

The seats for the poor were in the centre part of the church, and nearest to the pulpit and reading desk.

The sub-committee appointed previous to the restoration of the church, reported at a parish meeting on April 15th, 1857, that the sitting accommodation was as follows :—

Galleries	...	... 95 pews	...	465	sittings.
Ground	...	... 158 ,,	...	756	,,
Free Benches (narrow)			...	75	,,
Children	.	...	...	53	,,
		253		1349	(of which about 630 were free).

They stated "that there were a great many sittings *but*, so bad that they were practically worthless. It is not too much to say that there are at least 200 sittings in the church at present in which nothing but dire necessity would induce any person to sit."

The present seats, which were placed in the church at the restoration, are of oak (except where the contractor was allowed to insert chestnut, of which the greater portion of the actual seating is formed), of beautiful design and workmanship, the mouldings being remarkably clean and sharp : the ends have a sunk quatrefoil panel on the face, filled in with exquisitely carved foliage, copied from natural objects the holly, oak, strawberry, ivy, vine, hop, &c. ; the arm rests have ivy and other leaves carved on the face ; the backs of the seats are all framed, paneled, and very strong. The backs and fronts next to the passages are paneled, the tracery being of a very rich and elaborate design, and of excellent workmanship. The seating of the chancel is of a different design, having carved terminations to the mouldings on the ends : the fronts are of open tracery, of an early character. The children's seats are placed under the tower, and are of pleasing and substantial construction. The churchwardens formerly occupied a large square seat on the north side of the chancel, nearest the nave. At each corner of the seat was placed one of the four wands used by the churchwardens when the bishop visited the church. In lieu of this, they now occupy the front seat on the same side, but nearest the east window. Adjoining the former seat was that of the bailiffs and aldermen. The "vicar's seat" was nearer the pulpit.

At a parish meeting, held on February 4th, 1858, it was resolved, "That the whole of the sittings in the North aisle should be free and unappropriated for ever." The remainder (except those under the tower) are allotted to applicants from time to time, as occasions occur. This system of appropriation was the cause of much unpleasantness at first. "One party urgently pressed for an entirely free church," while another talked of "a suit for perturbation in the Ecclesiastical Court, and an action on the case at common law against the churchwardens for disturbing him in the use of his pew. The vicar, in a printed address, tried to cast oil on the troubled waters ; and the churchwardens, Messrs. T. Scott, W. Holyoake, E. Hadley, and E. Jackson, declared that the matter did not legally rest with them."* The grievance was quietly and peaceably settled, and is now, it is hoped, forgotten.

The present accommodation is for about 1050 persons, of which 550 are free.

In the vestry, in a massive carved oak frame, with a gilt inside border, is a tablet bearing the following :—

May V. MDCCCXLIX.

Presented to the Vicar and
Churchwardens of Bromsgrove,
for the use of the Parish Church,
A Font and Faldstool
By the Rev. John Day Collis, A. M.
Headmaster of the Grammar School of
King Edward the Sixth.

———

Also two carved oak chairs and
two stools for the Chancel by
William Wildsmith of this Town.

Rev. William Villers, A.M. Vicar.

Robert Heynes
Hugh Phillips } Churchwardens.
William Baker
William Llewellin

The faldstool is of oak, and has six pieces of old carved oak inserted into the new work, one of which is a representation of the Lord's Supper.

One of the chairs referred to above is on the north side of the communion table, the other is in the vestry, as is also one of the stools, the other being used by the organ blower.

* Noake's "Guide to Worcestershire."

In 1868, two seats for the use of the aged and infirm poor were placed in front of the pulpit and reading desk, the style of the work harmonising with the other sittings. The churchwardens' seat, by the font, was also added, at a cost of £3. In December, 1869, Mr. W. S. Batten presented to the church eight large-type Prayer Books, and the same number of Bibles, for the use of the poor persons occupying the kneelings near the prayer desk and pulpit. The oak kneeling desks were also the gift of Mr. Batten.

The Pulpit, Lectern, &c.

N January 2nd, 1744, a new pulpit, reading desk, and clerk's desk, standing one above another in the middle of the nave, completely hiding the view of the chancel and altar from the congregation, was placed in the church, at a cost of £41 13s. In the parish records, on January 2nd, 1744, it is ordered, "That it be inserted in this Book that during the churchwardenship of Mr. Will. Smith Mr. Will. Kimberley Mr. John Harsnot and Mr. John Wright the sum of £41 13s. was raised partly by a subscription of the parishioners for the erecting of a new pulpit &c. and partly by the Ground in the Church made convenient thereby for seats. And that the same has been expended and that an account thereof has been laid before the Parishioners at a parish meeting and that they are satisfied therewith." This is signed by Will. Phillips, vicar, and others. The pulpit, one of the description usually called a "three decker," was decorated with gold fringe and other ornaments, the cost of which was £20 16s. 9d. In December, 1776, the church was entered and robbed of the fringe and a surplice; and at a parish meeting held on December 15th, 1776, "twenty lones" were granted to the churchwardens, "in order to defray the charge of replacing the gold Fring and Tassells belonging to the pulpit cloth and Cusion and surplice &c. lately stolen from out of the Church and Vestry and towards defraying other necessary parts of their said office." Over the pulpit was suspended a Chinese sounding board, having a dove and gilt ball on the top of it. The removal of this dove and board seems to have offended the "Bird of Bromsgrove," for, in the "Bromsgrove Memorial," we read:—

"*Our* clergyman ; a word with you,
Just ground, a cutting word or two.
You, who have had the font remov'd,
Can *you* expect to be approv'd ?
Suffered the dove away to hop,
With our beloved pulpit top ;
That hole made lately through the wall,
Forgive you, sir, we never shall.

Put up, we will not, with your whims,
New tunes, new organ, psalms and hymns.

The people turn'd religion-mad,
No seats, no sitting to be had :
The lessons read by such a boy,
Without our leave, or reason why ;
(The man that cannot read so well,
Has faults to find and tales to tell),
By candle catechise the poor ;
Expenses hateful to endure."

The present oak reading desk, and the handsome oak pulpit, were placed in their present positions when the church was reseated, and the old one, described above, was, with the old pews, &c., sold by auction in the Crown Close. The pulpit is on the south side of and underneath the chancel arch, the reading desk occupying a similar position on the opposite side.

The door to the old clerk's desk is now in a partition in a house on Stoney Hill.

At the west end of the south aisle is a small oak lectern, with desk top and trunk lock, having an ancient volume chained to it : the whole being in good condition. The work is dated 1609, and is --

"A SERMON Made in Latine in Oxenford, in the raigne of King *Edward* sixt, by the learned and goodly Father JOHN JEWEL, late Bishop of *Sarisburie*, and translated into English by *R.V.* : Dedicated vnto the Bishop of *London*, as appeareth *in the commentarie of Master* CALVINE upon the Galathians, in English . 1 Cor. 9, 16 . *Wo is vnto me if I preach not the Gospell.*"

The upper part of the first page has been cut out by some ruthless hand, otherwise the work is in good order, clean and complete.

The handsome brass lectern now in use, was the gift of the late Miss Maria Sanders, and represents an eagle (the symbolic representation of the Evangelist St. John), with out-stretched wings, standing upon a ball supported by a twisted shaft on a circular base, round which is this inscription :—

" IN HONOREM DEI ET IN USUM ECCLESIÆ S. JOHANNIS BAPTISTÆ DE BROMSGROVE DD. D. MARIA SANDERS. A.D. MDCCCLXII."--(In honour of God, and for the use of the Church of St. John the Baptist at Bromsgrove ; given by Maria Sanders. A.D. 1862).

The Font, Reredos, &c.

THE baptismal font which was for many years in use in the church, was made by Jonathan Pinfield, a mason of Bromsgrove, and cost the parish 26s.! In the parochial accounts the following receipt is given : "Jany. 2nd. 1744.—Recvd. of John Wright, for making a font, the sum of one pound 6 shillings. pr. Jona : Pinfield.—£1 6s." It would be interesting to know what has become of this inexpensive and primitive piece of workmanship. This font originally stood in front of the organ gallery, but on March 30th, 1807, it was removed to the side of the monuments of the Shrewsbury family, at the east end of the north aisle. To the font was a lid surmounted by an eagle, and suspended by a brass chain from the ceiling.

The present font was presented to the church in 1847, by the Rev. John Day Collis, D.D., and bears this inscription—

" Ex Dono Johannis Day Collis, A.M., Scholæ Regis Edvardi VI. apud Bromsgrovenses Magistri. MDCCCXLVII."—(The Gift of John Day Collis, M.A., Master of King Edward VIth's School at Bromsgrove, 1847.)

The carving was executed by Mr. Irving, of Leicester.

The last christening at the old font took place August 29th, 1847, and the new one was brought into the church on September 22nd of the same year, the first christening taking place on the following Sunday, when the Rev. P. M. Stedman baptised " Emma, daughter of John and Ann Barley, Lickey End, nailer."

Some " few years " before 1799, Mrs. Moore, relict of Edward Moore, of Barn Green, presented a handsome marble communion table, and an altar-piece of oak, neatly ornamented, containing the Lord's Prayer, the Decalogue, and the Apostles' Creed, to the church. Its height, however, hid the lower part of the east window. She also presented an iron communion rail.

The present reredos, placed in the church at the restoration, is of Ancaster stone : the two sides are arcaded with marble shafts, the centre portion over the altar is in alabaster, diapered, with a sunk quatrefoil panel in the centre, with monogram I.H.C., &c. This is surmounted with paneling containing some coloured decorations, and medallions of our Lord and the Evangelists. Underneath are the words : "This DO IN REMEMBRANCE OF ME."

The altar cloth was the gift of Mrs. J. D. Collis. The altar railing* is of wrought-iron, with oak capping, the standards and ornamental parts coloured in ultramarine, and the leaves gilt. The altar table and two stools are of oak, of neat design.

---

* When the rood screens were ordered to be removed, it was found necessary to protect the altar from general intrusion, and hence the origin of " altar rails," which were first ordered to be put up by Archbishop Laud.

D

The communion plate is of silver, of very chaste description, each piece bearing the monogram I.H.C., and the chalice, in addition, the words, "Glory be to God on high." It was made some five or six years ago, out of the plate formerly in use, by Messrs. Keith and Co., of Denmark Street, London.

At a parish meeting, held December 15th, 1776, "It was agreed that the church-wardens for the time being should have the custody or keeping of the communion plate, &c. And in case any accident shall happen at the house or place where the churchwardens shall deposit shall be broken open and the Plate, &c., stolen or lost therefrom, the said churchwardens shall not be at any loss thereby, but it shall be made or repaid by the Parish."

In 1868, an oak box, lined with velvet, was bought for the plate, at a cost of £1 12s. 6d.

In 1548, the number of communicants was 1000.

The Windows.

ITH the exception of the beautiful windows at Great Malvern, Worcester-shire is very poor in stained glass. There is, however, a considerable quantity of fine old glass at the little church of Oddingley, and a few figures remain at several other places. Nash informs us that in the "first pane" of the great east window of Bromsgrove church was some ancient stained glass representing a bishop, "subscribed *St. Wulstan*," Bishop of Worcester. In the same window were some defaced coats of arms, one of which was Bishop Alcock's. Wolstan, who was surnamed "the saint," was born at Long Ichington, Warwickshire. He was Bishop of Worcester from 1062 to 1095, and was present at the coronation of William the Conqueror. In 1084, he began to build the present cathedral of Worcester ; three years afterwards he assisted in crowning William Rufus, and in 1088 opened his new cathedral, which was finished, and he held a synod there in 1092. Great encomiums are passed upon Wolstan, especially by William of Malmesbury, who wrote a book of his life and miracles. He was doubtless an extraordinary man, a persuasive and powerful preacher, though his attainments in literature were mean ; he was remarkably humble in an age when the prelatic character was distinguished for haughtiness : meek and patient, yet on proper occasions he wanted not spirit. He died January 19th, 1095, aged about 87, having held the see 32 years. He was canonized by Pope Innocent III., for the miracles pretended to be wrought at his shrine in Worcester Cathedral, and was the last Saxon Bishop of Worcester.

The arms of Bishop Alcock referred to were—Argent, on a fesse between three cock's heads erased sable, a mitre or. These arms are a good pun upon the bishop's name—Alcock. The mitre is sometimes omitted, as in glass at Malvern ; and in some examples the arms are surrounded with a bordure gules, charged with eight crowns or. John Alcock, Bishop of Rochester, was translated to the see of Worcester September 18th, 1476. He was President of the Council in the 1st of Edward IV., and afterwards Lord Chancellor of England. During the time he was Bishop of Worcester he confirmed the foundation of a perpetual chantry in Bromsgrove parish church by Alianore Stafford, the widow of Sir Humphrey Stafford, of Grafton, Knt., A.D. 1478. This fact may account for his arms appearing in the window. He was appointed to the see of Ely in 1486, and died October 1st, 1500, being buried in the Cathedral of Ely. No record appears to exist stating what has become of this old glass, unless, indeed, it met with that fate which Mr. Noake suggests in referring to other painted glass in the county : " When Horace Walpole tricked up Strawberry Hill, the introduction of stained glass into private houses was first made fashionable, and large prices were offered for the article by the London dealers, who sent their travellers all through the country. The village glaziers, being tempted by the lucrative offers, took advantage of every high wind, and, abstracting the finest quarries piecemeal from the church windows, laid the fault of the mutilation at the door of rude ' Boreas ' and charged the parish with repairs, which the church-wardens (good, easy souls) thought unavoidably necessary. '

We find this item in the parish accounts : " January ye 2, 1744-5 then Reseved of Mr. Smith and Mr. Kimberley and Mr. Horsnett & Mr. Right (Wright) ye Late Church Wardens ye sum of Eight pound and four shilling being in full for last Easter and keeping ye leades (leads) and windows of ye Church at Bromsgrove in Repaire and ye other New Windows wich I have to Reseve to make up my moneys to ye present churchwardens ye sume of ten shillings to make up my sume."

The five lancets of the great east window are filled with stained glass, containing subjects from the life of our Blessed Lord. The glass was supplied and inserted by Messrs. Lavers and Barraud, of London, and cost £263, which sum was collected by the exertions of the Rev. C. H. and Mrs. Jenner, and the ladies of the town.

The two windows on the south side of the chancel are filled with stained glass supplied by Messrs. Clayton and Bell, of London, as memorials to members of the late Mr. Benjamin Maund's family. The glass in the easternmost of these windows represents : First—St. Paul, seated, with a long straight sword in his right hand, and in his left a quill pen. Over his head, " PAUL SERVANT OF JESUS CHRIST."

Second—St. Luke, seated, with a book in his left hand, and over his head, "LUKE THE BELOVED PHYSICIAN." The lower part of the window has this inscription :

IN MEMORY OF JOHN MAUND : M.D. WHO DIED AT MELBOURNE, VICTORIA MDCCCLVII	AND WAS INTERRED THERE IN THE GENERAL CEMETERY (sic.) ·≍·≍·≍·≍·

The other window is similar in design, and has : First—a female at a faldstool, reading the Scriptures, and over her head the words, "BLESSED ARE THE PURE IN HEART." Second—another female figure, holding flowers, representing Charity, and the words, "CHARITY NEVER FAILETH." The lower part of the window bears the following :—

IN MEMORY OF SARAH WIFE OF BENJAMIN MAUND F.L.S.* DIED 1857.	IN MEMORY OF MARY WIFE OF OWEN MAUND DIED 1848.

The east window of the north aisle is filled with stained glass, furnished by Messrs. Clayton and Bell, and was the gift of the Rev. J. D. Collis, D.D. It represents our Lord blessing the children and healing the sick. The motto is—

FOR CHRIST'S LITTLE ONES   FOR CHRIST   FOR CHRIST'S POOR

Along the bottom of the window –

IN THE YEAR OF THE RESTORATION OF THE CHURCH , 1858 JOHN DAY COLLIS

The east window of the south aisle is to the memory of the late Mr. Thomas Day, of Bromsgrove, who for upwards of 20 years filled the office of clerk to the Board of Guardians, during which period his strict fidelity and wonderful habits of business, and the pains he took in tabularising all information useful for the various parishes of the union ; his kindness to the poor, the excellent advice he gave them, the way in which he bestowed his time, and employed his business talents, in promoting many good works for the education and social improvement of the inhabitants of the town and parish, demanded a substantial recognition on the part of his fellow townsmen and others. Accordingly, a project was set on foot for erecting some permanent memorial of his personal worth and record of his official services to the town and neighbourhood, and it was decided that it should take the form of a memorial window. To attain this object subscriptions were invited, and a meeting of subscribers was held at the Institute on February 25th, 1867, under

---

* Mr. B. Maund rendered Bromsgrove remarkable by the production of an horticultural work far surpassing anything of the kind ever attempted in a provincial town. On the 1st of January, 1825, Mr. Maund issued the first monthly part of his "Botanic Garden," illustrated with "accurately coloured plates of hardy and ornamental flowering plants," which immediately attained a large circulation, both in our own and in other countries. The work was completed in 16 vols., and is extremely rare. On the 1st of January, 1836, the same spirited scientific gentleman issued the first number of his "Botanist," being assisted by the Rev. J. S. Henslow, professor of botany, which work "contains plates and the description of tender and hardy ornamental plants," and, if possible excels its predecessor in style of execution.

the presidency of Lord Lyttelton. A statement of the position of the funds was presented by Mr. Thomas White, the hon. sec. ; the meeting adjourned to the church for the purpose of deciding which window it would be best to select to receive the memorial, and it was there resolved "that the east window of the south aisle should be selected." A plan for a beautiful window, comprising six subjects from the miracles of Our Lord, had been submitted by Messrs. Lavers and Barraud, of Bloomsbury, London, the cost of executing which would be £150, but by leaving out some of the elaborate details of the plan the cost was reduced to £130. It was resolved that the plan should be adopted, subject to the proposed reduction in the cost, and subject also to the consent of the Vicar, who was present at the meeting, and who at once, of course, gave the required consent. The funds at command not being sufficient, many of the subscribers increased their subscriptions, and the amount required was soon raised. A committee, consisting of the Rev. G. W. Murray, vicar, Rev. Dr. Collis, Dr. Fletcher, and Mr. T. White, hon. sec., was appointed to carry the resolutions into effect. The window was put into its place during the first week in the June following, and is an appropriate memorial to one whose life was in so many ways devoted to the service of his fellow townsmen.

The subjects of the window are Our Lord's works of mercy mentioned in St. Matthew xi. 5. Under the three upper scenes are the words—

| THE DEAF HEAR | THE DEAD ARE RAISED UP | TO THE POOR THE GOSPEL IS PREACHED. |

and under the lower ones—

| THE BLIND RECEIVE THEIR SIGHT | THE LAME WALK | THE LEPER IS CLEANSED. |

Along the bottom of the window we read—

| To THE GLORY OF GOD AND IN MEMORY OF THOMAS DAY OF BROMSGROVE | BORN SEPTEMBER 25 1809 DIED MAY 6. 1866 | ERECTED BY THE INHABITANTS OF THIS TOWN AND NEIGHBOURHOOD 1867. |

The relatives shortly after had placed beneath the window a brass plate, 21½ in. by 12½ in., which has the following :—

To THE GLORY OF GOD AND IN MEMORY OF THEIR LATE
MUCH RESPECTED TOWNSMAN, MR. THOMAS DAY,
BORN SEPTEMBER 25TH 1809, DIED MAY 6TH 1866.
THIS WINDOW HAS BEEN ERECTED BY THE INHABITANTS
OF BROMSGROVE AND THE NEIGHBOURHOOD, AS A TRIBUTE
TO DEPARTED WORTH, AND IN ACKNOWLEDGMENT
OF THE HONORARY SERVICES OF THE DECEASED, IN
PROMOTING EVERY GOOD WORK IN CONNECTION WITH
THE INSTITUTIONS AND CHARITIES OF THIS TOWN.

The amount received from subscriptions was £140 11s. 6d., which was disposed
of as follows :—

	£	s.	d.
Lavers and Barraud, for window	133	15	6
W. Brown, taking out old window and fixing new one	3	14	3
A. Palmer, for printing, advertising, &c	2	9	6
Carriage	0	12	3
	£140	11	6

The great west window is an excellent representation of the parable of the Wise
and Foolish Virgins, with the figure of Christ in the centre. In the lower part of
the middle compartment is the figure of an angel holding a scroll, on which are
the words—Saint Matthew ch. xxv. v : i–xii.

Underneath the window, on long brass plates, is the following inscription, in red
and black church lettering :

First line.—To the Glory of God and in affectionate memory of Olivia Emma,
wife of the Rev. Walter More-Molyneux, B.A., and daughter of the Rev.
G. W. Murray, M.A., Vicar of Bromsgrove.

Second line.—This window is dedicated by her husband. She was born
Sep. xxiii., 1847, Married July xiv., Died August x. 1868. "Watch therefore, for ye know neither the day nor the hour." Matt. xxv. 13.

Olivia Emma More-Molyneux.

Died August 10th, 1868.

Alas ! she's gone ; the young, the loved, the gay !
Gone like the sunshine of a summer's day ;
Gone in the happiness of bridal bloom ;
Her footsteps hurried to an early tomb.

Of what avail the tears so freely shed ?
Can they bring back the loved, the lost, the dead ?
Ah ! no—she sleeps the last long sleep of Death ;
Clasped in his arms, chilled by his icy breath.

But will she *never* wake again ?—this fair young thing—
Yes ! she will wake when the last trump shall bring
His startling call to rouse the sleeping dead :
She shall awake and leave her narrow bed :

Who died in faith, shall surely rise with joy,
To meet her Lord, triumphant, in the sky ;
And go with Him—a trophy of His love—
To live for ever in the realms above.

Then, tried and suffering mourners, cease to weep ;
Your loved one " is not dead ;" she does but sleep.
Look forward, in the hope to meet again,
Where shall be no more parting, no more pain.

" Bromsgrove Parish Magazine,"* September, 1868.

The *Bromsgrove Messenger* of July 2nd, 1870, has the following : " One more beautiful object has been added to the many with which our noble parish church is enriched, by the pious munificence of the Rev. H. W. More-Molyneux, who has filled in the large west window with exquisitely painted glass, as a sacred tribute to the memory of his late wife, whose lamented death occurred so soon after her marriage. The subject of the painting on the window is the 'Parable of the Ten Virgins,' and the work has been executed by M. Capronnier, of Brussels. It is the only work of the kind executed by that artist in this county, and the largest window erected by him in this country. The design and execution are excellent, and the 'story' of the parable is so well and so plainly told by the picture, that it *must* be 'read' at once by the most casual observer—if by any possibility there can be a 'casual observer' of an object so beautiful and attractive. The figures, of which there are twelve (thirteen)—the Redeemer, two angels, and the ten virgins—are life size, and there are smaller figures of angels in the upper lights of the window. The background and general ornamentation are appropriate and effective, and the rich and glowing colours in which the whole is depicted have a charming effect, and render the window 'a thing of beauty' and 'a joy for ever.'"

The subject of the window, the writer is informed, was taken from a fresco in a church in Herefordshire, and cost the donor upwards of £600.

At the restoration of the church, the whole of the windows (except the three then filled with stained glass) were reglazed with Hartley's rolled cathedral glass ; new saddle bars and stanchions, with *fleur-de-lis* heads, being inserted in each.

* In January, 1866, appeared the first monthly number of a "Bromsgrove Parish Magazine." It was issued to subscribers at 1s. 6d. per year, and contained much parochial information. In 1870 the payment was increased to 2s., and in December, 1871, the work was discontinued.

The Lighting and Heating.

REVIOUS to the introduction of gas into the town, in 1835, the church
was lighted, when necessary, by means of candles. In the nave,
suspended by a massive iron chain from a beam, was a large brass
chandelier, which was purchased on March 21st, 1773. at a cost of £22 15s. This
chandelier was removed on June 29th, 1854, by order of two of the churchwardens who were then in office, and placed in the tower gallery. Great difficulty
was experienced in its removal on account of its great weight, but the work was
successfully carried out by Mr. Jonathan Brazier, who made a platform on the
high pews, and a ladder being held perpendicularly by four men, he ascended
and unhooked the chandelier, and by means of ropes it was lowered to the
ground.

On Sunday, September 11th, 1836, the church was lighted for the first time
by gas. The cost of the fittings necessary for the church and churchyard amounted
to £126 15s. 6d., and of this sum £122 10s. was collected by subscription. In a
manuscript note the writer has met with the statement is made that there was not
a gas meter in the church till September 12th, 1847. (?) The arrangements for the
artificial lighting at present in use are by Mr. Skidmore, of Coventry. The brass gas
standards are beautiful in design and workmanship: those in the chancel have 24,
and those in the nave 16 lights each. In addition there is a suspended chandelier in
the chancel having 24 lights.

The "Bromsgrove Almanack" records that the first evening service in the church
was on May 22nd, 1836.

The church was formerly heated by means of ordinary coal stoves, for we
read that new stoves were purchased in 1844, at a cost of £21 10s. each, exclusive
of piping. and were used for the first time on Sunday, October 20th, in that year.
At the restoration of the church, in 1859, the stoves were done away with, and
the building heated by hot air on an improved plan, carried out by Mr. Harper,
of Birmingham.

The heating apparatus being found defective for the proper warming of the
church, was, in 1872, altered and improved, at a total cost of £122 17s. 4d. The
churchwardens, in a circular issued by them shortly afterwards, state that "they
hope the completion of the heating apparatus will add to the comfort of the
congregation."

The Musical Services, Choir, Organ, Organist, &c.

EFORE an organ was placed in the church, the musical portion of the service was supplied by means of fiddles,* &c. Amongst the last persons who played instruments in the church were : William Rose and Richard Byng, bassoons ; Joseph Smith, clarionet ; Perks Brothers, French horns. Flutes, fiddles, &c., were also used, but time has erased from memory the names of those who played them.

The choir was a voluntary one, consisting of ladies and gentlemen, who occupied the old " singers' gallery " at the west end.

By an indenture, bearing date July 10th, 1787, Simon Crane left a rent charge of 20s. per year, to be disposed of " in or towards accommodating the singing-loft in the parish church of Bromsgrove and the choir of singers to be there assembled at Divine worship, with instruments of music, books, instructing boys to sing, or in such other manner incident thereto as the said vicar and churchwardens for the time being or the major part of them should see fit, and to no other purpose whatsoever."

The first organ used in the church was placed in the " organ gallery "† under the tower, and in rear of the choir, in 1809. It was opened on July 9th, by Mr. B. Simms, at that time organist of St. Philip's Church, Birmingham, and cost £750, the amount being collected by subscription. Mr. Elliot, of Tottenham Court Road, London, was the builder. The first organist appointed was Mr. James Simms (a brother to the one above-mentioned), who held the office 44 years, at the expiration of which term he resigned. During the last nine years his son, Mr. John Simms, officiated for him, and at his father's resignation, a meeting was held at the Town Hall at which the son was appointed successor, but he, immediately on appointment, resigned, and Mr. J. B. Tirbutt, the present organist, was elected.

Mr. James Simms died June 24th, 1854, at the ripe old age of 84. A stone, near the north door of the church, is erected to his memory. The schemes of the

---

* " The introduction of the fiddle into the church was probably copied from the French. We are told that Charles II. established a band of 24 violins, in imitation of his brother monarch's band at Paris, which gave occasion to Dr. Urfey's famous song of ' 4 and 20 fiddlers all in a row.' The king was not content to keep his 'fiddlers' exclusively to the court, but introduced them into the sacred worship of the Royal Chapel. John Evelyn, in his diary, says : 'I went to the Chapel Royal, but soon came away, quite sick with what I had heard. The solemn organs did no longer play, but instead thereof, 4 and 20 fiddles, as though the devil himself had been among them. Made up my mind to go there no more, but to speak to the king about it.'"—Mr. J. Noake, in " The Rambler."

† On July 19th, 1809, £100 was voted from the parish rates towards the gallery.—" Bromsgrove Almanack."

special services on behalf of the Sunday schools, the choir, in aid of the organist's salary, and on other occasions, shew that he was a man of considerable ability, both as a writer and composer of music, many of the pieces performed at those services being his own production. Other members of his family appear to have been gifted in the like manner, for their names also appear in the schemes as writers or composers.

The remuneration to the organist was £30, paid out of the weighing machine fund, whilst such fund sufficed, after which the amount was made up by collections or other means. In the *Worcester Herald*, of May 10th, 1834, we notice the following advertisement :—

SACRED MUSIC.

On SUNDAY NEXT, MAY 11th, a SELECTION of SACRED MUSIC, from the most esteemed Authors, will be performed in BROMSGROVE CHURCH, under the direction of MR. SIMMS, Organist; when a Collection will be made in aid of his Salary and the support of the Choir.

The salary of the organist at the present time is £50 per annum.

The organ blower, Thomas Wainwright, wore the uniform appertaining to his office, viz., a green cloth coat with scarlet tippet, and tall silk hat with gold band.

The present organ is by Mr. Nicholson, of Worcester, and cost £335 and the one formerly in use. It is a splendid instrument, occupying a position at the east end of the north aisle. It has three manuals or rows of keys. The great organ has 10 stops, CC to G, 56 notes : 1, open diapason ; 2, ditto ; 3, stop diapason bass ; 4, clarabella treble ; 5, principal ; 6, harmonic flute ; 7, twelfth ; 8, fifteenth ; 9, mixture—three ranks ; 10, trumpet. The choir organ has eight stops, CC to G, 56 notes : 1, open diapason ; 2, viol di gamba ; 3, stop diapason bass ; 4, stop diapason treble ; 5, dulciana ; 6, flute ; 7, dulcet ; 8, cremona. The swell organ has 10 stops, CC to G, 56 notes : 1, bourdon ; 2, double dulciana ; 3, open diapason ; 4, stop diapason ; 5, flute ; 6, principal ; 7, piccolo ; 8, doublette ; 9, oboe ; 10, cornopean. The pedal organ, CCC to F, 30 notes : 1. open diapason, 16ft. ; 2, bourdon, 16ft. ; 3, spare slide. Couplers : Gt. to pedals, ch. to pedals, sw. to pedals. Sforzando pedals : Sw. to great, sw. to choir, ch. to great. Three composition pedals to great organ, three concussion valves. All the trebles are made of the best spotted metal.

The present choir, of which Mr. Charles Fowler is leader, consists of about 16 boys (who receive a small gratuity for their attendance), and gentlemen, who give their services voluntarily. They occupy four seats—two on either side of the chancel —nearest the nave, and wear surplices during Divine service. There is an annual collection in aid of the choir funds, and till quite recently the accounts of the choir were kept separate from those of the churchwardens, but they are now amalgamated. A choirmaster was formerly paid £5 per year, but the office was dispensed with some four or five years ago.

The Alms, Offertory, Churchwardens, &c.

N the vestry is an alms box,* probably of the 17th century, which was formerly fastened up in the body of the church. It is painted, and has on the front three trunk locks, underneath which, and at the back, are the words, painted in red—

Remember the poore:

And at the ends—

God loueth	Blessed is hee yᵗ
a cheerefull	considereth the
giuer : 2 : Cor :	poore : Psal : 41 : 1 :
9 : Cha : Ver : 7 :	

At a meeting of the parishioners, shortly after the restoration of the church (July 17th, 1859), it was decided, "That the money required for the celebration of Divine Service and for the expenses annually incurred by the Church Wardens, the organist's salary, the Lighting and Heating of the church, &c., shall be discharged by the weekly offertory."

At a meeting of the congregation, held in the vestry of the parish church, on July 28th, 1870, the Vicar in the chair, it was proposed by Mr. Jefferies, seconded by Mr. John Green, and carried unanimously, "That the weekly morning offertory be made, and that the collections in the afternoons and evenings on the last Sundays in the month be also made as at present ; that all moneys go to one common fund ; that the division of money for the poor, taken on an average of seven years, be arranged by the Vicar and Churchwardens ; and that, on not exceeding six Sundays in the year, the morning offertory be devoted to such purposes as the Vicar and Churchwardens may think proper."

Since July 16th, 1871, collections have been made at the close of each morning and evening service, and the amount given away by the vicar and churchwardens to the poor out of the offertory was reduced from £1 to 15s. per month, when a separate district was assigned to the new church of All Saints.

---

* An Act of Parliament, passed in 1536 (27 Henry VIII. c. 25), orders, under a penalty of 20s., the gathering and procuring of charitable and voluntary alms for the relief of the poor *with a box*, any Sunday, holiday, or other festival ; and further ordains that the money so gathered shall be kept in the common coffer or box standing in the church. In "Articles to be followed and observed according to the King's Majesty's Injunctions and Proceedings," and issued in 1549, is the following direction :—"*Item*. That after the Homily, every Sunday, the Minister exhort the people—especially the communicants—to remember the poor men's box with their charity." The disuse into which the alms box fell in the 18th century is shown by the painter-satirist, Hogarth, who, in one of his works, introduces the alms box with the aperture in the lid covered with a cobweb. There is no reason to believe the rebuke, thus conveyed, was undeserved.

The present poor boxes are of oak, and were placed in the church in 1868. At the conclusion of the evening service on the last Sunday in each month these boxes are opened by the churchwardens.

The collecting plates are of oak, turned, and are eight in number. Those formerly used were of pewter, and the collections—some four or five in number during the year—were made at the church doors.

It seems to have been the custom here, time out of mind, to elect *four* church-wardens annually on Easter Monday, and they—by virtue of that office—became "overseers." Two of the wardens are named by the vicar, and are called "vicar's wardens," and two are elected by the parishioners at the meeting—of which due notice is given—and are called "people's wardens."

Amongst the many duties which a churchwarden was expected to perform, years ago, was "to see that the Lord's day be duly observed; search alehouses on Sundays; and if they find any persons therein, during Divine service, they are to make them pay 3s. 4d., and also 1s. for being absent from church : and the master of the house shall forfeit 10s." 1 James I. c. 9.

In the parish books we find that it was decided, on October 23rd, 1673, "That the Four pounds levied upon several persons for not coming to church shall go to put out apprentices, and the Rents of the Flats and the interest of Mr. Edkins' gift, £10."

The churchwardens' expenses were defrayed by the overseers from 1796 to 1817, when the church rate was again allowed. At this period (1796) we find record in the parish books of the custom of the parishioners, at the conclusion of their meetings, to adjourn to some inn—the "White Hart," the "Dolphin," &c., and to regale themselves at the expense of the parish ; such entries as "good tap," "ale moderate," frequently occur.

The following are a few extracts from the parish books relating to the office of churchwarden :—

> 1683. It is agreed that no churchwarden shall charge more than 3s. 6d. at any visitation.
>
> 1684. November 7th.— It is agreed that all churchwardens shall give in their accounts one month after going out of office, and shall be reimbursed in two months if out of pocket.
>
> 1688. June 25th.—It is agreed that the "*prockters*" be allowed but 10d. at the visitation, and that no churchwarden shall have his levys abated.
>
> 1718. It is ordered that the churchwardens be allowed 2s. at any visitation in Bromsgrove.
>
> 1770. It is agreed to put Walter Creswell in the Bishop's Court for the levys and to bear the churchwardens harmless.

On February 14th, 1839, there was an anti church rate disturbance in the town, and a subscription list was started "to defray the law expenses attending the prosecution of Nicholas Hill and others for a church rate riot, Hill being one of the churchwardens," the amount subscribed amounting to upwards of £830. On January 31st, 1860, according to the "Bromsgrove Almanack," a meeting was held in support of church rates.

The Library.

HE vestry contains a valuable collection of 16th and 17th century books,* chiefly on theology. A register is kept of books taken away, when taken, by whom, and when returned. Many of these books are valuable, and at the present time are exposed on shelves; it is certainly desirable that some means should be taken to make them more secure. The works are as follow :—

Osiander Histor : Eccles : 1st to 4th Centuries. 1607.

    do.   do.   5th to 6th   do.   1607.

    do.   do.   7th to 15th   do.   1608.

    do.   do.   16th   do.   1608.

Origen contra Marcionitas, &c. 1673.

Histor : Papatûs, a Philippus Mornæus. 1662.

On Testaments and Last Willes. Swinburne. 1590.

The Interpreter, or Booke, containing the Signification of Words. John Cowell. 1637.

Clarke's Praxis. 1684.

    (This has a book label of John Waugh, Chancellor of Carlisle.)

Philip of Mornay's Booke concerning Trewnes of Christian Religion. Translated by Sir Philip Sidney.

Motives to Holy Living. 1688.

Descartes Principia Philosophiæ. 1656.

Les Plees del Coron :

    (This has book mark of John Waugh.)

Sir Thomas Ridley's Civile and Ecclesiasticall Law. 1634.

---

* Libraries were, at a very early period, collected and kept in connection with churches, which were furnished, not merely with the Scriptures in the original and in translations, together with books necessary for the church service, but with commentaries, homilies, catechisms, and theological works. These libraries were of great importance, and often were very extensive.

H. Grotii de Imperio Summarum Polestatum circa sacra Commentarius
    Postumus.   1648.

Pomponii melæ de situ orbis, &c.   1685.

Hierocles.   *(Greek and Latin.)*   1673.

S. Clementis Epist : ad Corinthios.   1669.

S. Petri Epist : Explic : Amesius.   1635.

Examen Responsionis Fausti Socini, per Joannem Junium.   1628.

Opus Caroli magni, &c.   1549.

Theophilus ad Autolycum.   1684.

Nemesius de Natura Hominis.   *(Greek and Latin.)*   1671.

Epist : IV., de Turcis, &c,   1674.

Salmasii Responsio ad Johannem Miltonum.   1660.

Quæstionum Juris Civilis Centuria.   R. Zouchei.   1660.

Theses Theolog :   Sedanenses.   1675.

Theses Theolog :   Sedanenses.   1683.

Prælectiones Theolog : per Joan Davenantium.   1631.

Opera Theolog :   Curcellæi.   1675.
      (Donation of Jno. Fitch, of Dorchester, 1689.)

De Monachatu.   Hospinianus.

Rationale Divinorum Officiorum.

Origenis Dialogus contra Marcionitas.   *(Greek and Latin.)*   1624.

Codex Canonum Eccles : Primit : a Beveregio.   1678.

Origenis Contra Celsum :   *(Greek and Latin.)*   1677.

Philosophia Vetus et Nova, 2 vols.   1684.

Orphan's Legacy.   J. Godolphin.   1685.
      (Has Jno. Waugh's book mark.)

Abridgment of Eccles : Laws.   J. Godolphin.   1687.

Exposition of Judiciall Lawes.   John Weemse.   Vols. 2 and 3.   1636.

Polit : Eccles : 2 vols.   Parker.   1616.

The Countrey Justice.   Dalton.   1622.
      (Book mark of John Waugh.)

De Jurisdictione Imperiali.   Schardius.   1566.

Origenis Opera, 2 vols.

Forbesii Opera, 2 vols.   1703.

Centur : Magdeburg : 8 vols.   1589.

S. Chrysostomi Opera, 8 vols.   1612.

S. Augustini Opera, 5 vols.   1616.

Jansenii Augustinus.   1652.

Chronicon Eccles : Græcæ Cyprii, &c.   *(Greek and Latin.)*   1679.

A Supplement to the Morning Exercise.   1676.

Theologia Speculativa, by R. Fiddes, B.D.   1718.

Nizolius.   *(Front part lost.)*

De Dieu in Acta Apost.   Ludovico.   1634.

Epiphanii Opera, 2 vols.   1682.

Goldasti Monarchia Imperii Romani.   1612.

Goldasti Politica Imperialia.   1640.

Cornelii a Lapide Opera, 3 vols.   1618.

Collectio Conciliorum.   Stephanus Baluzius.   Vol. 1.   1683.

Concordance.   Cotton and Newman.   1643.

Whitakeri Opera Theolog : 2 vols. in 1.   1610.

Foxe's Martyrs, 2 vols.   1631.

Cyrilli et Synesii Opera.   *(Greek and Latin.)*   1640.

Heptas Præsulum.   1639.

Hist : Rerum in Orien :   1587.

Origenis Omnia Opera, 2 vols.

Bulli Opera Omnia.   1703.

Bibliotheca Sancta, a Sixto Senensi.   1610.

Erasmi Adagia.   1539.

D. Chamieri Panstratiae Catholicæ, 2 vols.   1629.

The Soule's Conflict with it Selfe.   R. Sibbes.   1635.

The Sanctuary of a Troubled Soul.

On the last leaf of this book is written—

> " The truth in this I am sure is tould
> Dispise it not because its old
> Peruse it well and you will find
> A cordial fitted for the mind "

Many of the volumes retain their original bindings, whilst others have been rebound and trimmed. A large number of the works appear to have belonged to a " Tho : Tullie," as that name occurs very frequently on the first or second leaf of the books.

Charities at the Disposal of the Vicar and Churchwardens.

O far as this work is concerned, it would be out of place to deal with the charities of the town generally, and this notice is confined to those in which the vicar and churchwardens are particularly interested.

In 1701. "It is agreed that the church wardens shall provide a handsome 'table' to hold the charities of this parish."

In 1708. "It is agreed that the church wardens have 2 'tables' for the gifts of the charity school."

At the present time only one tablet is left, and that is in the vestry, and is as follows :—

A table expressing the names of those which have ben benefactors to the ffreeschoole & poore of Bromesgrove

The worthy Staffords doale $\overset{a}{xx}$ yerely for ever to y^e poore to be dealt at Christm. and Easter.

William Balis of Bromesgrove gent. gave : 2 : Closes called Chandlers, nowe being let at v^l pr. ann^n to be payd to the poore yerely for ever.

*William Sheldon gent: gave v^l the interrest thereof to remaine to the poore for ever.

*Robt. Caldwall of whitford gent : gave v^l the interrest thereof to remaine to the poore for ever.

Nicholas Lylly of Bromesgrove gent: gave $\overset{a}{xx}$ to be dealt yerely for ever, to the poore, and to be payed out of the land which he gave to Raynold Lylly in Bromesgrove. And also $\overset{a}{x}$ yerely to the freeschool given by the said Nicholas and Richard Tirier of Bromesgrove, and to be payd by John Lylly and his heires.

*— Palmer of Alcester Butcher gave x^l the interrest thereof to remaine to the poore for ever.

Henry Brooke of Bromesgrove upholster gave x^l the interrest thereof to remaine to the poore for ever.

*Thomas Wilkes of Bircott gave $\overset{a}{xL}$ the interrest thereof to remaine to the poore for ever.

Thomas Chance of the cittie of Worcester gent : gave xv^l the int. thereof to be payd to the freeschoole yerely for ever.

---

* These donations, amounting to £44 10s., are supposed to have been laid out at an early period, either in the purchase of the closes called "The Flats," or in part of the purchase of the land called "The Riddings," which formed part of the Linthurst Farm ; but there are no conveyances, or other documents relating thereto, now to be found in the possession of the trustees.

Ales Tomms of Bromesgrove widd: gave x̊x̊x̊ and Willia. Taylor of Ashborough
gave x̊x̊ both did (will?) the dole thereof should be dealt in yᵉ bread to yᵉ poore
at church yerely for ever.

in Aᵒ dni : { John Lylly / John Butler } { Richard Dureling / John Boweter } { Church / Wardens } 1636 :

Another table of benefactions, which was in the church at the time of the
Charity Commissioners' enquiry, in 1832, contained, amongst other donations,
that of Thomas Jolliffe, Esq., of Coston Hacket, £20.*

About 1845, a list of the charities was printed, a copy of which hangs up in the
vestry. With a few alterations and additions it is as follows :—

THE BROMSGROVE CHARITIES,

WHICH REQUIRE

THE ATTENTION OF THE MINISTER AND CHURCHWARDENS.

——o——

THE REV. JOHN WELCH, who died September 16th, 1800, bequeathed the sum of
£20, to be invested in the public funds, or real security ; the interest thereof
to be paid to the Vicar of Bromsgrove, or his Curate ; to be by them given
away yearly at Christmas, to such poor persons of that parish as they shall see fit.
The amount was formerly receivable at the Worcester Old Bank, on the 14th of
January and July, respectively.—At the Charity Commissioners' enquiry on July
2nd, 1879, the Vicar said this fund remained in abeyance for some time. It
now consisted of £23 18s. 8d. New Three Per Cents., from which he obtained
14s. 4d., distributed in small sums of 2s. each to poor widows. It was not
considered desirable to distribute this charity in this manner.

JAMES RIDGWAY, who died July 23rd, 1839, bequeathed the residue of his personal
estate, which amounted to £330 (£170 was invested with the Local Board on
mortgage of the town rates, and the remainder in Consols), to the Minister and
Churchwardens of Bromsgrove, for the time being, and their successors in office :
to be invested in funded or real security, and the interest thereof to be given
annually on the 21st of December, in bread, to the deserving poor of the said
parish.—At the enquiry, it was stated that the deed in relation to this fund could
not be produced, but Mr. Holyoake said the interest (£12 10s. 3d.) was regularly
spent in bread.

* See note page 42.

I

JAMES WILKINSON, who died March, 1821, bequeathed £2 annually; payable on the 14th of March, to the Churchwardens, out of a field on the Kidderminster Road, called Brick-Kiln Field (built upon by Mr. B. Sanders), to keep his tomb in Bromsgrove Churchyard in repair—to be cleaned and painted once in seven years; and the overplus to be expended in coals, and divided amongst the inmates of the Alms Houses in the said parish. In the year 1845 receivable of Mr. B. Sanders.—This charge is regularly paid by Mr. T. T. Sanders, on account of land on which Denmark Cottage is built.

JOSEPH SMITH, bequeathed the sum of £5 annually; payable out of the Clock House Estate, at Bournheath, in the parish of Bromsgrove, on the 1st of November, to the Minister, Churchwardens, and Overseers of the said parish; to be by them expended in "some Woollen Manufacture," the same to be "made up into garments," and distributed to some "poor widows, decayed persons, and fatherless children, within the parish of Bromsgrove, on St. Thomas's Day."—At the enquiry, it was stated that this charity was regularly paid, and distributed by the Church-wardens.

WIDOW ROBERTS, left £40 in trust, to be laid out in some convenient purchase of land or property, and, with the consent of the Churchwardens, to distribute the rent among twelve poor widows.—It appears that this sum was expended on the restoration of two houses in St. John Street, occupied by W. Duffill and another (?) and that the money has never been repaid; but a sum of £2, being interest at the rate of 5 per cent., is paid to the Churchwardens annually (10s. to each Churchwarden), and by them distributed, in sums of 3s. 4d. each, to twelve poor widows.

REV. THOMAS WARREN, of Inkberrow, in 1867, left £200 to the Bromsgrove Burial Board, to be invested by them; the annual income from which—after payment of repairs to the tombstone over the grave of his wife in the Bromsgrove Cemetery—was to be devoted to the purchase of warm clothing for poor people of the congregation of St. John's Church.—At the enquiry, the Inspector said that, according to the decision of Fitch v. the Attorney-General, this gift was strictly void. The money was stated to have been employed in the purchase of £212 4s. 4d. Three Per Cent. Consolidated Annuities, producing £5 15s. 10d., given away in flannel at Christmas. The Inspector suggested that this bequest should be handed over to the Consolidated Charities. Mr. Amphlett said the mode of administering was by tickets, inscribed with the names of each recipient, being handed over by the Vicar and Churchwardens to the members of the Burial Board.

MARY MACKEG, who died November 24th, 1832, bequeathed the sum of £200, less duty of £20, to be invested in the public funds, or on mortgage ; the interest thereof to be received by the Vicar and Churchwardens of Bromsgrove ; and after the payment for duly repairing the monument erected in Bromsgrove Churchyard, to the memory of Samuel Mackeg, the remainder to be by them distributed on St. Thomas's Day, to poor resident parishioners of the parish of Bromsgrove, in sums not exceeding three shillings to any one family in one year.—The money was invested in the purchase of land, at the Lickey End, paying 4½ per cent., the yearly income being £8 2s. The deeds are in the parish chest, and the amount is regularly received.

SIMON CRANE, by deed, dated July 10th, 1787, gave to the Vicar and Church-wardens of Bromsgrove for the time being, twenty shillings annually ; payable on the 28th of October, out of Houses situate near the centre of the south side of High Street, Bromsgrove, now the property of the Stourbridge and Kidderminster Banking Company ; to be by them expended in Musical Instruments and Books for the choir of Singers in Bromsgrove Church ; or, in the instruction of Boys to sing in such choir, after providing for the keeping of his brother's tomb in repair.

The Inspector subsequently read a summary of the charities, from which it appeared that the Churchwardens have in their keeping gifts to the number of 962, viz., 546 bread, 175 flannel, 124 sheets, and 117 dresses. These figures, it was stated, always remained about the same.

———————

OLD SWINFORD HOSPITAL.—The parish of Bromsgrove is entitled to send to this institution two boys, nominated by the parishioners in vestry, and recommended by the Vicar and Churchwardens. The lads are maintained, clothed, and educated in, and apprenticed from the institution.

EDWARD MOORE, Esq., of Barnt Green, who died in 1746, left an annuity of £5 per annum out of his estate, to be paid to the Vicar of the parish so long as daily Prayers shall be read in the said Parish Church, and in default thereof, the £5 to be given away in cloth to the poor of the parish.—The amount was secured (?) on an estate joining up to Twatling Street, and was for many years received in November, and expended in linen cloth ; but when the Earl of Plymouth purchased the estate no notice was given of the charge, when, upon a demand made, and a subsequent enquiry into the circumstances, it was discovered that the grant was void, under the Statute of Mortmain, the deed not having been enrolled, and the grantor having died within twelve months of the date.

The Belfry.

THE belfry, in the tower at the west end of the church, is reached by a spiral staircase, the steps of which, at the lower part, are cased in oak, on account of the worn condition of the stone. It contains an excellent peal of 10 bells, which bear the following inscriptions :—

Treble.   PURCHASED BY SUBSCRIPTION 1816

          J. LAWRENCE OF WHITFORD FIRST SUBSCRIBER

Second. T. MEARS OF LONDON FECIT 1816

Third.   THOMAS RUDHALL GLOCESTER FOUNDER 1773

Fourth. T. *(impression of a bell)* R. 1773 WHEN YOU US RING

                                 WE'LL SWEETLY SING

Fifth.   GOD PROSPER THIS PARISH A. R. *(impression of a bell)* 1701

Sixth.   IOHN WAUGH VICAR T. *(impression of a bell)* R. 1773

Seventh. REVᴰ Dᴿ WINGFIELD VICAR

          Wᴹ WARD THOMAS GREENING THOS WRIGHT

          JOSEPH GABB CHURCHWARDENS 1816 ⁂

          T. . MEARS OF LONDON FECIT

Eighth. JOHN CROMWELL RICHARD WILKES

          DANᴸ HARRIS THOˢ TAYLOR

          CH: WARDENS 1773

Ninth.   THE REVᴰ THOˢ FOUNTAIN VICAR

          INº AISHMORE C: WRIGHT I: BADGER

            & R: WILKES WARDENS 1790 ⁂

Tenor.   I TO THE CHURCH THE LIVING CALL

          AND TO THE GRAVE DO SUMMON ALL 1773*

The fourth and fifth bells are without canons. The fourth is a maiden bell. The ting-tang is dated 1816.

There appear to have been bells in the tower of Bromsgrove Church from a very early period, for on July 10th, 1691, "It is agreed that the Ringers shall have but 5 . on any Ringing day except the 5th of November† and then 6. 6ᵈ and the ringers shall not ring without the consent of the churchwardens." At this time there were probably five bells, for, on October 11th, 1695, "It is agreed to cast the five bells

---

* A great many of the bells cast by Rudhall bear this inscription.

† In 1705, "It is agreed that the Ringers shall have 10/- for ringing on the 5th of November;" and in 1718, "It is agreed that the Ringers have 10/- on the 5th November and King's Coronation and 6/8 on other ringing days."

into six the same being out of repair." In 1701, "It is agreed that Abram Rudhall shall new cast the *six* Bells and the Bell at the Town Hall and that the clock and chimes be repaired." Only one of these bells so recast (the fifth) is left in the tower. On March 21st, 1773, "It was agreed to have three of the Bells new cast and two new ones to make eight." On the same date, Thomas Rudhall, of Gloucester, was instructed to perform the work, the cost of which was £117 16s., towards which sum £33 15s. 4d. was collected by a town subscription. The bells which were new and recast were the third, fourth, sixth, eighth, and tenor. In 1790, the present ninth bell was recast; and in November, 1815, a subscription for adding two other bells—the treble and second—and for recasting the present seventh, was started, when John Lawrence, of Whitford, "first subscriber," gave £10. These bells, with the ting-tang, were cast by Thomas Mears, of London. On November 22nd, 1815, Mr. Thomas Paul, of Bristol, was agreed with by the inhabitants and churchwardens to "rehang, repair, and tune the bells, with the following amendments for different charges :"

	£	s.	d.
8 Pairs of new Brasses and turned Gudgeons	10	0	0
8 new rings to the Bell wheels with four iron stays and 2 coupling screw bolts to each	12	0	0
8 new guide wheels to receive the Ropes from the Bell wheels and stays to fix the same on	5	0	0
8 new ash stays, slides, and rests to support the Bells when up, each stay to be fixed to the stock with iron screw bolts	5	0	0
Repairing all the iron work of the hangings and Japanning the same	4	0	0
Workmanship	12	0	0
Tuning the 8 Bells	5	0	0
	£33	0	0

I agree to the above Thomas Paul

John Adams	George White	Benjamin Tilt
Will. Ward	John Rose	William Haden
John Watterson	James Tandy	
Tho. Amphlett	Thom. Wright	

The staging of the bells was again repaired in 1871, at a cost of about £25, and the first peal after the completion of the work was rung on Thursday, July 27th, 1871, to welcome Mr. William Holyoake, the senior churchwarden, and his bride on returning from their wedding tour. The formal opening ringing did not take place till Monday, September 11th, 1871, when ringers attended from Worcester, Birmingham, Chaddesley Corbett, and Belbroughton, and rung out merry peals during the greater part of the day. Later in the day about 40 ringers partook of a substantial repast at the Golden Lion Inn; the Rev. G. W. Murray, vicar, presided. There were also present—Rev. Ll. Jones (curate), Rev. J. B. Wilson, Messrs. W. Holyoake, A. Bennett, J. R. Horton, and S. Saywell, churchwardens, and others.

On February, 18th, 1703, it was agreed, "That Thomas Hemming, the sexton, shall have 25/- more than the clerk allows him for ringing the bell at 4 o'clock in the morning and at eight at night, to be payed yearly to him, or any one the church-wardens think proper." On December 2nd, 1730, it was agreed, "That William Taylor, Clerk, shall have 30/- per year for winding up the church clock and chimes and shall have 25/- for ringing the bell at 4 o'clock in the morning and 8 at night as allowed to Richard Hemming." The morning bell, for many years rung at four o'clock, and afterwards at five o'clock, is now discontinued altogether; but the curfew still

> Tolls the knell of parting day.

Every evening, at eight o'clock, a bell is rung for about five minutes; after which, on the tenor bell, the day of the month is chimed, as, for instance, on the first day of the month the bell is chimed once; on the second, twice; and so on every evening throughout the year, except on Sundays, when neither the eight o'clock bell or the day of the month is tolled. On Saturday evenings the bell is rung at seven instead of eight o'clock. The origin of this custom is that William the Conqueror, by his partiality for his Norman followers created many enemies, and to prevent them holding seditious meetings he ordered a bell to be rung every evening at eight o'clock, at which time all fires and candles were to be put out or covered. From that time till the present, upwards of 800 years, the eight o'clock bell has been known as the curfew, or cover bell. There is yet another trifling circumstance, which all may not have noticed. When a male corpse is about to be buried in our cemetery, "the passing" bell is tolled three times three, both at the commence-ment and conclusion of tolling time; and in the case of a female corpse, it is tolled three times two only. This custom has prevailed here probably for centuries.*

On December 5th, 1774, "It is agreed at this Vestry that Whereas there was at a former meeting by a sett of Ringers Agreed with the Church Wardings that if the parish could have Eight Bells they could Ring the Fixd Ringing Days in Every Year for three years without having aney pay from the church wardings for so Ringing untill the 29 May 1776 they having the privelidge and proffits for Ringing

---

* The tolling of bells at the decease of a person, and at funerals, was originally an expedient of a superstitious age to frighten away demons that were supposed to be hovering around to prey upon the spirit of the dead or dying. This superstition was widely extended during the dark ages. Bells were often rung with violence also, during a tempest, to frighten away demons, and avert the storms which they were supposed to raise.

for Weddings and on aney other Ocation untill the end of the Terme and whereas part of the same Ringers did Refuse and Neglect to ring on the 26th Oct. last Whe do exclude all such ringers from all Benefits that shall arise from Ringing and whe do chuse the under written to ring according to the former agreement and in case aney one of them Die the church-warding shall elect another."

Bromsgrove has long been noted for its change ringing, and in the bell-ringers' loft are four tablets recording some extraordinary feats in the campanological art, especially one on the 29th of December, 1788. To the general reader these tablets will not possess much interest, but to those acquainted with the mysteries of change ringing they will be welcome.

CHANGE RINGING.

On Monday Decr. 31st 1787 was rung at the Parish Church of Bromsgrove, by the United Society of this place, in 6 hours and 33 Minutes a Compleat Peal of Bob Major Containing 10192 changes, By the following Persons : J Ledbury Treble, C Ravenscroft 2nd J Ravenscroft 3rd G Thomson 4th J Dunn 5th T Brooke 6th W Johnson 7th B Tilt & R Brooke 8th

On the 29th of December 1788, was rung at the above Place a true Peal of Bob Major containing 12000 Changes in 7 hours and 38 Minutes, by the following Persons : J Ledbury Treble, J Tandy 2nd R Brooke 3rd J. Rose 4th C Ravenscroft 5th T Brooke 6th B Tilt & W Johnson 7th G Thomson & J Dunn 8th The above Peals were composed and conducted by Mr C Ravenscroft.

On the 26 of Decr 1816, Was rung at the above Place a true Peal of Grandsire Royal containing 5160 changes in 3 hours & 35 Min utes By the following persons : J Barrett treble, B Tilt 2nd J Rose 3rd T Rose 4th J Tandy 5th B Ravenscroft 6th J Skidmore 7th R Pearce 8th W Rose 9th G Rose Tenor. On the 18 of August 1817 Was rung at the above place a true Peal of Oxford Treble Bob Royal containing 5000 changes in 3 hours and 20 minutes, by the following Persons : R Brooke Treble, R Pea rce 2nd T Ravenscroft 3rd T Rose 4th J Rose 5th B Ravenscroft 6th J Skidmore 7th B Tilt 8th

J Ledbury 9th W Rose Tenor. On the 8th of Octr 1827, Was rung at Bromsgrove a true Peal of Bob Major comprising 3040 Cha nges, in 3 hours and 9 minutes : By the follow ing Persons, S Giles Treble, J Duffill 2nd E Pearce 3rd J Tandy 4th R Pearce 5th W Crump 6th J Ledbury 7th R Wright 8th. On the 30th of Octr 1827 Was rung at Bromsgrove, a true Peal of Grandsire Cators comprising 6111 Changes, in 4 hours and 10 minutes, By the following Persons : S Giles Treble, J Duffill 2nd J Rose 3rd E Pearce 4th W Rose 5th W Crump 6th R Pearce 7th Who composed and conducted the peal. R Wright 8th J Ledbury 9 T Facer tenor. On the 18 of Feby. 1828, Was rung at Bromsgrove a true Peal of Kent Treble Bob Major comprising 5,088 changes in 3 hours and 7 minutes By the following Persons : J Ledbury Treble, J Duffill 2nd E Pearce 3rd W Crump 4th J Rose 5th R Pearce 6th R Wright 7th W Rose Tenor. On the 21 of July 1843, Was rung at Bromsgrove a true Peal of Grandsire Tripples comprising 5040 cha nges, in 3 Hours & 4 Minutes, By the following Persons, J Duffill Treble R Pearce 2nd W Coley 3rd J Amess 4th Coley 5th J Higgs 6th I Overton 7th J Hall Tenor. On the 29th of Octr 1853, Was rung at Bromsgrove a true Peal of Grandsire Tripples comprising 5040 Changes in 2 Hours & 58 Minutes, By the following persons, M Wright Treble, W Duffill 2nd W Chattles 3rd R Wright 4th J Duf fill 5th J Robinson 6th I Overton 7th W Hill Tenor

CHANGE RINGING.

On Monday, Novr. 3rd 1856, Was
performed upon the Bells
of the Parish Church of
Bromsgrove, a true peal of
Grandsire Tripples contain
ing 5040 Changes, in three
Hours and one Minute, By
the following Persons :

W. Danby	Treble	J. Brain	5th
T Rose	2nd	W Duffill	6th
J Evans	3rd	I Overton	7th
J Duffill	4th	W Jones	Tenor

The above Peal was conducted
BY MR. W. DUFFILL.

CHANGE RINGING.

On Monday Jan'' 26, 1863, Was rung by the
Society of Change Ringers Bromsgrove,
with the assistance, of Messrs. B & J Bate
of Bellbroughton a true Peal of Grandsire
Tripples, containing 5040 Changes in 2 hour'
and 58 Minutes : By the Following Persons

William Danby	*Treble*	*Benjamin Bate*	*5th*
James Bate	*2nd*	*William Duffill*	*6th*
Joseph Rose	*3rd*	*Isaac Overton*	*7th*
Joseph Evans	*4th*	*Frederick Wright*	*Tenor.*

On Monday May 1ˢᵗ 1865, Eight of the
Society of Change Ringers Bromsgrove,
ascended the Tower of the Old
Church Kidderminster and succeeded
in ringing a complete Peal of Grandsire
Tripples, containing 5040 Changes in 3
Hours & 11 Minutes : By the Following Persons

William Danby	*Treble*	*Joseph Evans*	*5th*
Samuel Crowther	*2nd*	*William Duffill*	*6th*
Elijah Cramp	*3rd*	*Reuben Broomfield*	*7th*
Charles Hatton	*4th*	*James Parry*	*Tenor.*

N.B. There had not been a Peal rung upon
the bells of the Old Church since April 29ᵗʰ 1765.
*The above peals were conducted by W*ᴹ *Duffill.*

CHANGE RINGING.

On Tuesday, Feby 13th 1866, Eight of
the Society of Change Ringers
Bromsgrove ascended the Tower
of this Church and rung a true
Peal of Grandsire Tripples contain
ing 5040 Changes in 3 Hours and 2
Minutes, By the Following Persons

George Perrygrove	Treble	William Duffill	5th
George Bourne	2nd	Elijah Crump	6th
Joseph Evans	3rd	Reuben Broomfield	7th
Charles Hatton	4th	James Parry	Tenor.

CONDUCTED BY W. DUFFILL

On Monday, April 2nd 1866, Was rung a
true Peal of Grandsire Cators containing 5095 Changes in 3 Hours and 16
Minutes, By the Following Persons,

John Wood	Treble	Charles Hatton	6th
George Bourne	2nd	Reuben Broomfield	7th
Elijah Crump	3rd	William Duffill	8th
William Danby	4th	Isaac Overton	9th
Joseph Evans	5th	James Parry	Tenor.

. CONDUCTED BY W. DUFFILL

On Monday, October 18th 1869* was rung
a true Peal of Grandsire Cators con
taining 5004 Changes in 3 Hours and 15
Minutes By the Following Persons.

John Wood	Treble	Charles Hatton	6th
George Bourne	2nd	Reuben Broomfield	7th
Elijah Crump	3rd	William Duffill	8th
William Danby	4th	Isaac Overton	9th
Joseph Evans	5th	James Parry	Tenor.

CONDUCTED BY W DUFFILL

* The anniversary of the society.

G

In addition to the foregoing, there is a tablet with this inscription :—

In Memory of
Chas Ravenscroft
who died Septr 18 1812 aged 46 yrs.

Ah CHARLES ! thy ringing now is o'er
Thou'lt call the merry peals no more,
To Single, nor to Bob, direct
To give each Change its due effect,
Nor teach the inexperienced youth
The course to range with ease and truth
Of this no more, give up thou must,
And mingle with thy parents dust
Into its place thy Bell is come
And Ruthless death has brought *the* home.

The following rules,* made in November, 1875, are printed and hung up in the belfry :—

BROMSGROVE
PARISH CHURCH BELLRINGERS' RULES.

1.—That the Society of Ringers consist of Ten Members and Two Supernumeraries.

2.—That the Ringers shall appoint from among themselves a Treasurer, to whom all Monies shall be paid, and by whom it shall be divided amongst the Ringers ; and in case of any dispute, the matter shall be referred to the Vicar and Churchwardens, whose decision shall be final.

3.—That no person shall be admitted into the Society except by the Vicar and Churchwardens, and that any Ringer guilty of misconduct, particularly of making use of bad Language, or of intoxication while engaged in his duties at the Church, shall be reported to the Vicar and Churchwardens, who will instantly dismiss such offender from the Society.

---

* In the last century the rules of bellringers were often written in verse, and generally painted on a board and fixed in the belfry. As, for instance, in the belfry of Bredgar—

" My friendly ringers, I do declare
You must pay one penny each oath you do swear
To turn a bell over
It is the same fare ;
To ring with your hats on you must not dare
MDCCLI "

4.—That the Ringers shall undertake to Chime on Sundays, and to perform all other duties connected with the Bells, except such as belong to the office of Sexton.

5.—That the Ringers shall be required to appear in the Belfry on the Sabbath Day in clean and decent apparel, or be subject to a fine, the amount of which shall be determined upon among themselves.

6.—That any Ringer frequenting a Public-house on a Sunday be expelled from the Society.

7.—That all the Ringers attend Church regularly.

NAMES OF RINGERS.

1. William Duffill†
2. Elijah Crump
3. George Bourne
4. James Parry
5. George Hayward
6. Walter Rea
7. Oliver James
8. Thomas Albutt
9. Joseph Crawford
10. John Perry

SUPERNUMERARIES.
None.

The Clock and Chimes.

THE first known mention of the clock or chimes occurs in 1684, when it was "Agreed that Edward Carter the clerk shall have 20/- per year to take care of the Bells, ropes &c. and shall have 22/- per year to take care of the clock and chimes and 50/- per year to keep them clean." In 1705, it is "Agreed that John Spurstone (?) shall have £4 per year to repair and wind up the church and Town Hall clocks and chimes and keep them clean." In 1739, it is "Agreed to give John and Robert Butler £7 10s. per year to keep in repair the Bells, clock & chimes & clock at Town Hall in every particular." At a meeting held at the Workhouse, February 3rd, 1742, it is "Agreed to give William Southall £6 per year to keep the Bells, Clocks, chimes and Town Hall clock in Repair in

† Conductor, treasurer, and secretary.

every particular & and to give him 10ˢ 6ᵈ towards a new pinion wheel." In 1774, it is "Agreed to give Rich: Brooke £3 per year 'to wind up and clean and finde oyle for the clock and chimes.'" In Dr. Nash's view of the church from Hill Top, the dial of the clock is shown on the south side of the tower, and is square shaped. The present clock was made in 1752. Attached to it was a brass plate, bearing the following particulars :—

Clock made

1752

Dial-Plate Painted

1797

Churchwardens

Edward Kings

Willⁿ Connard

Joseph Duffill

Stephen Packwood

On July 6th, 1831, it was resolved, "That the present Clock Dial shall be taken to pieces, that the best of the boards shall be selected and with these the back of a new dial shall be formed and that to this back a new front shall be attached—formed of well seasoned one inch English oak." But at the suggestions of Mr. Maund and Mr. W. Taylor, it was resolved, "That instead of taking the old dial to pieces—that it shall be made true on its face and covered with one inch Honduras Mahogany." This was agreed to, and tenders were ordered for painting and gilding the dial. At another meeting, on July 12th, tenders were received from John Juggins (£4), and from William Woodhouse (£6), including a lead margin round the clock dial.

In November, 1848, new hands, &c., were put to the clock, at a cost of £27, and the dial was repaired, and afterwards painted by Samuel Clarkson.

The chimes still in the tower (unfortunately entirely out of order and repair), were made by Edward Draycott, a native of Bromsgrove, by trade a brushmaker, and were put up in 1775, at a cost of £100, which sum included the keeping of them in repair for three years. Draycott was ordered to be paid this sum on March 8th, 1775.—*Vide* parish books. In the report of a vestry meeting, held on March 4th, 1778, we read, "Whereas the Chimes are now much out of Repair ocassioned by one of the Bells being overturned by Reason of which they were Damaged by the Rope being Intangled in the work, Ordered that the present Churchwardens pay Edward Draycott the sum of Five pounds immediately after the Chimes shall be put in good order and that a further sum of Sixteen Pounds shall be paid him in Equal proportion for Four Years viz. £4 per annum. Provided the said Edwᵈ· Draycott keep the chimes in good order to the End of the said Term of Four years from the date hereof."

In 1837, the chimes were repaired by Thomas Bingham, of Birmingham, and the "Easter Hymn" and "Life let us Cherish" were added at this time. The second part of the latter tune was put on by Joseph Rose, in 1844. At the church restoration about £100 was spent on "the clock, chimes, and belfry;" and in 1868, the chimes and clock were put in order by Messrs. Gillet and Bland, of Croydon, at a cost exceeding £146. Towards this sum £25 17s. was collected privately, and the remainder was carried to the General Church Expenses Fund. After these repairs had been executed, the chimes were again heard on March 19th, 1869, when the whole series of tunes was run through. They were set to play a different air every twenty-four hours, the arrangement being thus—

Sunday...................... Hanover, or the 104th Psalm.
Monday .... Easter Hymn.
Tuesday .... National Anthem.
Wednesday .... Money Musk.
Thursday.................. Life let us Cherish.
Friday .... 113th Psalm.
Saturday .... From Morn till Night, or Maggie Lauder.

To the two first a symphony was arranged by the late Joseph Rose. Shortly after (July 26th), the chimes rope broke, and the weights (15½ cwt.) fell with a crash to the floor, doing some injury. It was ordered that the defect was not to be repaired till Mr. Gillet had been communicated with. The result of the communication was the substitution of a new steel rope, about the middle of the August following.

Considering that so much money was spent upon the chimes in 1868, and that they have not played for eight or ten years, there is reason to suppose either that the work of reparation was badly done, or that the chimes were nearly useless when the outlay was made. The money would have been of much greater service as a nucleus for providing an entirely new set, on a more approved principle, and one in which the strain upon the barrel is not so great.

The old clock now in the vestry was formerly fixed in the centre of the front of the west gallery.

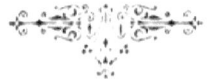

Arms and Monuments.

CONSIDERABLE local and historical interest is attached to the monuments to be found in the church. Adjoining the south wall, on the west side of the south doorway, is a well executed and decorated monumental effigy of Mr. George Littleton, counsellor of law. (Plate II.) He is represented in a reclining position, his elbow on a cushion and his head resting on his hand. He is arrayed in his serjeant's gown, with a ruff round his neck, and a roll in his right hand. The figure rests upon an altar tomb, beneath a semicircular arcade, at the crown of which are the initials, G. L.; above is a horizontal entablature, supported at the angles by columns of the Corinthian order; skulls, torches, hour-glasses, and various other devices complete the design. In an escutcheon at the top his arms are quartered thus: 1, *Littleton;* 2, *Westcote;* 3, *Quatermain;* 4, *Burley;* quartering all *Shrewsbury's* arms, and the arms of *Paston.* On the right side of the monument, Littleton's arms quartering Shrewsbury's single coat; and on the left, Littleton empaling Argent a lion rampant Sable debruized with a fesse counter-compony Or and Azure. Under the arch, on the right, Littleton empaling Talbot; on the left, Littleton empaling Stanley, and these quarterings: 1. Argent on a bend Azure three stags' heads cabossed Or. Stanley. 2. Or on a chief indented Azure three plates. 3. Azure three hunters' horns stringed Argent. 4. Gules a chevron between three hurts Or, a mullet on the chevron. 5. Or, three chevronels Gules. 6. Sable six fleurs-de-lis, three, two, and one; the field replenished with cross croslets fiché, a canton Ermine. 7. Azure three fusils Or. 8. Sable a chevron between three lozenges.

At the back of the arcade, on an oblong panel, in incised gilt lettering, is the following verse :—

> " QVI LEGES HÆC, LEGES FATORVM DISCE TVORVM,
> QVAS IPSI NEQVEVNT LEGVM VITARE PERITI.
> ECCE LYTELTONVS TVMVLO CONCLVDITVR ISTO
> QVI LEGVM PATRI LYTELTONO SANGVINE IVNCTVS,
> IVNCTIOR INGENII EST STVDIIS & DOTIBVS IISDEM
> IVDICIS VT TITVLO PARITER IVNCTISSIMVS ESSET
> NON INCERTA FIDES ET SPES CERTISSIMA MANSIT,
> INVIDA SVRGENTI SI VIVERE FATA DEDISSENT."
> GEORGIVS ISTE EX ROGERO PATRE
> OBIIT QVINQVEGENARIVS 28° MAII 1600.

Plate II

Mr GEORGE LYTELTON

Which translated reads :—

> " Child of this earth, one instant pause, to view
> The doom pronounc'd against thy sinning world.
> The old, the young, the wise, the beautiful, .
> Must perish all, and still the fairest first.
> Lo ! Littleton lies here, conjunct in name
> With him, the father of our British law :
> In name alike, but far more close resembling
> In mind, in thought, in talents, in pursuits.
> Oh ! certain fame had shed around her honours,
> Had given his name to rise pre-eminent,
> Defying death,—but envious fate forbade."

George Littleton was the eldest son of Roger Littleton, who was the fifth son of John Littleton, by Elizabeth, daughter and coheiress of Sir Gilbert Talbot, of Grafton, and Anne his wife, coheiress of Sir William Paston. By the will of his uncle, Sir John Littleton, Knight, he inherited the manor and farm of Grovelly, in the parish of Cofton Hacket, and some land near Barnt Green, in Bromsgrove parish, called Pynton Fields. He died without issue, May 28th, 1600, in which year the monument was erected, and it was repaired and redecorated in 1864. Originally it stood within the communion rails on the south side of the chancel, and was enclosed with iron railings, which were taken down and sold during the time the Rev. John Waugh was vicar (1754–1777).

The tomb is a fair specimen of the Elizabethan style of ornamental architecture, and by its inscription and display of heraldic decoration, forcibly recalls to the mind the well-known words of Gray—

> " The boast of heraldry, the pomp of pow'r,
> And all that beauty, all that wealth e'er gave,
> Await alike th' inevitable hour ;
> The paths of glory lead but to the grave."

On the north wall of the chancel, at the extreme west, is a neat and very handsome marble monument to the memory of John Hall, D.D., the only son of John Hall, vicar of this parish from 1624 to 1652, and grandson of Richard Hall, of Worcester, clothier, by Elizabeth, née Bonner, his wife. Dr. Hall was Prebendary of Worcester in 1676, and was a scholar of Pembroke Hall, Oxford. He was also master of Pembroke College for 45 years, and was consecrated Bishop of Bristol in 1691, in the reign of William and Mary. He died at Oxford, February 8th, 1710, aged 77 years. On the monument is a long Latin inscription, composed by Rev. William Adams, M.A., once a student of Christ Church, Oxford, and Rector of Staunton-upon-Wye, Herefordshire. The following is a translation, made by Rev. Ll. Jones :—*

Translation of the Epitaph on Bishop Hall's Monument,

IN THE SANCTUARY OF BROMSGROVE CHURCH.

———

Here lies buried
JOHN HALL, DOCTOR OF DIVINITY.
Born in this town, only son of John, Vicar of this Parish :
He was Rector of St. Aldate's Church, Oxford ;
Master of Pembroke College ;
Lady Margaret's Professor of Divinity ;
Chaplain to King Charles II. ;
And, at length, in the reign of William III. and Mary, Bishop of Bristol.
A man of a mind capacious and sublime, of a judgment refined and most acute,
Who united a knowledge of languages with elegant literature,
The polite arts with thorny and recondite sciences,
And, when united, consecrated them to religion ;
Amidst his multifarious learning, modest, humble, holy.
His college, over which he successfully watched for xlv. years,
He taught by his precepts, he ruled by his example, he rendered distinguished
by his dignity,
He improved it by new buildings, and a new master's lodge ;
And, having added to its Scholarships, Fellowships, and Revenues,
He enriched it with a most valuable selection from his own library.
While he strictly insisted upon virtuous conduct in others, he likewise liberally
rewarded it.
Advanced to the Episcopate by the unanimous consent of Divines,
He made a timely refutation of Romish and Socinian errors,
So as more firmly to establish the faith of the Church of England ;
In his lectures and scholastic disputations
Clear, ready, subtle, vigorous ;

---

* The Rev. Llewellyn Jones was Curate of Bromsgrove from May, 1864, till June, 1874, when he was appointed Vicar of Little Hereford. Previous to leaving Bromsgrove he was presented with a handsome testimonial by the inhabitants. He accepted the Bishopric of Newfoundland in February, 1878, was consecrated by the Archbishop of Canterbury in St. Paul's Cathedral, May 1st, and preached his farewell sermons in Bromsgrove Church, previous to departing for his see, May 12th, in the same year.

And, though a lover of peace, yet a strenuous defender of the truth.
In the care of souls he was faithful and unwearied,
And this care, even when raised to the Mitre, and broken by old age, he did not
lay aside.
Mindful of others' salvation because mindful of his own ;
Distributing not merely solid food to adults,
But to the young and tender also the sincere milk of the Word.
Faithfully and constantly explaining the principles of the Gospel,
He equalled the primæval Preachers of the Church, who (as it were) rose again
in him.
Amidst Parish Priests, a most consummate Divine ;
Among Bishops, a most useful Parish Priest ;
Worthy indeed of double honour,
Who, as a laborious shepherd, and wise clergyman,
Served his flock by ruling them, and ruled them by serving them.
In his frequent sermons at Court, at Oxford, in his addresses to the clergy and
laity,
An elegant, eloquent, deep, familiar preacher, according to the genius
of his hearers,
He gained the praise and veneration of all.
Becoming all things to all men, that he might by all means win some to Christ.
He earned dignities, without asking courtiers for them ;
Those, however, which were spontaneously offered, he retained with honour,
Only not refusing them, in order to benefit as many as possible ;
Riches he neglected, unless to spend them on the poor—
To those his house was ever a ready refuge and a treasury,
Amongst these he divided his patrimony.
Making abundant provision—for this neighbourhood especially—
So that when dead he might support those whom he daily fed while alive.
He made the poor his residuary legatees,
In order to find treasure in heaven.

He died at Oxford, Feb. 4, 1710, in the 77th year of his age.

Under the inscription is a Death's head, above which are his lordship's arms (Sable, crusuly argent, three talbot's heads erased of the last langued gules), empaled with the arms of his see ; near the top is a group of cherubs' heads, well executed, and over this is an urn, from which issues a golden flame. From the ceiling is suspended the pastoral staff, as appertaining to a shepherd over Christ's flock ; and also the double-pointed mitre, which was probably introduced as an episcopal ornament about the

9th or 10th century. This monument was originally fixed to the opposite wall, and had over it an oak canopy. Dr. Hall, by his will, bearing date March 19th, 1708, directed that the sum of £800 should be laid out in the purchase of an estate, and £20 of the annual profits arising therefrom be expended in the distribution of clothes, between November 1st and February 2nd, to the poor men and women in the parish of Bromsgrove, who had not received parochial relief; the recipients not to be the same persons for two consecutive years. The value of the clothing to each man was not to exceed 13s.; to each woman, 7s.; unless otherwise directed by the executor, Mr. John Spilsbury,* of Chadwick, who, in conformity with the will, purchased, March 11th, 1811, a farm called Urloxhey, at Elmbridge, in the parish of Dodderhill, and raised the value of the clothing to 18s. and 12s. respectively. The trustees of inheritance were directed by the bishop's will to meet annually on September 23rd, and upon the death of one-third of their number to appoint others to fill up the vacancies thus occasioned. The will also directed that the residue of the profits, after the expenditure of £20 in clothing, was to be laid out by separate trustees in the distribution of Bibles yearly in the parishes of Bromsgrove, Kidderminster, Worcester, Stourbridge, Bewdley, and Droitwich; the trustees of distribution, 10 in number, were to meet at Kidderminster annually, on August 12th, and when reduced by death to three, were to elect others within three months. The administration of this charity was the subject of a long discussion at the Charity Commissioners' enquiry in the Town Hall on July 2nd, 1879.

Dr. Nash says, there was in the church, some years ago, a stone to the memory of "Johannes Hall, A.M., hujus ecclesiae vicarius, ob. Aug. 19, 1652, Anna uxor ejus ob. Jan. 1, 1658," the father of Dr. John Hall. Among the archives of the Dean and Chapter of Worcester is a letter from Charles I., dated February 1st, 1643, directing them to turn out J. Hall, Vicar of Bromsgrove, a rebel, and to admit Anthony Fawkner, to supply his place. Mrs. Phœbe Hall died August 4th, 1717, aged 82.

* John Spilsbury, M.A., was, during the Protectorate, the incumbent of this church. After the Protector's death, and his son's abdication, and at the passing of the Act of Uniformity, he was ejected from his "living," but continued to labour privately in the town as long as he lived. In the sessions rolls we find that in 1654, Edward Sheldon and Nicholas Hill deposed "that upon the 20th day of August the deponents were objecting against one Mr. Spilsbury, who desired to be minister of Bromsgrove, that he had a low voyce: one Humphrey Potter then answered that if he had a low voice he had a *true* voice; unto which Mr. Joseph Amige, now minister of Bromsgrove (as these deponents conceiveth), answered and said, 'Soe have I;' unto whom the said Potter replied, 'Noe, for you have toukl lies in the pulpit,' or words to that effect." Mr. Spilsbury died June 10th, 1669, aged 71 years. He was exceedingly valued by Dr. Hall, whose sister and heiress he married. The bishop ordinarily visited him once a year, and continued some weeks at his house, and when he died made his only child his heir, viz., John Spilsbury, who was for several years pastor of a congregation of Dissenters at Kidderminster, and the father of the worthy Francis Spilsbury, minister of Salters Hall. It is stated that Dr. Hall resided for some time at the "Little Broomhouse."

Plate III

SIR HUMPHREY STAFFORD & HIS WIFE ELEANOR.

At the east end of the north aisle is an alabaster monument to Sir Humphrey Stafford, of Grafton, son and heir of Sir Humphrey Stafford, of Grafton, knight, by Elizabeth his wife, daughter and heiress of Sir John Burdet, knight, displaying a full length recumbent figure of a knight, arrayed in the superb armour of the period ;

Cased from head to foot in panoply of steel.

His head is covered with a conical basinet or helmet, encircled by a rich jewelled wreath, called an *orle*, which was introduced during the reign of Henry IV. for the purpose of contracting the heavy pressure of the jousting helme, worn over it at tournaments. (Plate IV., figure 1.) The basinet is attached to a gorget (a piece of armour worn round the neck, the origin of that which officers now wear when on duty), the fastening being covered by an ornamental border (Plate IV., fig. 2), which is succeeded by the breast plate and back piece ; the shoulders are covered with pauldrons, and the arms and hands protected by brassarts, elbow pieces, vambraces, and cuffed gauntlets, all likewise of plate. Round his neck is suspended the collar of SS. (Plate IV., figure 3), a cognizance introduced by Henry IV., being the initial letter of his favourite motto "Soveragne." Beneath the head is a jousting helme, the crest of which is a boar's head (Plate IV., figure 4), couped upon a wreath mantling and doubling.* The thighs, legs, and feet are incased in cuisses, genoiulleres, jambs, and sollerets pointed at the toes ; rouelle spurs were originally fastened to the heels, but the straps alone of these remain. The bawdrick or girdle, horizontally disposed about the loins, formerly bore the arms of Stafford, within a border engrailed, and an anelace or dagger on the right side : this is now missing, as also the sword, which was suspended on the left side from a belt buckled in front, and crossing the body diagonally, a fashion which had fallen into disuse on the introduction of the bawdrick, in the reign of Edward III. but was, during the 15th century, again revived. At the feet reclines a greyhound.

> Outstretch'd together are express'd
> He and my lady fair :
> With hands uplifted on the breast
> In attitude of prayer ;
> Long visaged, clad in armour, he,
> With ruffled arm and bodice, she.

By the side of Sir Humphrey reposes the effigy of his wife Eleanor, represented in the fashionable dress of her time, viz., a surcote or low bodied gown, fitting close to the shape, with light drawn sleeves ; over this a mantle, open in front, and fastened across the breast by a cordon hanging down. The hair is gathered into a network of an orbicular shape, divided in the middle, mitre-like. (Plate IV., fig. 5.)

---

* When a knight was equipped for the tournament, he wore a wreath upon his helmet, which was generally composed of two skeins of silk, of different colours, twisted together, and answering to the principal colours of the device of his shield.

Round her neck is a double chain. (Plate IV., figure 6.)* Her head is supported by two angels, and a dog and griffin crouch at her feet. The sides of the tomb are divided into square recessed compartments (Plate VI., fig. 1), containing quatrefoils, in the middle of which are small shields ; to these were affixed armorial bearings, but none of them are now discernable. According to Nash they bore the following :— Or a chevron Gules and canton ermine ; Stafford ; quartering Azure, a chief Gules, over all a lion rampant Argent ; Hastang : and empaling Azure a cross Argent ; Aylesbury. The tomb also bore the arms of Palgrave and Burdet. Stafford was heir of Palgrave, and Palgrave heir of Burdet. The inscriptions are worn away. Eight of the compartments originally completing the sides of this tomb now form the front and end of a long seat or sedilia on the south side of the sanctuary.

In the 18th year of the reign of Edward IV., Eleanor, the widow of Humphrey Stafford, founded in the church a chantry of one chaplain, who was daily to say mass at the altar of our lady for the good estate of the king and queen, herself, Sir Humphrey her husband, and Humphrey, Thomas, Elizabeth, Anne, and Joyce, their children. For the support of the chaplain, she granted to Thomas Lytelton, Justice of the Common Pleas, John Catesby, serjeant-at-law, and others, an annual rent of 10 marks, issuing out of her manor of Dodford, in Northamptonshire, with intent that they should pay the same to the chaplain of the said chantry by two equal portions, at Lady-day and Michaelmas. She presented the chaplain, and the Bishop of Worcester gave him institution, and after her death the lords of Dodford presented. Thomas Harding, the first chaplain, was succeeded by Thomas Lancastre, in 1504. Roger Chant (1511) and Thomas Blackweye (1512) also held the office. The deed of the foundation is worded as follows :—

"To all trewe christen men to whom this present writyng indentyd shall come, Alianore Stafford, wydowe, sometyme wyff of Humfrey Stafforde of Grafton, yn the county of Worcestre knyght, sendys gretyng yn our Lord everlastyng. Know ye me the seide Alianore yn my pure wydowhode and lawful power, unto the lovyng and worshepyng of allmyghty God, and of his blessed moder our lady Sainte Mary, and all the saintes of heven, to the augmentation of dyvyne service, and to the helthe, refreshing, and relievyng of the soule of the said Humfrey late myne husbande, and of myne, and of all cristen soulys, by the licence and auctorite of the most cristen prince, Edwarde, by the grace of God, kyng of England, and of France, and lord of Ireland ; and also of the assante of all other having interest in this partye ; to have made, founded, and stablyshed, and by these presentes make, found, and

---

* Mr. Fairholt observes that the earliest ornament for the neck perceived upon the sepulchral effigies and brasses of the middle ages "is a simple double chain of gold, like that worn by the wife of Sir Humphrey Stafford (1450) in Bromsgrove Church, Worcestershire, engraved by Hollis."

Plate IV

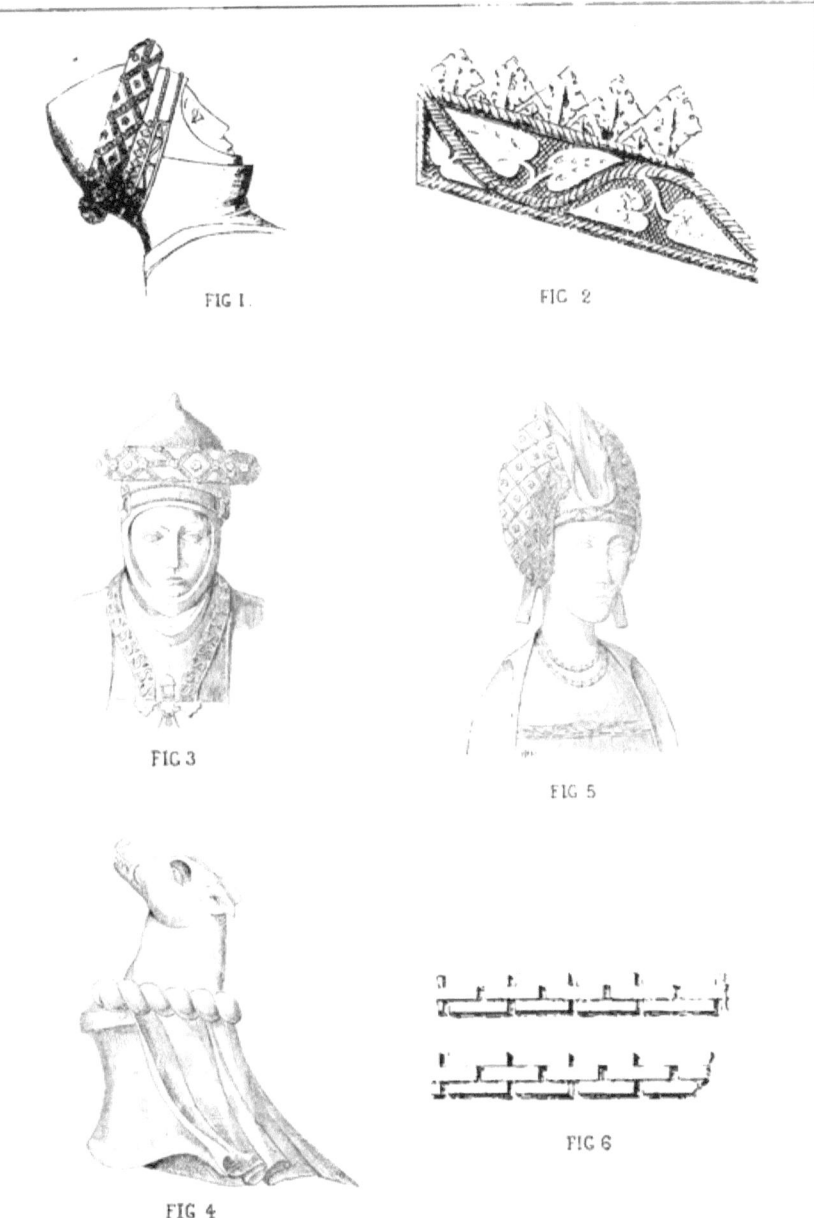

FIG 1.

FIC 2

FIG 3

FIG 5

FIG 4

FIG 6

stablyshe, a chauntrye perpetual of one chapellayn perpetually to doe dyvyne service in the parryshe churche of Bromesgrove, in the seide countye of Worcestor, and atte the auter of our lady in same church dailye to sey masse for the good estate of the seide most cristen prince, and the queen, and of me the seide Alianore, with Humfrey, Thomas, Elizabeth, Anne, and Joyeux, children of the seide Humfrey late my husband and me, during our lives; and for our soules when we be decessed; and for the soule of the said Humfrey Stafford, and for all christen soules. And to the saide chauntrye, by vertu of the lycence above seyde, to have named and presented Thomas Hardyng cappellayne; and to hym, as much as in me is, have graunted and assigned, to have and to hold, to hym, and to his successours cappellayns doyng dyvyne service in the same chauntrye, in the manner and forme hereafter written. And I will that the seyde Thomas Hardyng and his successours in the same chauntry, shall be named and called chappellaynes of the seide Humfrey, knyght; the which chapellaynes, and everych of them, shall dewly kepe and observe, as moche as thym belongith, my wyll and ordinaunces in the articles here following expressed and declared. Fyrst, I woll and ordeyne by these presentes, that the successours of the seyde Thomas Hardyng, chappellaynes of the seyde chauntrye, and everyche of them from the date of these presentes to be admittyd, shall be presentyd by me whyles that I lyve, and after my decesse by the lordys of Dodforde for the tyme beying, unto the bishop of Worcestre, or to his vycar for the tyme beying, within a moneth after the decesse of everyche of the said chappellaynes, and by the same bishop or his said vicare, yn the same chauntrie to be ynstituted, as a chappellaine perpetuall oweth to be, in kepyng of the said chauntrie. And yf hit happen that I the saide Alianore in my lyf, and the lordes of Dodford aforesaide after my decesse, present nat a convenient and able prest to the said chauntrie, within the tyme of a moneth after the decesse of any of the said chapellayns; than I woll that the said bishop of Worcestre for the tyme beying, or the priour of Worcestre, the see beying voyde, present unto the saide chauntrie an able prest, to be instituted in the fourme aforesaide; the ryght and pryvilage of presentation of the said chauntrye to me, and to the lordes of Dodforde for tyme beying, allwey saufe and reservd: when hit shall happen the seide chauntrie then next to be voide in manner and fourme aforesaide. Also I wyll and ordeyne that the saide Thomas Hardyng chapellaine and his successours chapellaynes in the said chauntrie, and everyche of thym, shall dailye and continually be resident in propyr person entending upon the same chauntrie; and daylye say masse, and other dyvyne service, after the use and constitution of the chirche, as the tyme requires, devotly, as God woll graunte theym grace witheouten fraud or negligence. And that every chapellain of the sayde chauntrye, for the tyme beying every Sonday and other festivall dayes, yn his surplice att his own charge pourved,

shall entend the quere of the said parrishe church of Bromesgrove at the first
evensong, matyns, masse, and other canonical houres, with the vicare of the
parryshe : and other ministring divyne service thear. Also I will, that every
chapellain of the said chauntrye in their masses, and other orysons and devocyonnys,
specially pray for me, and all my children, whiles we be alive, and for the soul of the
seyde Humfrey, late my husband, and for my soule after my decesse ; and for the
souls of all my children ; and for the soules of all the benefactours of the sayde
chauntrie, and for all cristen soules : and also there shall yerely kepe the obytte
of the said Humphrey late my housebond, with also myne conjunctly when I shall be
decessed, with placebo, and dirage, and masse of requiem be note, after the
devote usage of holy chirche. Also the said Thomas Hardyng chapellain, and
his successours chappellains in the saide chauntrie, successively, all and every thyng
to the same chauntrie in any wise belonging or perteyneth, as bokes, chalices,
vestments and other ornaments whatsomever, beyng nowe, or what hereafter shall be
purveyde for the behove of the same chauntrie at ther proper costys, expenses, and
charges shall kepe, conserve and susteyne. And yf it be happen any of thym to be
empeired, hurt, lost, or wasted everych of them for his tyme, shall provyde for
the renewyng and repairynge of theym well and competentlye, and theym sufficiently
repared and made shall leve unto his successours withouten diminucyon of theym or
every parcelle of theym. And the said Thomas Hardyng, and everyche of his
successours, chapellains, in the said chauntrye, at their incommyng and institution
yn the same chauntry, shall make a clere and a true inventory by wrytyng endented
of all maner thyng found by him, or theym, or any of them, receyvd, perteygning, or
belongyng unto the seid chauntrie for the tyme beinge with the scalys of eithir
of them scalyd. Also that the seide Thomas Hardynge, nor his successours,
chapellains to the said chauntrye, nor any of theym, yn no maner wise attempte to
do enythyng that may be prejudiciable to the seyde churche of Bromesgrove, or the
parson or vicare of the same chirche pryveley or openly, but every of them shall
dewely entend the monysshyng and advertisements of the said vicare, and hym obey
in all thinges lawfull and honeste for a chauntry prest to doe concerning divine
service, at such time as they aught to entend hit. And ther, nor noon of theym,
shall not meddle nor entermete theym with the cure or governaunce of the said
churche, nor of the parishe : bot yf hit be at the special request of the seyde vicare,
or his depute for the tyme beying. And then yf ther goodely may and woll for their
one meryte and charitable example of other, they may help to supporte their charges
with their good will, and by noon other dewty, or constrainte otherwise then above
is expressed. Also the seide Thomas Hardyng, nor noon of his successours,
chappellians aforesaide, shall not be absente from the seide chauntre past 15 daies,
continuelly, or in the yere past 40 dayes by severall dayes ; and that with cause

reasonable. Also yf the seyde Thomas Hardyng or any of his successours chapellains in the seide chauntrie, thorough age, infirmyte, or other cause, resonable, withouten fraude, fallen thorough Goddys visitacion, where-thorough he ys not of power, and may not doe dyvyne service, and acomplyshe the observaunce of the saide chauutrye, as is aforesaide, he shall not therefore be put removed from his saide chauntrye, bot there to contynue his lyf, during assiduell prayour for the founders and other abovesaide, dulye keping and observyng other articles, of this present ordinaunce after his possibilyte. Also yf the saide Thomas Hardyng, or eny of his successours chapellains in the same chauntrye, be evydentley noted of unclene and vicious lyvyng, and dishoneste conversacyon and demeanyng, or yf he be suspended or irregulier, or use eny thing to clerkes by the lawe inhibyte, and he be thereof convicte, whereby he is not nor may not be of power nor of abilite to observe the premisses; or yf he doe eny thing in prejudice of this present fundacyon, or make waste or destruction of bokes, chalyces, vestiments, or of any other ornaments, or of eny londes or tenementes yn eny wise belongynge or perteigne, or hereafter shall belonge or perteigne unto the said chauntrye; then he, as unable, hys offence so declaring him, shall be remoeved and deprived by the same; and another chapellain of good and vertuous disposicion, and conversation, to be admitted and instituted in the said chauntrye in the fourme abovesaid. And as for the fyndyng and sustenation of the saide chapellain perpetuall doyng dyvyne servyce in the said chauntrye as is aforesaid, I have graunted to Thomas Lytelton oon of the kynges justices of the common place, John Catesby, oon of the kynges justices att the lawe, Richard Jourdan late vicar of Stoke, now vycar of Hull, John Bowdok and Richard Harpecote of Bromesgrove aforesaid, and other nowe decessyd, an annuel rent of ten mark, to be had and perceyvid in, and of my mannour of Dodford in the counte of Northampton, and in and of all other my landes and tenements in the toun and feldes of Dodford aforesaide, at the festes of the annunciacion of our Lady and Sainte Mychell the archangell, by even porcions; with a clause of distresse, to thentent that the same Thomas Lytelton, John Catesby, Richard Jourdane, John Bowdok, and Richard Harpecote, and their heyres, when the chauntrye were stablished and founded, and the kynges licence thereupon inpetred and obteyned the seyde annuel rent of ten marks shuld gyve, graunte, and conferme, to the chapellain of the said chauntrye, and his successours, chapellains, in the same, after the tenor and effect of the fundacion thereuppon made, as by my dede and wrytyng thereof made unto theym more plenely is expressyd and declared. Wherefore; accordyng to thentent of my saide graunt touching the chauntrye aforesaid by me creatyd, founded, and establysshed, by the auctorite and lycence above specified, for a comfirmation of the same, with a perfyte and entier fundacion; as well for the forsaide chauntrie as for the fyndyng and sustentacyon of the saide perpetuell prest; at the instance of my prayer and request, the said Thomas Lytelton, John Catesby, Richard Jourdan, John Bowdock, and Richard Harpecote, by their dede thereuppon to be made and sealyd, have promyssed to geve and graunte to the said Thomas Harding nowe chapellain of the said chauntrye, and to his successours chapellains in the same doyng dyvyng service, as is abovesaid, the foresaide annuell rent of ten marks perpetually, to be had and perceyved in the maner and form hereafter followying :—

"To all faithful servants of Christ, to whom this present indenture cometh, Thomas Litelton, Justice of the Common Pleas, John Catesby, King's Serjeant-at-law, Richard Jordan, formerly vicar of Stoke, now vicar of Doderhill, in the county of Worcester, John Bowdock, and Richard Harpecote, of Bromsgrove, in the aforesaid county of Worcester, greeting in the name of the Lord,

"Whereas Eleanor Stafford, widow, formerly wife of Humphrey Stafford; of Grafton, in Worcestershire; soldier, deceased, by her writing triparted and indented, dated the fifteenth day of March in the thirteenth year of the reign of Edward the fourth (post Conquestum), hath granted to us the aforesaid, 'Thomas,' 'John,' 'Richard,' 'John,' and 'Richard,' and to others now deceased for herself and her heirs a certain rent of six pounds thirteen shillings, and four pence, the aforesaid annual rent to be had and received yearly by us, and by our heirs and assignees, from and in her manor of Dodford in the county of Northampton, also in and from all other lands and tenements in the Town and fields of Dodford aforesaid in the county aforesaid, on the feast of All Angels and of St. Michal the Archangel, in equal portions, with a clause of distress, according as contained in the same deed, With this intent that when a chantry of one chaplain, shall have been erected and stablished in the Church of the Parish of Bromsgrove aforesaid in the said county of Worcester by the abovementioned Eleanor, that we the said 'Thomas,' 'John,' 'Richard,' 'John,' and 'Richard,' should grant the said annual rent to the aforesaid Chaplain and to his successors, chaplains of the aforesaid Chantry, having and receiving the said annual rents for the aforesaid Chaplain and for his successors, chaplains of the aforesaid Chantry as is fully set forth and declared in the aforesaid deed. And whereas the aforesaid Eleanor having lately obtained, with that of others, the licence and authority of the King for herself or for any other person or persons holding her authority, or that of any other person or persons acting in this matter to make found stablish create, and erect in the aforesaid Church of Bromsgrove, a perpetual chantry, consisting of one perpetual chaplain, and the said chaplain and any successor of the said chaplain to be called the Chaplain of Humphry Stafford formerly of Grafton, according as it is clearly set forth in the said letters patent: and the same Eleanor has made, founded, erected, created, and stablished the said Chantry, by virtue of the abovementioned licence, and has named and presented Thomas Harding, Chaplain according to the manner and form of the foundation of the said Chantry as is plainly set forth in the foundation aforesaid. Be it known therefore that we the aforesaid, Thomas Littleton, John Catesby, Richard Jordan, John Bowdock, and Richard Harpecote withe the will and pious intention of the said Eleanor, and by virtue of the letters patent of his Majesty the King, and of others interested in this matter, have given and granted to the said Thomas Harding, Chaplain of the aforesaid Chantry; viz. of Humphrey Stafford formerly of Grafton, Soldier; an annual rent of six pounds, thirteen shillings and four pence to be had and held by him and his successors, Chaplains of the aforementioned Humphrey Stafford, Soldier, holding service in the holy Chantry aforesaid, according to the foundation executed by the said Eleanor. And if the said annual rent of six pounds thirteen shillings, and four pence, be behind, in part or in whole not paid, beyond the term in which it should be paid, then it shall be lawful for the aforesaid Thomas Harding, Chaplain, and for his successors Chaplains of the aforesaid Chantry, or their assignees, or any one of them, to enter into the lands and tenements aforesaid, or any allotment, and to distrain, and it shall be lawful for them to carry away drive and lead and retain in their power those things taken in distress, to take full satisfaction and payment of the rent aforesaid, together with arrears of the same, and expenses of distraint occasioned and sustained.

"In witness of the above writing, we place our seal to one part of this our indenture to remain in the possession of the aforesaid Thomas Harding and of his successors, Chaplains of the aforesaid Chantry. And the said Thomas Harding having affixed his seal to the other part, it remaineth in the possession of the aforesaid Eleanor and of the gentlemen of Bedford abovementioned.

"Dated this 20 day of April in the 18th year of the Reign of Edward the fourth (post Conquestum.")*

"And that this my present foundacion ordinance, and endewmente, as well touching the chauntrye aforesaide, as for the sustentacyon of the said Thomas, chapeleyne, and his successours chapeleynes, doyng divyne service in the same chauntrie, as is aforesaid, shuld hereafter be the more fermely kept and conserved, and obteyne it entier and continuell strength, I have made dowble this same by parties endented ; of the which I woll that on oon partey remaine in the keping of the reverend father in God the Abbot of Evesham, and his successours, and the other party to remaine in the keeping of the said Thomas Hardyng, chapeleyne, and his successours chapeleyns in the forsaid chauntrie, perpetually. And moreover, for a perpetuall remembraunce and plenar confirmacyon thereof, I woll that these presentes be in the registres of the reverend father in God, John by the grace of God, bishop of Worcester, diocesane of the place, and of the venerable parsonnes of the chapitre thear, clearly written and registred. Exhorting furthermore and chargyng on Godds behalve, and our lady Sainte Marie, with all the Saints of hevyn, and upon my blessyng, and under the dredful sentence of Goddes judgement in the last daie of venjaunce, that noon of my heires, childeren, kyn, or allye, nor any other, this my present foundacion, will, and ordinaunce, made in forme abovewritten, thei nor noon of theyme, yn no maner wise lett, distourbe, or impugne, or in any article hereof interupte, dissolve, or adnulle. In wytness of all and sundry things abovesaid, I the foresaid Alianore to the partyes hereof have put my seal.

"Gyven the first day of Aprill in the yer of our Lord 1478, and of the reigne of kyng Edwarde IV. after the Conquest the 18th."—*Nash.*

* Translated from the Latin. "Post Conquestum" signifies "after the Conquest," to show date, as it was not common to place the year on a deed.

In the Augmentation Office, in certain "Certificates of Colleges and Chauntries, &c., 61, No. 10. Temp. Hen. 8. and Edw. 6." mention is made of "The Parishe of Bromsgrove wherein be of houselyng people the number of M. (1000)" "There is one Chaunytre called Stafford's Chauntery w'in the said parishe." And, under the head of "The namys of the Governors Maisters and Incumbentis," we find, "Thomas Jamys Chauntery prist there hath yerely paid out of the man' of Sorford in y' Countie of Northampton in y' nature of a Kent Charge vj^li xiij^s iiij^d unde pro ^xmis^* dno Regi xiij^s iiij^d."

That part of the church assigned as the chantry is supposed by Dr. Nash to be the present vestry.

Judging from the size and length of the figure (6ft. 9in. from the helmet to the toes), Sir Humphrey must have been a fine, well-built, stalwart man. Connected with this monument are some marvellous traditions. A legend, still preserved in this neighbourhood, and carrying us back to the time when Bromsgrove formed part of the great Forest of Feckenham, says, that Sir Humphrey Stafford killed a wonderful wild boar that lived in an enchanted castle, and destroyed all that passed that way ; that he released the lady whose effigy lies beside him from enchantment and the power of the boar ; and that he, as an act of piety, built the church in which he lies, and an abbey near it.

The late Mr. Jabez Allies was at much pains to produce the ballad of "The Jovial Hunter," also connected with this monument. There appears to have been several versions of this ballad, two of which are here given :—

" Sir Robert Bolton had three sons—
    Wind well thy horn, good hunter ;
And one of them was called Sir Ryalas,
    For he was a jovial hunter.

" He rang'd all round, down by the wood side—
    Wind well thy horn, good hunter ;
Till up in the top of a tree a gay lady he spy'd,
    For he was a jovial hunter.

" Oh ! what dost thou mean, fair lady, said he —
    Wind well thy horn, good hunter ;
Oh ! the wild boar has killed my Lord and his
        men thirty,
    As thou be'st a jovial hunter.

" Oh ! what shall I do, this wild boar to see—
    Wind well thy horn, good hunter ;
Oh ! thee blow a blast, and he'll come unto thee,
    As thou be'st a jovial hunter.

" Then he blow'd a blast full north, east, west,
        and south,
    For he was a jovial hunter ;
And the wild boar heard him full into his den,
    As he was a jovial hunter.

" Then he made the best of his speed into him,
    Wind went his horn, as a hunter ;
And he whetted his tusks as he came along
    To Sir Ryalas, the jovial hunter.

" Then the wild boar, being so stout and so strong—
    Wind well thy horn, good hunter ;
He thrashed down the trees as he came along,
    To Sir Ryalas, the jovial hunter.

" Oh ! what dost thou want of me, the wild boar,
        said he—
    Wind well thy horn, good hunter ;
Oh ! I think in my heart I can do enough for thee,
    For I am a jovial hunter.

* Decumis Domino.

"Then they fought four hours in a long summer's
  day—
Wind well thy horn, good hunter ;
Till the wild boar fain would have gotten away
From Sir Ryalas, the jovial hunter.

"Then Sir Ryalas draw'd his broad sword with
  might—
Wind well thy horn, good hunter ;
And he fairly cut his head off quite,
For he was a jovial hunter.

"Then out of the wood the wild woman flew—
Wind well thy horn, good hunter ;
Oh ! thou hast killed my pretty spotted pig ;
As thou be'st a jovial hunter.

"There are three things I do demand of thee—
Wind well thy horn, good hunter ;
It 's thy horn, and thy hound, and thy gay lady,
As thou be'st a jovial hunter.

"If these three things thou dost demand of me—
Wind well thy horn, good hunter ;
It 's just as my sword and thy neck can agree,
For I am a jovial hunter.

"Then into his locks the wild woman flew—
Wind well thy horn, good hunter ;
Till she thought in her heart she had torn him
  through,
As he was a jovial hunter.

"Then Sir Ryalas draw'd his broad sword again—
Wind well thy horn, good hunter ;
And he fairly split her head in twain,
For he was a jovial hunter.

"In Bromsgrove Church they both do lie—
Wind well thy horn, good hunter ;
There the wild boar's head is pictur'd by
Sir Ryalas, the jovial hunter."

Another version of the ballad is—

"As I went up one brook, one brook—
Well wind the horn, good hunter ;
I saw a fair maiden sit on a tree top,
As thou art the jovial hunter.

"I said, fair maiden, what brings you here ?—
Well wind the horn, good hunter ;
It is the wild boar that has drove me here,
As thou art the jovial hunter.

"I wish I could that wild boar see—
Well wind the horn, good hunter ;
And the wild boar soon will come to thee,
As thou art the jovial hunter.

"Then he put his horn into his mouth—
Well wind the horn, good hunter ;
And he blow'd both east, west, north, and south,
As he was a jovial hunter.

"The wild boar hearing it unto his den—
Well wind the horn, good hunter ;
He whetted his tusks, for to make them strong,
And he cut down the oak and the ash as he came
  along,
For to meet the jovial hunter.

"They fought five hours one long summer's day—
Well wind the horn, good hunter ;
Till the wild boar he yell'd, and he'd fain run away,
And away from the jovial hunter.

"Oh ! then he cut his head clean off !—
Well wind the horn, good hunter ;
Then there came an old lady running out of the
  wood,
Saying, you have killed my pretty, my pretty
  spotted pig,
As thou art the jovial hunter.

"Then at him, this old lady, she did go—
Well wind the horn, good hunter ;
And he clove her from the top of her head to
  her toe,
As he was the jovial hunter.

"In Bromsgrove Churchyard this old lady lies—
Well wind the horn, good hunter ;
And the face of the boar's head there is drawn by,
That was killed by the jovial hunter."

It is supposed by many that Bromsgrove was formerly known as *Boarsgrove*, but this appears to be but fiction, concocted to fit in with the fable with which Humphrey Stafford is so closely connected, for the town was called Bremesgrefa in Anglo-Saxon charters, and Bremesgrave in Domesday Book. The crest of the Staffords is a *boar's* head, and the device adopted by the town authorities being a wild boar, has probably strengthened the popular idea that the town was once called *Boarsgrove*.

The Staffords of Grafton were a branch of the baronial house of Stafford, which acquired the manor of Grafton in the reign of Edward III., in right of the marriage of Sir Ralph Stafford with Maud, eldest daughter and co-heiress of Sir John de Hastang. Sir Ralph was succeeded by his son, Sir Humphrey, who married Elizabeth, daughter and heiress of Sir John Burdett, by whom he had issue Sir Humphrey Stafford, of Grafton, who, with his brother William, were slain whilst fighting against Jack Cade and the Commons of Kent, in the 28th of Henry VI. (see Shakespere's *Henry VI.*), and being buried here, form the subject of this notice. In Hook's "Lives of the Archbishops," we find Humphrey Stafford's death referred to as follows: "As the archbishop (John Stafford) and his noble kinsman (the Duke of Buckingham) drew near the camp (of Blackheath) they saw the effects of the late battle in the bodies of many of their friends and kinsmen who had fallen in the fight, and who had been stripped of their armour. All the precautions and discipline, at that time prevalent in armies, were strictly observed ; and with much military pomp they were ushered into the presence of the captain. There a sight awaited them which they might well have been spared : a sight which at once declared the fate of Sir Humphrey Stafford, who, with his brother William, had not, as they had hoped, been made prisoners of war, but had died in battle. The captain stood before them, arrayed in the splendid armour of their kinsman. There was no mistaking the armour, of which Sir Humphrey had been so proud, 'his brigandine set with gilt nails, his salet and his spurs.' There was nothing to complain of, for these were the spoils of war ; but still the sight was a sad one." He had issue, by Eleanor, his wife, daughter and co-heiress of Sir Thomas Aylesbury, of Milton Keynes (by Katherine, his wife, daughter and co-heiress of Sir Laurence Pabenham), a son, Sir Humphrey, of Grafton, who fought under the banners of Richard III., at Bosworth, and after the defeat of his party fled for security to Colchester, in Essex. Not discouraged, however, by his former ill-fortune, he undertook, with the help of his brother Thomas, to raise some men for the assistance of Lord Lovel. When this nobleman abandoned his project, the Staffords took refuge at Colnham, in Berkshire. The Judges of King's Bench did not long

Plate V.

SIR JOHN TALBOT AND HIS TWO WIVES

permit this place to extend its protection to traitors, for Humphrey was attainted by Act of Parliament, in November, 1485, and executed at Tyburn ; but Thomas was pardoned. A tradition prevailed that he was drawn upon a hurdle from the Foregate, or Northgate, of Worcester to the Cross, and there put to death. It is, however, believed that Tyburn was the scene of his execution. This last Sir Humphrey married Katherine, daughter and co-heiress of Sir John Fray, knight, and had issue, Sir Humphrey, who removed to Blatherwick, in Northamptonshire, where his descendants continued until the line ended in two co-heiresses, Susannah and Anne, sisters of William Stafford ; the former married, in 1699, to Henry O'Brien, and the latter, in 1703, to George Evans (Lord Carberry).

Adjoining the monument of Sir Humphrey Stafford, is one to the memory of Sir John Talbot, of Grafton, knight, son* of Sir Gilbert, with his figure all armed except the head, under which is a helmet and wreath ; about the neck a collar of SS., with a cross patee dependent (now broken off), and at his feet a Talbot. On his right hand is the effigy of his first wife, Margaret, and on the left that of his second wife, Elizabeth. Mr. Fairholt, in his "Costume in England," writes : "They are exceedingly interesting examples of a style of costume that completely disappeared in the ensuing reign, after retaining its ascendancy for more than half a century. The diamond shaped head dress (Plate VII., fig. 1) worn by the first lady may be considered as the latest form of that peculiar fashion ; the hair beneath is secured by bands or ribbons ; the gown is low in the neck, displaying the partlet, with its embroidered border, and the gold chains so fashionable with the upper classes at this time ; it is secured at the waist by a loosely-fitting girdle, and is held up in front by jewelled bands passing round the loins, displaying the petticoat beneath ; the sleeves are wide, shewing the pleated and puffed under ones, with the ruffle encircling the wrist. A crimson mantle envelopes the back part of the figure, falling over the shoulders and hanging to the feet ; and the entire dress is interesting for its display of the modification and variation adopted since its introduction to fashionable society. The companion-figure wears her hair parted in front from the centre in the simplest manner, and she has a close fitting cap of dark cloth or velvet, encircled with a border of gold lace and rows of gilt beads (Plate VII., figure 2) ; it takes the shape of the head, and was frequently worn with a point descending to the centre of the forehead. A long gown with a turn over collar, envelopes the entire figure ; it is open in front down the entire length, being secured by ties at regular intervals, and having no girdle at the waist ; small puffs are on the shoulders, from whence descend long hanging sleeves, ornamented by diagonal

---

* Grazebrooke says he was half-brother ; but Nash, who gives a pedigree of the family, states that he was a son of Sir Gilbert.

stripes, reaching to the knee, through which the arm was never placed. Ruffles decorate the wrist; but the entire dress is exceedingly, not to say unbecomingly, plain."

On several parts of the monument are quartered arms ; and round the tomb this inscription :—

> "Hic jacent corpora Johannis Talbot militis, et dominae Margaretae primae uxoris, atque dominae Elizabethae uxoris secundae, filiae Walteri Wrochelei arm. qui quidem Johannes obiit decimo die Sept. anno dom. mccccl. quorum animabus propicietur Deus. Amen."

Or, in English—Here lie the bodies of John Talbot, soldier, and of Margaret his first wife, and of Elizabeth his second wife, the daughter of Walter Wrocheley, esquire. The above John died on the 10th day of September, in the year of Our Lord 1550. May God have mercy upon their souls. Amen.

Underneath this *was* another inscription, but the letters, which were in relief, have been cut away. This fact caused considerable comment during the Shrewsbury Estate trial, in 1859. The inscription, as given by Dr. Nash, was—

> "The lady Margaret bare to him three sons and five daughters ; and the lady Elizabeth bare to him four sons and four daughters."

The size of the tomb is 6ft. 6in. by 4ft. 8in., and at the sides are these arms : "Three piles, a canton Ermine. Wrottesley. Quarterly—1. Azure a lion rampant and bordure plain. Talbot *alias* Bellissimo Earl of Shrewsbury. 2. Gules a lion rampant and bordure engrailed. Rhees ap Griffith *alias* Talbot modern. 3. Bendy of ten. Talbot ancient. 4. Barry of ten Argent and Azure an orle of martletts Gules Valence. 5. Gules a Saltire with a martlet. Nevile. 6. A bend between six martlets. Furnival. 7. Or, a fret. Verdon. 8. Two lions passant. Strange of Blackmere. 9. A lion rampant. Lovetot. Quarterly—1. A fleur-de-lis between three Moore's heads. Troutbeck, *alias* Moore, quartered by Troutbeck. 2. Three piles. 3. Two chevrons, in a canton a cross patee fitche. 4. A lion passant."—*Nash.*

In "Nash's Worcestershire," there is an engraving of this and Humphrey Stafford's monument, in which the sides of the tombs are represented as being alike, but this is an error. (Plate VI., figures 1 and 2.)

These monuments originally stood in the centre of the chancel, and were removed to their present positions by order of Mr. Waugh, a former vicar, about the year 1742. At this time the monument of Humphrey Stafford was shortened, in order to correspond with that of Sir John Talbot, and the effigies now overhang at either end.

Plate VI

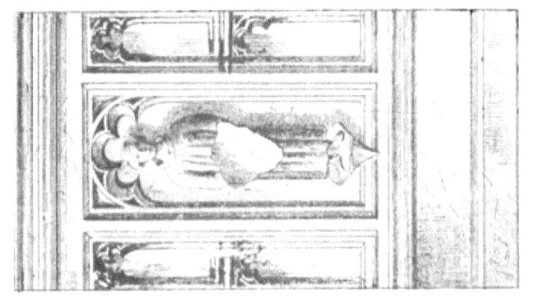

PANEL SIDE OF TOMB IN CHANCEL
FIG 3

PANEL SIDE OF TALBOT TOMB
FIG 2

PANEL SIDE OF STAFFORD TOMB
FIG 1

On the wall, at the foot of these tombs, are two brasses, bearing the following inscriptions : —

"HERE LYETH THE BODY OF
DAME BRIDGET TALBOT, DAUGH
TER TO SIR JOHN TALBOT
THE ELDER OF GRAFTON AND
WIFE TO SIR JOHN TALBOT
OF CASTLE KING IN IRELAND
WHO DIED 1619"

(Size 28½in. × 15in.)

"HERE LYETH THE BODY OF DAME MAR
GARETE LYGON, DAUGHTER TO THE
AFORESAID SIR JOHN TALBOT AND
SISTER TO THIS DAME BRIDGET
TALBOT THAT LIETH HERE
AND SISTER TO THIS SIR ARNOULD
LYGON OF BEAUCHAMP'S COURT,
DIED FEBRUARY 24, 1632"

(Size 25½in. × 13in.)

The lettering on the former is in relief, and on the latter it is incised. Both are very good specimens, for the date, and are in a fair state of preservation. Dr. Nash, writing in 1781, says, "Some few years since the chancel was repaired, and a handsome communion table, &c., given by Mrs. Moore, relict of Edward Moore, of Barnt Green, in this parish, esqr. The monuments that were formerly in the chancel were carelessly placed in different parts of the church. Some of those belonging to the Talbots were removed to the north side of the church."* At this time the above-mentioned brasses were preserved in the vestry, having been taken up from the floor of the chancel. They were afterwards placed in their present positions.

* In "The Beauties of England and Wales," we find the following :—"The body of the church has three aisles ; the windows contain some very good painted glass ; there are several handsome monuments of the Talbots, of Grafton, now the Earls of Shrewsbury, and one of Counsellor Lyttelton, of the Hagley family ; but we are sorry to observe, that during the repair of the chancel, some years ago, some very improper changes of the monuments and brasses took place. It were well, indeed, if an Act of Parliament were to take place to prevent the *barbarous beautifyings*, which are so often executed by the orders of as *barbarous* churchwardens. Surely, even now, the bishops or archdeacons, in their visitations, might look into these matters, if the resident clergy will not."

Formerly there was in the floor of the chancel, on the fifth stone from the vestry
door, and at the foot of the communion steps, this inscription :—

Sacred to the Memory of
Catherine Talbot daughter of John
and Lady Jane Clifton of Lytham Hall
in the county of Lancaster, and wife of
John Talbot, Esqre Brother to Charles
15th Earl of Shrewsbury, she departed this life
at Grafton the 14th of May A.D. 1791
aged 23 years
R. I. P.

The vault underneath this stone was opened July 23rd, 1857, with the object
of obtaining information on some points raised at the Shrewsbury trial. The
inscription found on the coffin plate was :—

THE HON^{ble}
CATHE^E TALBOT
Died May 14th
1791 Aged 24
R. I. P.

The stone was probably removed at the restoration of the church.

The Talbots, Earls of Shrewsbury, are descended, in the female line, from the
Kings of the Britons and Princes of Wales ; the Earl of Charlemagne ; the Norman
line in England ; the Kings of the Scots and Picts ; the Saxon line of England ; the
Plantagenet line, and several houses of Emperors.

Referring to the Talbots of Grafton, Mr. Shirley says : "No family in England
is more connected with the history of our country than this noble race ; few are
more highly allied. The Marches of Wales appear to be the original seat ; afterwards we find the Talbots in Shropshire, in Staffordshire (where their estates were
inherited from the Verdons, in the time of the Edwards), and lastly in Yorkshire, at
Sheffield, derived from the great heiress of Neville Lord Furnival." The first of
this great historical family who possessed the Manor of Grafton was Sir Gilbert
Talbot, K.G.,* second surviving son of John, second Earl of Shrewsbury, who
obtained, in recognition of his great services, a grant from King Henry VII. of the
Manors of Grafton and Upton Warren, and several other estates in Hanbury,
Bromsgrove, King's Norton, and elsewhere, which had been forfeited to the Crown
on the attainder of Sir Humphrey Stafford. "Sir Gilbert died in the year 1517,

---

* Sir Gilbert Talbot was Sheriff of Shropshire at the time of Richmond's invasion, and guardian
of his young nephew, the Earl of Shrewsbury, at the head of whose retainers, amounting to 2000
men, he joined Richmond at Stafford. He had command of Richmond's right wing at Bosworth,
and to him the heroic young Earl of Surrey delivered up his sword. He was badly wounded in the
fight, but survived it, and was made a Privy Councillor and a Knight of the Bath by Henry VII.

Plate VII

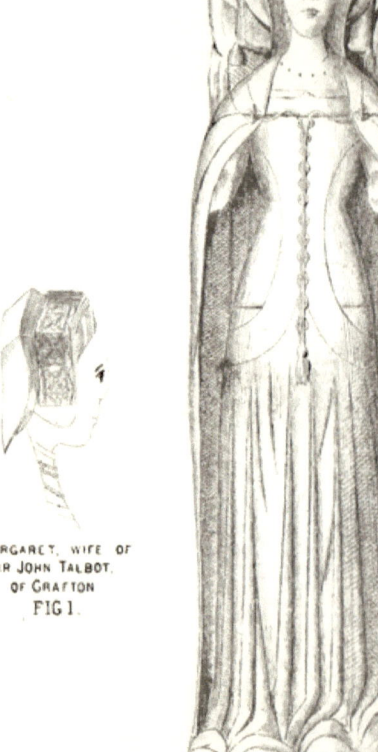

MARGARET, WIFE OF
SIR JOHN TALBOT,
OF GRAFTON
FIG 1.

ELIZABETH, SECOND WIFE OF
SIR JOHN TALBOT,
OF GRAFTON
FIG 2

ELIZABETH, WIFE OF SIR GILBERT TALBOT
OF GRAFTON
FIG 3

having had issue by his first wife, Elizabeth, daughter of Ralph, Baron of Greystoke,
a son and successor, Sir Gilbert Talbot, knight, who died in 1542, leaving, by Anne,
his wife, daughter and co-heiress of Sir William Paston, three daughters, his
co-heiresses, viz., Elizabeth, wife of John Lyttelton, of Frankley; Mary, wife of
Thomas Astley, of Patshul; and Margaret, wife of Robert Newport, of Rushock.
He also had issue, by Elizabeth Winter, widow, whom he appears to have afterwards
married, several natural children. Sir Gilbert was succeeded by his half-brother, Sir
John Talbot (whose monument we have just noticed), called 'of Albrighton,' who
was twice married: first, to Margaret, daughter and sole heiress of Adam Troutbeck,
by whom he was father of John Talbot, *of Grafton*; and secondly, to Elizabeth,
daughter of Walter Wrottesley, of Wrottesley, county of Stafford, by whom he had
issue, John Talbot, *of Salwarpe*. John Talbot, of Grafton, succeeded, and was
grandfather of George Talbot, of Grafton, who succeeded his kinsman as 9th Earl
of Shrewsbury, but, dying without issue, was succeeded by his nephew, John, as
10th Earl, from whom the late Bertram Arthur, 17th Earl of Shrewsbury, was
descended. On the death of the latter, in 1856, unmarried, the earldom was
claimed, and after a protracted enquiry (during which this monument was often
referred to), adjudged, in 1858, to Earl Talbot, of Ingestre, who proved his
descent from John Talbot, of Salwarpe, half-brother of John, of Grafton. This
John, of Salwarpe, married Olive, third daughter and co-heiress of Sir Henry
Sherington, of Lacock, county Wilts, and was succeeded by his eldest son,
Sherington Talbot, of Salwarpe, Lacock, and Rudge, the male descendants of
whose eldest and other sons by his first wife eventually became extinct, and
whose son by his second wife, William Talbot, of Whittington Hall, and Stourton
Castle, in Staffordshire (near Stourbridge), was father of William Talbot, D.D.,
Bishop of Durham, &c., whose son, Charles Talbot, Lord High Chancellor of
England, was created Baron Talbot, of Hensol, in 1733, and was direct ancestor of
the successful claimant, Henry John, 3rd Earl Talbot, who thus became 18th Earl
of Shrewsbury."—*Grazebrooke's* "Heraldry of Worcestershire."

At the north-east end of the chancel is a beautiful raised tomb of alabaster,
in the Perpendicular style, on which reclines the figure of Elizabeth (Plate VII.,
figure 3), daughter of Ralph, and wife of Sir Gilbert Talbot, of Grafton, Knight of
the Garter, second son of John, second Earl of Shrewsbury. She died about the
year 1490, and is represented in the costume of the period, which consists of a
surcote or low bodied gown, hollowed out at the sides, and fitted to the shape; over
this is a mantle, open in front, and fastened across the bosom by a cordon, attached
on either side to a fermail. The head dress consists of a close reticulated coiffure,
originally ornamented with jewels or precious stones, as were also the neck and
bosom. The jewels have long since vanished, but the holes into which they were

fastened are plainly to be seen. The hands and arms, which were enveloped in tight drawn sleeves, and clasped in the usual attitude of prayer, have been broken off and taken away. The two angels also, that supported the cushions on which the head reposes, and the two dogs, against which the feet rest, have, unfortunately, been much mutilated. The monument is an elaborate work of art, and adorned with images of men, in the compartments at the side and end, holding escutcheons; but the arms, Barry Argent and Azure three chaplets Gules, once painted on them, are worn off. (Plate VI. figure 3.)

On the north wall of the church, on the east side of the doorway, are tablets, bearing inscriptions as under :—

In affectionate Remembrance of
JOHN HORTON (for 55 years Surgeon of this Town) he died
March 11th 1852 aged 80 years
also of JANE WINIFRED HORTON (his wife) she died
Feby 17th 1832 aged 54 years

———

Children of the above
ANN HORTON, died Septr 4th 1819 aged 11 years
JOHN HORTON. died May 6th 1821 aged 21 years
MARY HORTON, died June 23rd 1824 aged 18 years
The above lie buried in a Vault near this place

———

THOMAS HORTON (Surgeon of Bromsgrove) buried in
a Vault in the Churchyard, died Novr 6th 1832
aged 27 years

———

Also of 3 Children who died in their Infancy

Near this Place
are deposited the Remains of
Ann, the Wife of THOMAS MORGAN
and Daughter of
MR. RICHARD WALKER
(late Surgeon of this Town)
She departed this Life ye 26th July 1805
Aged 36 years
She was an affectionate Wife
A most indulgent Mother
a sincere Friend
And an exemplary Christian.

To
The Memory of
MRS. MARY LOWE
who
After having spent
a Long Life
of True Religion
and Virtue
Expired
Generally Lamented
on the tenth Day
of January
A.D. 1791 Æ 82.

The family of the Lowes, in the early part of the 17th century, were the largest landowners in the parish of Bromsgrove, and lived at Chadwich, another branch residing at Perry Hall. The last of the latter family sold Perry Hall to Edward Knight, of Wolverley, who afterwards made large additions to his property in the neighbourhood, including Barnesley Hall, Red Cross, the Cotton Factory and land around it, Townsend Farm, Lowes Hill, Shop Close, &c. The estates, however, on the death of one of the family, were thrown into Chancery, and disposed of by order of that Court, by public auction, at the Golden Cross Hotel, May 25th, 1853.

The Chadwich property went, by marriage, to Henry D. Jeffries, of Worcester, who sold it in 1776 to John Hutton, of Birmingham, stationer.*

Humphrey Lowe, of Chadwich, served the office of High Sheriff of this county in the 27th of Charles II. The Lowes, of Bromsgrove, were a branch of the Lowes, of The Lowe, Lindridge Worcestershire, springing from Humphrey (who died 1637), youngest son of Henry Lowe, of The Lowe. He had two sons : Thomas, who died unmarried : and Humphrey, of Bromsgrove, who married Rebecca, daughter of Benjamin Joliffe, of Cofton Hackett, and was grandfather of Thomas Humphrey Lowe, who married, in 1780, Lucy, the elder of the two daughters and co-heiress of Thomas Hill, of Court of Hill, Salop. A Roger Lowe, of Bromsgrove, gent., was fined £10 for not taking knighthood at the coronation of Charles I., and his name appears in the list of disclaimers at the Visitation of 1634 : but he is not mentioned in the pedigree of this family, given by Burke, in his "Commoners and

---

* In the "Life of William Hutton," written by himself, this purchase is referred to as follows :—"I bought the Manor and Estate of Chadwich, for £4500, upon a promise, from an attorney, of supplying me with what money I should want. I let it for £300 a year, and kept it one year : when it appeared that I could not fulfil my bargain, because my attorney had deceived me ; nor the seller his, because in some places he had charged near twice as much land as there really was. He was pleased that I had procured a tenant at an advanced rent, and we mutually agreed to dissolve the contract. My family rejoiced, but I lamented."

Landed Gentry."   On January 10th, 1655, a Mr. Lowe, of Bromsgrove, was robbed
of £120 in silver, and a considerable sum in gold, about twelve o'clock at night, by
10 horsemen, who bound him and his family and got off undiscovered, but were
afterwards taken.

Outside this Wall
lie the Remains
of the late CHRISTOPHER BELL
who died June 12, 1690 Aged 52 Years

Also of PHŒBE BELL Sister of the above
who bequeathed Land in trust for
the benefit of the Poor of this Parish
and who died June 19th 1710.

At the expence of the Trustees of the
General Charities this Monument was
repaired and removed into the Church
in the year 1826 the better to com-
memorate the good deeds of the
above PHŒBE BELL the produce
of whose land now
amounts to £23 pr Annum.

This tablet was originally fastened against the wall at the east end of the chancel.
Phœbe Bell, by will, dated 30th April, 1706, devised to Humphrey Lowe and
four others, all of Bromsgrove, "her meadows, closes, parcels of arable land or
meadow ground, in the parish of Bromsgrove, part of two common fields, called
Church Field, and Great Perry Field; in trust that they should, at Christmas yearly,
dispose of the rents in clothing such of the most honest, and industrious and
religious poor ancient men and women of the town of Bromsgrove, who, through
age, infirmity, or other calamity should be the greatest objects of charity."   Part of
this land was exchanged for other land in 1803.

The arms of this family were Argent, on a chevron between three escallops
gules two barrulets (or rather bars gemelles) of the field, on a chief of the second a
hawk's lure between two falcons of the first.

"In 1632," says Grazebrook, in his "Heraldry of Worcestershire," "there was
printed at Douay a curious work, called 'The testament of William Bel, of Temple
Broughton, left written in his owne hand, sett out above 33 yeares after hys death,
with Annotations by his sonne Francise Bel, of the Order of Freers Minors of the
College of Dovvay,'" 12mo.

This William Bell was "cruelly martyred" at Tyburn, 11th December, 1643.   In
his will he gives an account of his ancestors and family, and of the lands held

by them in Worcestershire, from the time of Edward I. The name was originally
de Belne, afterwards shortened to Bel, or Bell. It is asserted that the Manors of
Bromsgrove and King's Norton belonged to this family. W. Bel, the martyr, came
to London as a law student, and shared the "chamber and bed of that worshipfull
gentleman, Mr. George Shirley (Hotten)." A Mr. Bell was *deputy steward* of the
Manor of Bromsgrove in the reign of Elizabeth, but none of the name appear
as *lords* of either Bromsgrove or King's Norton. A family of the name was,
however, anciently seated at Bell or Belne Hall, in Belbroughton.

In Memory

of Eliz. the widow of JOHN a younger branch
of the PERROTTS of BELL HALL in this County
she was Born in 1645, dyed in 1707 and was
Buried near this Stone.

Descended

from a family not more Distinguished by its
Antiquity and affluence, than its Steadiness &
Sufferings in the Cause of CHARLES the first
which in the year 1641, became a Defence of
the Religion and Liberties of ENGLAND.

Her Father

was JOHN BROOK Esquire of HASELOVER in
the County of STAFFORD, whose Grandfather
ROBERT, married LUCY the Daughter &
Co-heiress of THOMAS STANLEY. Second Son
of EDWARD Earl of DERBY, by DOROTHY
Daughter of THOMAS, Duke of NORFOLK : &
her mother being an heiress Descended from
RICHARD son of EDMUND Lord (& brother to
RALPH Earl of) STAFFORD, Inherited his Estates.

And of her Daughters who lie near her
LUCY the widow of JOHN BRADLEY of COLBOURN
BROOK in the County of STAFFORD Gent : who
Died in March, 1744 Aged 75.

And

ELIZABETH the widow of SAMUEL SMART of
this parish Gent : who Died March 1752. in
the Eighty first year of her age.

This stone was originally fixed over the vestry door.

John Perrot was the second son of William Perrot, the son of Humphrey Perrot, who was the purchaser of Bell Hall. This John Perrot removed from Belbroughton to Pedmore, near Stourbridge, where he died in 1728, and was buried at Belbroughton, for on a plain blue stone in the chancel floor is this inscription—

JOHANNES PERROT NUPER
DE PEDMORE IN COM
WIGORN ARM OBIIT 8 DIE
MARTII ANNO DOM 1728
ÆTATIS SUÆ 76.

Under Neath
Lyeth the Body of Mary
Palmer Widow departed
This Life September y 29
1727 Aged 76.

Here also Lyeth the Body
of Thomas Palmer Late of
this Town Apothecary
Departed this Life the 30
day of July 1728 Aged
47 years.
As he Lived Worthily Esteemed
So he died Generally Lamented.

This tablet is cracked across the middle.

In addition to the foregoing, according to Nash, there were formerly in the church the following:—

"Richard de Harcy and Elizabeth his wife, died 1500, whose souls God pardon."

"Mr. Thomas Sheldon, died May 2, 1612."

"Thomas Corbin, mercer, son of John Corbin, gent., died April 14th, 1729, aged 25."

"Elizabeth, widow of Leonard Simpson, Esq.,* died February 6th, 1718, aged 89. Sarah Simpson, their daughter, died August 31st, 1729, aged 63."

---

* Leonard Symson, of Bromsgrove, was a J.P. for Worcestershire in 1660, and his name occurs in Penn's list of "those who were to find horse," and also in the list of Worcestershire gentry given in Blome's "Britannia," 1673. His arms were: Per bend nebulée Or and Sable, a lion rampant counterchanged.

" Edward Mitton, gent., younger son of Henry Mitton, of Shipton, in the county of Salop, Esquire, buried October 15th, 1719."

"George Mortimer, lieutenant in his Majesty's regiment of horse, commanded by the Earl of Oxford, died January 30th, 1697, aged 33."

Towards the west end of the church was a cross-legged knight, which Dr. Nash says was "covered with the floor of a seat," and which Mr. Noake, in his "Rambler," says "is supposed to be near a fathom deep in rubbish, somewhere at the west end."

In the south aisle was the portraiture, in brass, of Edward Blundell,* all armed, with his beaver open. On the right hand, his wife ; and, between them, their arms : Party per pale a chevron counterchanged.

In the chancel were two stones, bearing the arms of Dineley.† The one to the memory of Ann, wife of William Chaunce (or Chance), daughter of Mr. Christopher Dineley ; the second to the memory of her sister Elizabeth, wife of Mr. Thomas Russell.

Mr. Noake, in "The Rambler," says, "A very ancient stone effigy, apparently that of a female, was dug up some time ago in the north aisle, and is now placed in the sill of one of the windows : it is too much defaced to admit of its age being ascertained, but the statue must have been the tenant of an older edifice than the present church." This effigy is now lying outside the church on the ground near the north doorway, and is much more defaced than when first unearthed.

* Grazebrooke, in his "Heraldry of Worcestershire," referring to the family, says : "William Blundell and Juliana his wife, about the reign of Henry II., did give their lands in Stoke to the Monks of Worcester. This family of Blundell came in with the Conqueror, and is mentioned in the roll of Battle Abbey. One of this name and family was escheator of the county, 14 Henry IV. They continued here till the reign of Henry VII., and have monuments in Bromsgrove Church and St. Alban's, in Worcester."—(Nash, citing Habington, ii. 379.)

† Thomas Dineley, of Withall Chapel, or, as he often spelt his name, Dingley, was a man of very considerable learning, and very ingenious in drawing with his pen, and wrote a very neat hand. He attended Sir George Downing in his embassy to Holland, in the year 1671. Dr. Nash says : "I have seen two volumes of his drawing with a pen, now in the possession of Sir Edward Winnington, at Stanford : the first contains drawings of houses and monuments in England and Wales, the second sketches taken in his travels through Holland, Flanders, &c. To the drawings are annexed short accounts of the places, houses, and inscriptions on the monuments. The first volume was drawn after his return from Holland, about the year 1676. His schoolmaster was James Shirley, poet laureate, whom he mentions with great respect."

In the middle aisle of the church lay one of the ancient family of Barnesley,* of Barnesley Hall. There was also a brass plate, on which was an inscription, but this, like the figure, has disappeared.

At the lowest step of the chancel lay William Chaunce, who died May 3rd, 1622. His descent from Barnesley was shewn by the arms of that family on his tombstone —a cross, between four roses.

Here lies the Body of
Mary Allen
Wife of Thomas Allen Esqr
She departed this life
the 22 of May 1790
and
Also of the said Thomas Allen Esqr
who died March 12 1795
aged 68 years

‡ In Memory
of GERRARD BARRINGTON Esqr Major
of the Regiment of Buffs who died
the 23rd of June 1751
In the 64 Year of his Age
He was much Lamented for his Benevolence
Both in Public and Private Life

‡ Here lyes the Body of RICHARD
Hanbury Gent. who died ye 18 Dec.
1724.

* Barnsley Hall, which Habingdon styles "the seat of ancient gentry," is pleasantly situated on the skirt of the Lickey Hills. In the time of Edward I, it was called Brandeley. Afterwards it obtained the name of Barndesley without much variation, and then of Barnsley. There is reason to suppose that a family of the same name lived here from a very early period, though no authentic evidence fixes it sooner than the reign of Edward III. They were descended from the Ardens, of Park Hall, in Warwickshire. Barndesley Hall was in the possession of a Mr. Barndesley in the time of Queen Elizabeth, and William Barnesley, of Barnesley Hall, gent., entered his pedigree at the visitation of this county, in 1634. The property at one period belonged to the Lowe's, who sold it to Edward Knight, of Wolverley. Mr. Noake says : "One of the Barnsley family bore a commission in the army, and was on the continent in the German wars ; he there procured an extraordinary large thigh bone, 23 inches long and 22 inches in circumference. It was preserved in the old Hall, and when the house was pulled down, in 1769, the present house was built and the bone hung up in it. Mr. C. Creswell, who now resides at Barnsley Hall (1845), informs me that twenty years ago some surgeons examined the bone and pronounced it human."

Here lieth Interred
John Houghton, Draper
by Mary his wife was buried
-- Day of Feb. Anno Domini
1701 aged 82 years

‡ Here lieth the Body of
Peter Capelin Gent. who
Departed this life the 17
Day of July Ano Dom. 1709
Aged 66 years

‡ Here Lieth ye body of Mary
The Wife of Peter Capelin
Late Cittyzen of London
Gent. Dec'd who Departed this
Life the 5. day of May Anno
Dom. 1718 aged 60 years.

In Memory of
John Woodcock apothecary
who departed this life
September 2nd 1769 aged 62 years

Also in Memory of Ann the wife of
John Woodcock who departed
this life January 13th 1772 Aged 63 years

Also of William the son of John and
Ann Woodcock who departed this life
October the 9th 1776 aged 6 months

Also of John their son who departed
this life August 11th 1713 aged 11 years

Also in Memory of Anthony Woodcock
Surgeon son of the above John and
Ann Woodcock who departed this life
June 27th 1797 Aged -- years

And of Dorothy wife to the said
Anthony Woodcock who departed this life
the 13th April 1791.

‡ Here Lyeth The Body of
James Newnam* Gent. Lineed
In Chagley Parrish Who Was
Born the 5 of August Anno
Dom. 1632 Departed This Life
The 16 of April Anno Dom. 1685

Here Lyeth Alsoe The Body
Of Mary His Wife Who
Was Born The 14 of June
Anno Dom. 1638 Departed
This Life The 6 of July Anno
Dom. 1658.

‡ Here Lieth the body of
SAMUEL SMART
Gent : who departed this life
the 19ᵗʰ of March 1732
Aged 74.

‡ Here lieth the Body of
Samuel Smart Junʳ·
Who Departed this Life
The 25 day of April
1714 in the 13 Year of his
Age.

‡ Here lieth the body of
Susanna Smart, Sister
To yᵉ Said Samuell Smart
Junʳ· who Departed this
Life the 19 day of July
1714 in yᵉ 20 Year of her
Age.

---

* James Newnham, of Chaddesley, whose name appears in the list of disclaimers in the
visitation book of 1682-3, was probably the father, by Joan, his wife, of Humphrey Newnham, of
Winterfold, who married, at Clent, in 1693, Dorothy Cox, and had issue James Newnham, of
Winterfold, who was High Sheriff of the County in 1743.

‡ Here lieth the body of
A. S.
Who departed this life
The 24 February 1700
aged 17

Here lieth the body of Susanch
Smart y* daughter of Samuel Tyler
Late of Shottery Gent. now deceased
And the wife of Mr. Samuel Smart
she departed this life *of* Friday the
foure and Twentieth day of April
1704 and in y* 44 yere of her age.

Here lieth the body of
Dameris Walker widow
daughter of Samuel
Tyler of Shottery in y*
County of Warwick
Gent: Dec'd departed
this life the 16 day of
May Anno Dom. 1710
aged 49 years.

In addition to the above, several of the Vicars of Bromsgrove were buried within the chancel, and had flat stones placed to their memory, but few of them are now traceable. There is one to the family of Rev. William Phillips, near the priests' entrance to the chancel, and another on the north side to the memory of Rev. Walter Powell (?) Curate of Bromsgrove. Many of these stones were taken up from the floors, and those having ‡ opposite to them are now lying outside the church, the greater part of them being very much defaced.

The Churchyard.

In Worcestershire there's not a churchyard found,
With such a handsome pathway leading round ;
Full sixty trees, whose branches far extend,
O'erspread the way, from summer's heat defend,
Prevent the falling rain, draw forth the breeze,
And cause a pleasant walk beneath the trees ;
Whose grove-like aspect, to the distant eye,
And in the midst a spire ascending high,
The traveller admires when passing by,
A view like this, perhaps, he had not seen,
Where'er his travels formerly had been.

*Joseph Facer.**

NE of the objects which immediately attract the attention of a visitor
to the church is the splendid belt of lime trees by which it is
surrounded. These trees, 57 in number, are not noticed in the
engraving of the church in Nash's "Worcestershire" (1799), and are supposed
to have been planted by Charles Brooke,† by direction of one of the Crane family,

---

* Author of "A Morning's Walk in Bromsgrove Churchyard."

† THE BROMSGROVE NIMROD.—Perhaps that universal instinct or cosmopolitan propensity, the
love of hunting, was never more strikingly individualised than in the person of Mr. Charles Brooke,
of Bromsgrove, who is as well known to all who assist at the meets of fox hounds in this neighbourhood as the Stoke chimney, or even the Lickey itself. That remarkably ubiquitous personage, the
"oldest inhabitant," informs us that Mr. Brooke has followed the hounds on foot from a period to
which memory runneth not ; and therefore the reader will not be surprised to learn that his life has
exceeded by a year the period assigned in Holy Writ as the limit of human existence. He enjoys
truly a green old age ; and though his shoulders have been squarer, he is still as stout and agile as
many men at 45 or 50. Mr. Brooke was for six years quartermaster-sergeant in the local militia,
and during his service as a feather-bed soldier, he had many hard marches. For example, on one
occasion having marched with the regiment from Worcester to Bromsgrove it was ascertained that a
return connected with his office was missing, and back he marched same day, not merely to
Worcester, but to Ledbury. On the next day he marched to Hereford, there missed the General, and
had to march 13 miles further, and return the same distance that night. Next day he marched
from Hereford by way of Redmarley, Upton-on-Severn, and Worcester to Bromsgrove, and thus
completed a march in full regimentals of 120 miles in three days. Mr. Brooke, on retiring from the

in 1792, or a few years before Dr. Nash's history was published. It is said a bottle of port wine was deposited at the root of each tree, but it would be more reasonable to suppose that it was consumed by the parties engaged in the planting.

In connection with one of these trees a curious story has gone abroad, and during the present year (1880) a gentleman from the north of England came here to verify what he had heard, viz., that there was, springing from the root of one of the trees, a splendid stream of water, clear as crystal. It is impossible to tell how the story got into circulation.

In the churchyard are three yew trees—an old one nearly opposite the south door, and two, not so old, on the north side, near the boundary wall. Mr. Noake, in his "Rambler," referring to yew trees in churchyards, says: "Some suppose that they were intended to furnish bows for archers, before fire-arms were invented; others, that the yew was selected by the early Christians to supersede the cypress, which was the Pagan emblem of annihilation, while the former, by its perpetual verdure, symbolised that everlasting life which was the great reward held out by the new faith. It is, however, certain that the yew tree, now so fallen in value, seven centuries ago was in higher estimation than even the oak. With its tough, sinewy arms were won the red fields of Cressy, Poictiers, and Agincourt, where the archers' shafts, old Froissart tells us, fell so thick and continuous that they seemed like unto snow, neither hauberk nor head-piece being able to withstand their passage."

Between the lich gate and the priests' entrance on the south side of the chancel, was an old sun dial, erected in 1773, denoting the spot where formerly stood a large

profession of the sword, changed his spontoon for a constable's staff, and his hard marches into a careful perambulation of the parish of Bromsgrove. He so well and truly performed his office of constable during eight years as on several occasions to have had the honour of the thanks of her Majesty's Judges of Assize; and when he retired from its arduous duties, it was with regret alike of the magistrates and the inhabitants. He now enjoys his ease, possessed of a small independency, and he dresses something like a gamekeeper; in fact, we for a long time imagined him to be in the service of some neighbouring gentleman in that capacity. For 30 years he kept greyhounds, and was a regular attendant at all the coursing meetings within a reasonable distance of Bromsgrove, and he frequently has walked from Bromsgrove to Croome, followed the coursing all day, and walked back at night. During the last hunting season he met the hounds at Mr. Croydon's Mill Pool, and after a long chase occupying nearly the whole of the day, was in at the death, along with Major Clowes, Mr. G. W. Biggs, Mr. F. Taylor, Mr. Brock, and the huntsman, and received the brush from the Major. The hounds found at Mill Pool, the fox took for Hindlip through the Droitwich canal, then for Oakley, and ran for some time in the wood, then to Oddingley, again to Oakley, next to Hadzor, and for Hanbury through the Worcester canal, and was run into and killed near Summer Hill, at Hanbury. A subscription has been set on foot for taking a portrait of this sportsman; and an excellent picture, which gives the mild and cheerful features of the old man to the life, has been executed in crayons by Mr. Dalton, of Birmingham, and is now to be seen at the Bell Inn, Bromsgrove. The veteran has been painted with the brush in his hand presented him by the master of the hounds.—*Worcester Herald*, April 26th, 1851.

ancient cross.* The brass dial was stolen, and a reward offered for the discovery of the thief. Over the south porch was another sun dial, at the top of which were the words, "We shall," the latter part of the name of the instrument completing the sentence, thus—"We shall (dial) die all." This was removed at the restoration of the church.

The churchyard originally was bounded by a stone wall, 248 yards in length, and was kept in repair, prior to the year 1600, by the following yields :—

The Town Yield.....................repaired 80 yards from "The stayers"
                                towards the Litchgates.
Burnford Yield ....repaired 14 yards.
Woodcote   „   ....   „   9   „   and 1 foot.
Timberhonger Yield ....   „   10   „
Fockbury Yield ....   „   16   „
Catshill   „   ....   „   26   „
Barnsly   „   ....   „   17   „
Chadwick and Willingwick Yield   „   22   „   and 2 feet.
Gannow Yield.....................   „   8   „
Shepley   „   ....   „   15   „
Burcot   „   ....   „   13   „
Padstone   „   ....   „   12   „
" The Comandery"   ....   „   5   „

A new wall was built round it in 1815, the work being commenced March 27th.

The churchyard was enlarged about the year 1824, by the addition of a piece of land on the north side, which belonged to the "Crown Hotel," and included the cellaring where drinkables were stored, chiefly for supplying the "bowling green" adjoining, the site of which is occupied by the present National Schools. The cellar has been utilised by conversion into two vaults, the one belonging to the Dipples, and the other to the Compsons. The size of the cellar was about 16ft. by 10ft. 6in.

---

* There were several other crosses in the parish. In front of the Town Hall stood a great high cross, which was removed in 1732. There was a large round stone in the centre of the Kidderminster Road, at the point where the lane from Red Cross passes over it to Whitford. The stone had a hole in the middle of it, and was said to have been used as the socket hole into which the Papists placed the cross carried by them in their processions. At Shepley was a like stone, called "Sheply Cross." At the upper end of the Lickey Common, about three miles from Bromsgrove, was another, called "Stone Cross." In Hanover Street we read on a stone in the wall of one of the houses—

                    Neare
            St. John° Cro°°
            Hanover
            Street
            Anno dom°¹
                1715.

It is supposed that St. John Street formerly extended further, and that at the junction of the streets a cross stood to the memory of St. John the Baptist, after whom the street is named and the parish church dedicated. At the upper end of High Street stood a cross known as "Welch Cross."

Tombs and Gravestones.

Those num'rous hillocks, silent though they be,
They loudly speak of man's mortality;
With ceaseless eloquence they plainly teach,
In silence, stronger than divines can preach.
The child, just come to breathe the vital air,
The father's hopes, the mother's tender care,
Cropp'd in the bud, is number'd with the dead,
Quickly cut down, before its blossoms spread.
The growing youth, who thought of years in store,
And fancied coming joys, when months were o'er;
By Death's resistless arm is snatched away
From kindly friends, to mourn his shorten'd stay.
The full grown youth, whose blood with vigor flow'd,
Whose bosom with enchanting pleasure glow'd;
Who promis'd lengthen'd life, and lasting bloom,
Has found a faded and a breathless doom.
The middle-ag'd, their busy work is done,
Their restless, cank'ring cares for ever gone;
Their darling hopes, their fondest joys destroy'd,
They've left that earthly bliss, they ne'er enjoy'd.
Here hoary-headed, tott'ring, trembling age,
Quite tir'd of life's deceitful, painful stage;
With failing eyes, with pale and wrinkled face,
Within this ground, is now allow'd a space.

Joseph Facer.

IN the following description of the most interesting tombs and stones in the churchyard the inscriptions are given as accurately as possible, with such notes on the respective families as are available.

On the top of the north boundary wall is an old stone figure, called "Tom Thumb's," or "Tom's" monument. It has on a tunic, or mantle; the hands are placed in the attitude of prayer, but the features are entirely gone. It may have formed the lid to some coffin. Connected with this figure is an extraordinary tradition. It is said that the individual represented sold himself to his Satanic Majesty for certain considerations, some of which were to be advantageous to the seller in his sojourn through this life. The final stipulation, however, was that when he died he should not be buried either in or out of the churchyard; but this was

evaded by his giving orders to be buried under the boundary wall, and the figure
placed on the top of the wall over his remains. The story is very like that of the
man who signed a pledge not to drink any alcoholic drinks either inside or outside a
house, but who regularly got drunk standing on the sill of his own door.

As the churchyard has been enlarged, and the boundary wall removed some
20 yards from its former position, it would be interesting to know to what extent
Tom's bargain is affected.

In a manuscript note on this figure, dated 1778, it is referred to as that of
"a woman, with the arms, face, and breasts very much defaced. How long it has
been there is not known; it is said to belong to the Hughbourne's (Huband's), of
Ipsley."* The length of the stone is four feet, and the width one foot, and it
has been spoken of as that of a deformed dwarf. Which of these assertions (if
either) is correct, must be left for the reader to decide.

Our churchyard, so far as the writer is
aware, does not possess any early incised cross
slabs, and only one example of the raised cross
slab or coffin lid. This is near the lich gate,
at the top of the steps leading from St. John
Street. It is now in an upright position, and,
like very many of the gravestones, has been
removed from its original situation and placed
beside the path to support the bank. The lower
part of the stone is inserted in the ground, so
that the upper part only is exposed to view.
The length of the stone is four feet, its breadth
at the head 25 inches, and at the foot 22 inches.
An engraving of it is here given, showing the
"St. Andrew's Cross" united with the "Christ's
Cross," the reason for which it is difficult to
conjecture. A slab, very similar in design to
this, and ascribed by the Rev. Edward L. Cutts,
in his "Manual for the Study of the Sepulchral
Slabs and Crosses of the Middle Ages," to the 13th century, is to be seen in Elford
churchyard, Staffordshire. The stone has two small holes, about an inch in diameter
and about the same in depth, in the upper part.

* The Worcestershire branch of the Huband family (which is of great antiquity in Warwickshire), was founded by Anthony Huband, fourth son of Nicholas Huband, of Ipsley (who died in
1544), by Dorothy his wife, daughter and co-heiress of Sir John Danvers, knight. A baronetcy, now
extinct, was conferred in 1660-1 on John Huband, of Ipsley. An account of the family is given in
Dugdale's "Warwickshire."

In the churchyard is a large stone tomb, inclosed with tall iron rails, having a very clumsy figure of a man lying thereon, in a night-gown and cap, his head on a cushion, his hands on his breast. The heavy, clumsy appearance of the figure may be accounted for by the fact that it was cut by a working miller, who evidently mistook his calling when he turned his attention to stone carving. On the side of the tomb a brass shield was leaded into the stonework, bearing this inscription :—

Erected
To the memory
of
Wm. Chance, gent.
obiit Feb. 5
1768
Æt. 82.

The shield was stolen,* and no inscription now remains on the tomb.

On the sides and ends of another tomb is the following, the ages being worthy of note :—

(Side.)

Here lyeth the Body of Richard Palmer
of the Parrish of Solyhull in the County
of Warwick he departed this life ye 8 day
of February 1710-11 aged 69
Mors omnibus Communis.

Jacob Wilson died December 30th 1795 aged 64
Mary Wilson died May 11th 1797 aged 62
Ann Wilson died August 8· 1803 aged 74
Elizabeth Carpenter died April 15th 1826 aged 78.

(End.)

Lazarus Wilson died July 5th 1784
aged 85 years
Mary his wife died Nov. 7th 1786
aged 79 years.

(Side.)

Richard		June ye 6· 1705		17 weeks
Richard	departed	Feb. ye 4th 1707	aged	16 weeks
Anne		Feb. ye 1st 1708-9		11 weeks
Martha		Mar. ye 20th 1709-10		12 weeks
Joseph		Jan. ye 7th 1713-14		22 months
Benjamin	departed	October ye 13th 1717	aged	11 weeks
Sarah		August ye 16th 1720		6 years & 15 weeks
Thomas		Feb. ye 27th 1720-21		10 days

* On November 24th, 1829, three bodies were stolen from the churchyard.

In Memory of Ann the Wife of
Mr. Joseph Palmer who departed this
life the 15 Day of April 1729 aged 53

Also in Memory of the aforesaid
Mr. Joseph Palmer who departed this
life the 10' day of November 1763
aged 82 years.

The Palmers were a Warwickshire family. The Richard Palmer first mentioned was the only son of Robert Palmer (by his second wife), of Blockley, in this county, who was the second son of Richard Palmer, and younger brother of John Palmer, of Compton, in Warwickshire. To the memory of a Dudley branch of the family there is also another long railed-in tomb in the " new ground."

Many of the ancient and most interesting lettered stones are at the east end of the church. What appears to be the oldest *lettered* stone is shown on plate viii., figure 2.

The latter part of the inscription on this stone is not plain. A family of Wannertons flourished at Hagley about the beginning of the 16th century.

Not far from this is the stone shown on plate viii., figure 1.

This John Callowe, a list maker by trade, lived at, and was owner of, the Black Cross Inn, and a field called "Shurnell." At his death the property passed to his son William, a shoemaker. In his will this *item* appears : " I give and bequeath unto all my nephews and nieces the sum of *one shilling* each, to be paid by my executrix hereafter named." The property passed to the Hunts, and by them was sold to William Shenstone, alderman of Bromsgrove, who died August 1st, 1779. He had a son, Richard, also an alderman. In the churchyard are gravestones to members of the family.

Near the top of the church steps is a stone (on which nearly every boy in the parish appears to have sharpened his knife or slate pencil), to the memory of

Mary daughter of M. W.
Biggs ob! 5ᵗʰ Aug. 1685. aged 18.

———

A quondam beauty here is laid in dust,
And (tho' but young) was prudent, pious, just :
So modest, gracious, meek, so void of hate,
No injury she could retaliate.
But tears to earth, her sighs to heaven sent,
Ne'er bitter language shew'd her malcontent :
She pious counsel, dying, gave to all,
To be with Christ she longed, and her soul
Is now at heaven, in whom every grace
Was proto varnish'd with an angel's face.

A Matthew Biggs, his wife and two children, paid poll tax in 1690.

Plate VIII

FIG 1

FIG 2

Here
Lieth the body of Charles Clack
who departed this life
September the 13th 1761.

———

A loving Husband a Father Dear
A Faithful Friend lies Buried here
His acquaintance miss him since his Fall
His Relations miss him most of All.

On a curious stone, with a **Death's head and cross-bones** on the top : –

In Memory of
Alice wife of Thomas Hemus
who died July 26th 1686.

Also Elizabeth their daughter
died September 27th 1683.

Here Lyeth the Body of Frances the
wife of William Porter Mercer who De
parted this life November the 1st 1685.
And also John his son Mar. the 13th 1685.

———

"Blessed are the dead which die in the Lord."

On the back of this stone are lines recording the death of Abraham Pritchett, of the "Lower Dolphin," on March 15th, 1796, aged 52, and his wife Elizabeth in 1807. The present "Bell Inn" was called the Lower Dolphin, to distinguish it from the "Upper Dolphin," or "The Dolphin." The Bell Inn was known in the first place as the "White Swan;" it was afterwards altered to the "Lower Dolphin;" but when the property was purchased by William Rose, he, after his appointment as clerk of the parish church, went to live at the house, and altered the sign to that of the Bell, selecting the latter name from the fact of his being one of the change ringers at the church. The fields in the rear of the house are known as "Pritchett's Fields," and the site of the old bowling green is now occupied by the College School (Mr. Saywell's).

William Porter issued a halfpenny token in 1668.

O.   WILLIAM PORTER   ...   HIS HALF PENY
R.   IN BROMSGROVE 1668   W. P.   ½

Over the priests' entrance, on the outside wall of the chancel, is a tablet :—

Under these 3 stones, are
interred the Body's of Thomas
Porter, of Bromsgrove, Mercer, who
died in the year 1673, being the 73rd
year of his age. And of Mary his
wife, who died November the 13th
1702, being the 86th year of her age
And of Samuel their Son, who died
November 1st 1703,
With several other of their children.

"Blessed are the dead which die in
the lord." Revelations 14th Vr 13th

Thomas Porter issued a halfpenny token in 1668.

O.   THOMAS PORTER ...   HIS HALF PENY
R.   IN BROMSGROVE 1668 ...   T.P. conjoined.

On the south wall of the chancel was a tablet to the memory of Samuel Porter, who died in 1703, leaving two estates at Stoke Prior, of which the rent was then £56 11s. 2d., for 99 years, to be distributed among such poor of the parish as received no pay. The term expired in 1803.

There are numerous stones to the memory of members of the Brooke family :—

Here Lyeth Buried the Body of Roger
Brooke who departed this life the 19th
Day of February Anno Domini 1704
aged 68 years.

He is not dead but sleeps, No Good Man dies
But like the sun that sets next day to rise
With Brighter beauties, so after Deaths short night
The just shall reign with Christ in Endless Light.

On a tomb to the memory of William Blackford are these lines :—

Encomiums on the Dead are empty Sounds and
Mockery, the last great Day alone will wipe
the colouring off, and Mans true state without
a veil, will stand disclosed to view.

On a stone, the lettering of which is scarcely visible :—

Pale death will hardly find a Nother
So Good a wife so kind a Mother
In all her actions so discreet
Was She who here lies at your feet.

SACRED

To the memory of

Arthur Macnally & Anne his wife

Arthur Macnally	Anne Macnally
Died May 17th 1817	Died Sep. 26th 1831
Aged 72	Aged 76

Requiescant in Pace.

I know that my Redeemer liveth
And in the last day I shall rise out of the earth
and in my flesh (in this very flesh) which death
will reduce to dust, I shall see my God.
This my hope is laid up in my bosom.

On a stone to the memory of one Humphrey Coley, who died August 25th, 1727, aged 63 :—

Dear Friends weep not for me i pray
though sudden death snatched me away
my debts are paid my grave you see
wait but awile you'l be with me.

At the foot of a stone, dated 1714 :—

Here lieth a Child Virtuous and good
Her choice was Here to Ly and sleep
Whilst her friends behind
Lament & weep.

In Memory of

Ann the wife of William Penn who departed

this life Decr yr 16th 1787 aged 41 years.

Good people all that read these lines
On Heavenly things now fix your mind
Repent in time make no delay
For no one knows their dieing day.

Here lyeth yr Body of

Mary the Daughter of

George Fownes by Mary

his wife Shee Departed

this life July the 7th 1721

Aged one year.

I but began to live that I might die
And only dyd to live eternally.

On a stone to the memory of Mary, wife of Richard Stanton, who died December 16th, 1801 :—

> Beneath this stone confined lies,
> Till God shall call the dead to rise,
> A faithful friend, a kind relation :
> We hope through Christ she hath salvation.

Sacred

To the Memory of Ann

Wife of Richard Wilkes

who departed this Life the 24th day

of May 1804 aged 74 yrs

> In life beloved in death for ever dear
> O Friend O Partner take this parting tear
> If life has left me aught that asks a sigh
> Tis but like thee to live like thee to die.

Also to the Memory of the above

Richard Wilkes

who died the 8th day of April 1811

in the 80 year of his age.

> Here lies the just and truly honest man
> Say more I dare not and say less who can.

Sacred

To the Memory of Dorothy Lowis

who died 22nd of February 1827.

aged *100 years.*

She was the daughter of

William Baker Esqr of Londonderry

and grand-daughter of Major Baker

who was governor of the city and

commanded the forces when attacked

by the army and friends of James 2nd

after the battle of the Boyne.

Here is also interred James Mitchell

who died December 24th 1821

aged 61 years.

The above is, we believe, the greatest age recorded in the churchyard ; as a contrast we have—Ann, the daughter of Stephen and Mary Lilley, "Departed this life February the 16th 1748 aged *2 Hours.*"

On a stone to the memory of the wife of William Green, who died December 22nd, 1813:—

Peace to her pious shade intomb'd lies here
The best of Women and of Friends most dear
Farewell dear partner, best of wives adieu
May Christ prepare us all to follow you.

Sacred

to the memory of

James Mercer (Leiutenant

of the 4th Royal Veteran Battalions)

who departed this life Augt 26th 1822

Aged 62 years

Also five children who died in their
Imfancy

Also Ann Wife of the Said James
Mercer died Decr 21st 1825 aged 50 years
Leaving a Son and Daughter to deplore her
irreparable loss, as a most indulgent Parent, and
an affectionate Friend.

Sacred

To the Memory of

William Crawford

who died suddenly at the Crown Hotel

February 22nd 1833 aged 39 years.

O reader stay and cast an eye
Upon this grave wherein I lie
For cruel death has challeng'd me
And soon alas will call on thee
Repent in time, make no delay
For no one knows their dying day.

Hark from the tombs a doleful sound
My ears attend the cry
Ye living men come view the ground
Where you must shortly lie.

On the ground near the south chancel wall are stones to the memory of the Cullwicks, who for many years kept the Crown Hotel.

On a stone near the great east window, erected to the memory of Robert
Kimberley (who died July 31st, 1659), and other members of his family : –

Float not on Earthly things, Seek joys Above,
In Blissful Mansions of Eternal Love.

A John Kimberley, who died in 1500, was buried in a brick grave in the chancel.
—The above-named Robert Kimberley, described as "Alderman of y° parish of
Bromsgrove," was descended from Robert Kymberley, who in 1563 was appointed
head master of King Edward's School, Bromsgrove.   He was of the same family as
"Samuel Kimberley, Doctor of Physick," who was brother to Solomon Kimberley,
"a famed preacher in the University," and Chaplain in Ordinary to King Charles II.
William Kimberley, churchwarden of Bromsgrove in 1744, and who is described as
"gentleman," was also of this family.   Descendants of the family are still living
at Bromsgrove.

Mary Benson, who died July 1st, 1749, aged 29, was—

Grateful to her friends, just to her
Mother, Dutiful to her Parents,
And ever Faithful to her God.

At the top of this stone is a representation of the sun resplendent, and at the
bottom a Death's head.

On a stone to the memory of John Corbett, of the Bank House Farm, who died
in 1848, aged 67, is the verse : —

His hour was come, no power on earth could save
"The good old man" that rests within this grave :
Nor did he wish to live :—prepared to die,
His soul was gathered to the saints on high ;
So falls to earth at last the ripened grain
To perish not ; but rise, and live again.

"His peaceful old age, was an evening
without a cloud."

Here was Interred the
Body of Thomas
Holliman died the
10 1716 aged near 24 y

Passenger stand still & behold this stone
where thou may'st read of one so quickly (gone)
who gives thee warning never to delay
Finishing all thy work whilst it is day
that thou & he may'st come to meet at last
And be with God and all the Godly blest.

Sacred

To the Memory of Samuel Grove
who died Feby 28 1837 aged 50 years.

A Faithful Friend, a Husband Good
Beloved by all his Neighbourhood
He labour'd hard until his Death
And then to Christ resign'd his breath.

On a stone to the memory of the widow of John Milward, afterwards married to George Stonehall, but buried in the grave of her first husband, are these lines :—

While unconscious the danger which shortened my day
The pathway of Pleasure I trode
In an instant my spirit was summon'd away
And I stood in the presence of God.
In an instant I sank 'neath the shadow of death
And eternity around me arose
O Reader ! remember that life is a breath
And a breath may bring thine to a close.

She fell down dead, near Dyer's Bridge, on the Worcester Road. None of the lines are now readable, nor is any date visible.

To the memory of Thomas Mannaley, who died May 3rd, 1819. He was stabbed by a currier, near the Town Hall, and from whence he succeeded in getting as far as the "Shoulder of Mutton," in St. John Street, opposite which house he died :—   . . . Beneath

The overhanging roof of yon gashed tree,
A gravestone tells the melancholy tale
Of man, by fellow-man's unnatural hands,
Hurried unbidden, and, perhaps, unready,
Before the bar of the Omniscient Judge.'

On the stone is the following verse :—

Beneath this stone lie the remains,
Who in Bromsgrove street was slain,
A currier with his knife did the deed,
And left me in the street to bleed ;
But when archangel's trump shall sound
And souls to bodies join—that murderer
I hope will see my soul in heaven shine.

William Smith, late of Finstol, who died March 31st, 1796, aged 86, was—

Plain in his dress, in all his words sincere
In all his actions just, his concience clear.

* The lines quoted are by the late Mr. J. H. Seroston. The stone is near the boundary of the churchyard, on the east side, and near to one of the lime trees, in which the initials T M, and a cross underneath, are deeply cut.

M

To the memory of Edward Hill, who died January 1st, 1800, aged 70 years :—

> He now in silence here remains,
> Who fought with Wolfe on Abram's plains,
> E'en so will Mary Hill, his wife,
> When God shall please to take away her life.
>
> 'Twas Edward Hill their only son,
> Who caused the writing on this stone.

Here Lieth the Body of John
Harris who died August
the 30th 1745 aged 60 years.

> He was a Loving *husband*
> Likewise a Faithful friend
> *He* lived a sober *Life*
> And made a Godly End.

Also five children of Edward
and Mary Braine.
All those tender Branches were
Born and Buried within 5 years.

Here also Lieth the Body
of Mary the wife of John
Harris who died July
the 25th 1753 aged 70.

> Mercy, O Lord I ask
> this is the total sum
> For Mercy Lord is all my suit
> oh Let thy mercy come.

Here also was buried
the body of the said Mr
John Higgs who departed
this life the 11 Day of Sep
tember 1724 aged 73 years

> 2. Timothy 4 chap. 7. verse
> I have fought a good fight
> Have finished my course
> I have kept the faith.

Here was buried the
Body of Elizabeth the
wife of Mr. John Higgs
She departed this life ye
28th Day of December
1708.

The wife dying first, the stone was probably erected to her memory, and the first part left to record the husband's death.

John Gilbert Butler, who was buried October 18th 1652, is described as—

> A honest neighbour
> A Loving frend
> Godly in his life
> Hapy in his end.

There are other stones to the memory of this family, having coats of arms on the top, but much defaced.

Sacred

to the Memory of Mary, wife of
Joshua Peart, who died May 18th 1795
aged 67 years.

Also Susanna his *second* wife who died
July 8th 1814 aged 74 years.

Also Leonora his *third* wife who died
February 6th 1819 aged 81 years.

Also Sarah Wilkes Sister of the above
Susanna Peart who died July 19th 1819
aged 70 years.

Also the above Joseph Peart, he died
July 28th 1825 aged 87 years.

Mark the perfect *man* and behold the upright : for the
end of *that* man *is* Peace.   Psalm 37th and verse 37th

Mr. Peart belonged to an old Baptist family. At his death he left an endowment towards the support of the minister for the time being of the Baptist Church, Bromsgrove; and the same is now received towards the stipend of the minister of the New Road Baptist Chapel.

On a stone to the memory of Thomas Sanders, who died January 4th, 1700, his wife dying June 3rd, in the same year, is a Death's head, with an hour-glass on either side, and scrolls which bear the following :—

The glass is run   Good people all
Our Sand is spent   in time repent.

Here lyeth the Body of Mr
John Smith of Dodford was
Interrd July the 9th 1729 aged 50 years.
Also Elizabeth his wife was here Interrd
January the 9th 1728-9 Aged 41 years.

Death a short space did Man and Wife divide
To live without her he a little tried
Found it *to* hard a task and then he died
In all Relations They Behaved so Well
You'l scarcely Match Them with a Paralell

Also William the 11 Son Departed
This life Sep ye 13 1758 aged 49 years.

In Memory of
Ann
wife of Thomas Burns
of Edingburg
Writer to his Majesty's Signet
who died 14 Nov.ʳ 1814.

On a stone, the upper part of which has crumbled away :—

Fair well vain world I've seen Enough of thee
I value not what thou can'st say to me
Thy smiles I court not, nor thy frowns I fear
My days are past, my head lies quiet here
The faults you see in me beshure to shun
And look at home there's plenty to be done.

Here Lyeth
the body of Frances
the wife of Jonathan Pinfield
who departed this life Oct
yᵉ 3ᵈ 1746 aged 39 yʳˢ

A dear wife I have lost
Which was my whole delight
Lord instruct me all my dayes
That I may walk upright.
Afflictions sore long time she bore
Phisicians weare in vain
Till death seiz'd as God was pleas'd
To ease her of her pain.

This stone is erected
to perpetuate the memory of
James Ridgway
who died on the 23 day of July
1839 aged 70 years,
And who by his daily labour
and economy accumulated
the sum of £330 which
he bequeathed by his will
to the
Poor of this Parish.

The interest of this money was to be given away in bread, annually, on St.
Thomas's Day, to the deserving poor of the parish.

There are several stones to the memory of the Carpenter family. On the stone of Richard, who died in 1681, is cut—

> I did resist and strive with death
> but soon he put me out of breath.

To the Memory of Thomas Scaife
late an Engineer on the Birmingham and Gloucester Railway
who lost his life at Bromsgrove Station, by the Explosion of
an Engine Boiler, on Tuesday the 10th of November, 1840.
He was 28 years of age, highly esteemed by his fellow workmen
for his many amiable qualities, and his Death will be lamented
by all those who had the pleasure of his acquaintance.

The following lines were composed by an unknown Friend
as a Memento of the Worthiness of Deceased :—

My *engine* now is cold and still,
No water does my *boiler* fill ;
My *coke* affords its flame no more,
My days of usefulness are o'er.
My *wheels* deny their wonted speed,
No more my guiding hands they heed ;
My *whistle*, too, has lost its tune,
Its shrill and thrilling sounds are gone ;
My *valves* are now thrown open wide,
My *flanges* all refuse to guide,
My *clacks*, also, tho' once so strong,
Refuse to aid the busy throng.
No more I feel each urging breath,
My *steam* is now condensed in death.
Life's *railway* o'er, each station post,
In death I'm stopped and rest at last.
Farewell, dear friends, and cease to weep,
In Christ I'm SAFE, in Him I sleep.

This stone was erected at the joint expence
of his fellow workmen, 1842.

Sacred
To the Memory of
Joseph Rutherford
late Engineer to the Birmingham and Gloucester
Railway Company,
who Died Nov! 11th 1840, Aged 32 years.

Oh Reader stay, and cast an eye
Upon this grave wherein I lie
For cruel death has challeng'd me
And soon, alas, will call on thee
Repent in time make no delay
For Christ will call you all away.
My time was spent like dew in sun
Beyond all cure, my glass is run.

This stone was erected by his affectionate
Relict 1841.

On the top of each of the two last-mentioned stones a railway locomotive is carved.

> Here Lye Sleeping in the dust the
> Bodies of Father & Mother & *to* Sons

Thomas Fayting	⎱	April	+	+
And Frances his wife	⎰	August	+	+
Also John Fayting	⎰	Novem 23	+	
and George Fayting	⎰	April 29, 1680.		

The family of Fayting, according to the *Magna Britannia*, was seated at Woodcote for "above five hundred years." Of this family was Nicholas Fayting, Mayor of Worcester in 1695.

> Jeremiah Clark
> B. M. late of Worcester
> departed this life March 11th
> 1809 aged 66 years.

Clark was for many years conductor of the music meetings here and at Worcester. During his lifetime Bromsgrove was the focus of all the musical talent, both vocal and instrumental, for miles round the country.

When the cholera visited the town, in 1832, from which 18 persons died, the pleck of ground at the north-west corner of the churchyard was set apart for their burial. A tomb on this plot bears the following :—

> Beneath
> lies the body
> of
> Eliza Susanna Jacob
> The beloved wife of
> The Revd Stephen Long Jacob
> Vicar of Woolavington-cum-Puriton
> in the County of Somerset.
> She died of Cholera
> at the house of her son The Rev. G. A. Jacob
> Head Master of the Grammar School of King Edward VI.
> Bromsgrove
> August 10th 1832
> aged 56 years.

> "The righteous hath hope in His death."

The old worsted factory was used as an hospital, but no one died there.

There are numerous stones to the memory of the families of Corbin, Shenstone, Wilkes, Clark, Chellingworth, and others; John Chellingworth died in 1708, at the age of 92. Amongst other names mentioned are the following :—

DIPPLE.—Mention is made in Domesday Book of a family of the name of Dipple residing at Bromsgrove, and as there are families of the same name still living here, in all probability they never became extinct; they are therefore one of the oldest families in Worcestershire.

TILT.—Joseph Tilt is described as a "leather dresser."

KNIGHT.—William Knight, "butcher," died July 7th, 1787.

SANDERS.—In the early part of the 18th century, an extensive bell foundry was carried on by Richard Sanders, on the site now known as the Foundry Yard. According to the dates found on various bells cast by him, he seems to have commenced business about 1703, and continued till about 1738, during which period he did a large trade, judging from the extent of his work. His most successful cast was the famous octave of St. Helen's, at Worcester, distinguished as being a maiden peal, from the fact that none of them required any chipping or filing to give them the proper tone, and for their curious inscriptions in honour of Queen Anne and Marlborough's victories over the French. These eight bells were cast out of five previously existing ones, and are dated 1706 and 1712. We also find bells from this foundry in the towers of various other churches in the county, including Dodderhill, Droitwich, Eckington, Oddingley, Upton Snodsbury, Hanbury, Wolverley, St. John and St. Nicholas, Worcester, and Norton, near Evesham. But his business was not confined to this county only, for his bells are to be found at Alveston, Salford Priors, Tanworth, and Wootton Wawen, in Warwickshire, and at Welford, in Gloucestershire. The oldest bell the writer has met with bearing Sanders' mark is in the tower of Upton Snodsbury church, and dated 1703. None of the bells in Bromsgrove church appear to have been cast by him.

BROOKE.—Sanders seems to have been succeeded in the foundry business by William Brooke, for on the second bell at Upton Warren we read, "William Brooke of Bromsgrove made me 1743." We also find the bells of the latter founder at Meriden and Shustoke, in Warwickshire.

SAUNDERS.—Some of the members of this family lived at "The Lodge, in Grafton Manor."

The burials generally took place at the close of the afternoon service on Sundays, and upon one occasion as many as 11 coffins of various sizes are known to have been placed in the middle of the church on forms, where they remained till the service in the church was concluded.

In 1773, "The Parish Umbrella," for the use of the clergyman at funerals, was purchased for £3. It was kept in the vestry. A box was made, and carried from grave to grave for the officiating minister to stand in to read the burial service. It was first used November 19th, 1806.

The churchyard contained about 600 gravestones, tombs, and flat stones in 1778. —*Lacy*, MS.

The two following inscriptions are mentioned by Nash as being in the church-yard, but they cannot now be found :—

" In memory of the dead,
From the year 1618 to 1739, lieth buried near to this
stone, 19 bodies of the present family o' the Clanes o'
Cateshill, and on the 15th of March '42, was interred
Hannah the wife of William Chanes, gent., she was aged
42 years and 5 months."

On a flat stone :—

"This stone is devoted
by his friend T. Nash*
to the memory of
John Bagley Esqre
a native of the City of Worcester,
and Lieutenant of the Militia of this County
at its first formation.
Of sense superior to vulgar feelings,
he disclaims your pity and lamentations
over his grave.
Rejoice rather, benevolent reader,
that a life of 63 years spent in serving
to the utmost of his power
his country, his friends, and mankind in general,
was terminated in this town,
January 10th 1784,
by a dissolution as easy and happy
as his days had been social, joyous, and innocent.
Go thou and imitate him !
by abhorring to give pain,
and studying to impart pleasure
to thy friends and fellow creatures
whether happy or distressed."

* An ingenious apothecary, of Bromsgrove.

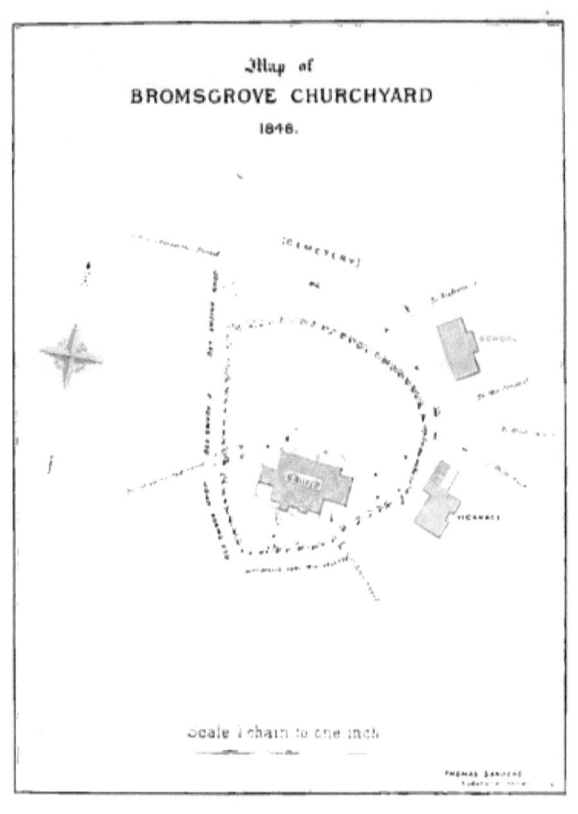

Map of
BROMSGROVE CHURCHYARD
1848.

Scale 1 chain to one inch

The course of the paths have undergone numerous alterations. In 1705, "It is agreed that the churchwardens shall not be allowed anything for cutting the paths in the churchyard." Plate IX. is a plan of the churchyard in 1848 : and at a parish meeting, held May 26th, "it was agreed that the paths marked A, should be stopped," and on April 9th, in the year following, "it was further agreed that the path marked B should be stopped up, and that that marked C should be opened in lieu thereof." There was also a path on the west side of the churchyard called the "Gentleman's Walk," on the other side of the lime trees to the present one. At the church restoration the ground and walks were lowered and soil removed.

The Author cannot close his description of "God's acre" without expressing his feelings of regret at the manner in which the stones marking the last resting place of the dead have been disturbed from time to time, and of the daily mischief done in the churchyard, chiefly, he fears, by the children attending the National Schools. Surely,

> These tombs and letter'd stones,

which

> Unfold the age and name of those who once had life,

ought to be respected, and steps taken to preserve them from mutilation by thoughtless hands. Some years ago handbills were issued, offering a reward for information which should lead to the conviction of offenders in this respect, and it would be satisfactory to see the "Burial Board" take up the matter now, with a determination to put a stop to the evil.

The Patronage of the Church.

 HERE was a church in Bromsgrove at the time of the compilation of the Domesday Book. Nash says: "The patronage of the church continued in the Crown till 16 Henry III., when that Prince conferred the church with all its appertinances on the Priory of Worcester,* 'for the salvation of his

---

* Charta of King Henry 3rd, in the matter of the Church at Bromsgrave.

Henry, by the grace of God, King of England, Lord of Ireland, Duke of Normandy and Aquitaine, Earl of Anjou, to Archbishops, Bishops, Abbots, Priors, Earls, Barons, Justiciaries, Sheriffs, Governors, Officers, and all Bailiffs, his liegemen, greeting :—

Know ye that we, in the face of God, and for the safety of our immortal soul, and for the soul of our Lord and Father, King John, and for the souls of all our Ancestors and heirs, have granted and given, and by this our Charter have confirmed, for us and our heirs for ever, to the Prior and

N

soule, the soule of his father King John, and the soules of his ancestors and
successors,' on condition that the prior and monks should celebrate the anniversary
of King John, and his own after his death.   Hubert de Burgo, Earl of Kent, Walter
de Beauchamp, Godfrey de Craucumb, and others were witnesses to this donation.
It was confirmed by Pope Gregory 9th."†   Habingdon says : " King Henry 3rd
gave to y" Priory of Worcester, for his own soule and the soules of his father,
ancestors and successors, the patronage of Bromesgrave, whereon attendeth the faire
chappell of Kingsnorton, with other chappells, a parish containing soe many and soe
great freeholders, as if it exceedeth not it equalleth the best in this shire."

Monks of Worcester, the Church of Bromsgrove, with all that appertaineth thereunto, to be held
and kept by them in free and perpetual alms, so that, so far as concerneth us and our heirs, they may
hold the said Church for their own special purposes—solemnizing every year the anniversary of King
John our father and of ours after our death, every year for ever.

Wherefore we do firmly promise and desire, for ourself and for our heirs, that the aforesaid Prior
and Monks, and their successors, may have and hold, for ever and ever, the aforementioned Church,
well and in peace, freely and quietly, with all that appertaineth thereunto, and that they may hold
the same for their special purposes – as far as concerneth us and our heirs, and for the solemnization of
the anniversary of King John our Father, and of our anniversary after our death, every year for ever
and ever, as aforesaid.

Witness this,

He. de Burgo, Earl of Kent, our Justiciary
Walter de Beauchamp
Godfrey de Craucumb
John, son of Philip
Galfrid Dispenser
Galfrid de Cano
Henry de Capella, &c., &c.

Given under the hand of the Reverend Father Padolf, Bishop of Chichester, our Chancellor, at
Worcester, the twenty-first day of May, in the sixteenth year of our Reign.   1232.

† I, Gregory, Vicar of the Church of Christ on Earth, servant of the servants of God, to my beloved
sons in the Lord the Prior and Members of the Church at Worcester, of the Order of St.
Benedict, greeting and blessing in the name of the Lord.   In as much as that which is sought of
us is lawful and just, equity and justice demand that, by a due discharge of the duties of
our office, it should be brought about.

Wherefore beloved in the Lord, concurring in affectionate assent to your just requests, We
confirm and by the present indenture validify to you and in you under the apostolic government of
your Church, the patronage of the Church of Bromsgrove, which our much beloved son in Christ,
the renowned King of England, Patron of the said Church (with the additional consent of William
de Bleys, of blessed memory, our Bishop) has conceded, so that thereby ye may hold it lawfully and
in peace.

Therefore let no man infringe upon this our deed of ratification, or dare to contravene it, for if
any man presume to attempt this, let it be known that he will, thereby incur the wrath of Almighty
God and of his blessed Apostles Peter and Paul.

Given at Orbitello, Tuscany, 26th day of April, 1237, in the eleventh year of our pontifical
Reign.

To quote further from Nash : "Upon the death of William de Furnell,* the last rector, William de Bleys, Bishop of Worcester, confirmed the King's gift, and at the same time assigned the chapel at Grafton to the sacrist of the church of Worcester, instead of 10 marks which the sacrist used to receive from the church at Bromsgrove for finding tapers to burn at the tomb of King John in Worcester Cathedral. The bishop reserved an annual payment of ten marks to the infirmary, and three marks towards the pittance on King John's anniversary ; and instituted a vicarage, to which he admitted Richard de Wynchcomb† on the presentation of the Prior and Convent. The vicarage consisted of the whole *alterage* of the church at Bromsgrove, and chapel at King's Norton, the best mortuary, the tythe of hay growing at Bromsgrove

* To all the Sons of Holy Mother Church ; who may hear or read this present writing. William of Bleys, by divine permission Bishop of Worcester, greeting ;—

We wish it to be known unto ye all, that the living of Bromsgrove having been vacated by the death of William Furnell, formerly rector of the same, at the request of our master the King, who hath given over the patronage of the said Church to the Prior and Monks of Worcester, in pure and perpetual gift, for the safety of the soul of King John, of blessed memory his father, whose body lieth in the Church of Worcester. We give and confirm to the said Prior and Monks, for their peculiar uses to be held, the above mentioned Church of Worcester, and furthermore with the agreement of the said Prior and Monks we have assigned to the Sacrist of Worcester, the Chapel of Grafton, which is a chapel of the Church of Bromsgrove, in lieu of ten marks per annum, which sum should be paid to the said Sacrist from the aforementioned Church of Bromsgrove, for the purchase of tapers for the tomb of the said King John.

Furthermore we assign ten marks to the Infirmary of Worcester, to be received yearly from the said Church ; and three marks to be used for a pittance on the day of the anniversary of the said King John. The whole of the residue we assign to the support of strangers and paupers applying to the above infirmary, excepting the perpetual vicarage which we institute in the said Church, with the assent of the aforesaid Priors and Monks. Save also to us and to our successors in the said Church both Pontifical and Parochial authority.

In proof of the contents of the present writing we confirm them by the affixing of our Seal in presence of these witnesses—

      Master Matt. de Grimell
      William de Tynton, gent., of Remesey
      W. de Thywe
      R. de Buckingham
      Master W. de Myll, gent., of Bredon
      J., Vicar of Hampton, of the monastery of Anketil
      Richard de Compton
      Gilbert Lyndes
      [Clergy and others.]

† To all Sons of Mother Church to whom this Indenture cometh, William de Bleys, by divine permission Bishop of Worcester, greeting in the name of the Lord, —

Be it known unto all of you, that on the presentation of Richard de Wynchcomb by Our beloved Sons in Christ, with Prior and Monks of Worcester, we have admitted the chaplaincy and perpetual Vicarage of the Church of Bromsgrove to the aforesaid Richard de Wynchcomb.

The said Vicarage consisteth in all the alterage of the aforementioned Church of Bromsgrove and of the Chapel of Norton, with the principal Mortuary, and with tenths of hay growing within the precincts of Bromsgrove only, and with a certain house at Bromsgrove, and another at Norton,

only, a house at Bromsgrove, and another at King's Norton. In 1380, Richard
Tewe, the vicar, sued for the tythes of hay arising from the meadows and other
places in Bromsgrove and its villages, and the tythes of pasture and hay appertaining
to the chapel at King's Norton. His claim was disallowed by John Blanchard,
Archdeacon of Worcester, Robert de la More, LL.D., John Malvern, precentor, and
Thomas Lench de Wych, proctor of the Consistorial Court, to whom the controversy
was referred, May 3rd, 1380. Their sentence was confirmed by the bishop, August
17th following, Walter de Cooksey and others being witnesses. It should seem that
this determination only affected the tythe hay of King's Norton, the tythe hay of
Bromsgrove being granted by the original endowment, and has ever since been paid.
Robert de Belne, Vicar of Bromsgrove, for the benefit of himself and his successors,
exchanged with the Prior and Convent, his patrons, the place of habitation where his
predecessor Henry dwelt, extending in length from the High Street, Bromsgrove, to
the entrance to the churchyard on the east, and to a path which leads from the said
High Street to the gate of the Prior and Convent's court, and in breadth from
the High Street to a water-course called Spadesborne on the west, for a messuage
which Nicholas de Prestford held of the Prior, with a portion of land which was
part of the Prior's garden, extending in length from the said garden, near the
churchyard, to the said path which comes from the High Street, on the upper part,
and on the lower part near the fish pool, and in part near the water-course of
Spadesborne. Godfrey Gifford confirmed this exchange by his deed, dated at
Alvechurch, on the day of St. Valentine the Martyr, 1292."

The house first alluded to, occupied the site of that in which Mrs. Davenport
now lives. It is not probable that much, if any, of the old house remains, although
some of the old stonework of the cellar certainly indicates the existence of a house
prior to the present one. This house was exchanged for the present vicarage
grounds. The fish pool referred to in the deed was a sheet of water in the Crown

In acknowledgment of these presents the aforesaid Vicar shall perform all proper and customary
duties in the aforementioned Church.

And that this our admittance and canonical precept may continue in due force for ever, save to us
and to our successors pontifical and parochial authority. We confirm the above writing in all its
contents by the affixing of our seal.

As witness,

Galfrid, Canon
Richard, Monk
W., Archdeacon of Worcester
Matthew Grimell
William de Tewe
Robert de Buckingham
Masters, Richard Compton, Gilbert Lyndens

[The Clergy and others.]

Close, from which the ecclesiastics residing in Holy Lane obtained their supply of fish. The pool was in existence, though of much smaller extent, till about the year 1836.

Holy Lane retained its name till October, 1852, when, by order of the Bromsgrove Local Board, the streets were renamed, and it obtained its present appellation of Church Street.

"In the 12th year of Edward II. reign an enquiry was made whether the Prior of Worcester held anything in Bromsgrove which was not in frank almoin; and it was found that he held 6 ox gangs of land and certain tenements of the glebe and endowment of his church time out of mind, and therefore not subject to tailage. A manor in Bromsgrove belongs to the parsonage. A court baron was formerly held by the Prior and Convent. The tenant of their manor was bound to receive the cellarist and steward of the priory during the court keeping at his own charges. The Prior and Convent granted a lease of the parsonage and its premises to John Greene, 5 Ed. IV., for 20 years, by which the tenant was obliged to entertain the cellarist, the cook, and the steward, with their servants, twice in a year, at the times of holding the court, and to provide food for their horses. The Dean and Chapter are now lords of the manor."—*Nash's* "Worcestershire."

The Manor House belonging to the Rectory Manor is situated on the west side of High Street, and till recently was occupied by Mr. Joseph Milton. It is a stone building, and was held in lease by Lord Windsor from the Dean and Chapter of Worcester, but the lease has now expired. Lacy, writing in 1778, in his MS., says: "The Rectory Manor has a court held twice a year, pays a yearly chief rent, but at death it pays no heriot. The Rectory Manor was formerly part of Feckenham Forest, and is now parcel of the Manor of Bromsgrove; was granted, some time before the Reformation, to St. Mary's Monastery at Worcester, in which church it still continues, and is leased, together with the rectorial tythes, to the present Earl of Plymouth, who also rents the glebe lands under the said church."

The old rent of the parsonage of Bromsgrove was £26 per annum, to be paid to the coquinarius (cook, or purveyor of food); all escheats and fines were reserved to the cellarist. In the Parliamentary survey, taken 1649, it is said to have been worth £125 16s. 8d. more than the rent. According to Nash, the rectorial tithes were purchased by Other Windsor, Earl of Plymouth, about the year 1768, of the heirs of James Cocks, being a lease for 21 years, renewable under the Dean and Chapter of Worcester. The last lease expired at Michaelmas, 1879, and the tithes are now collected by the Ecclesiastical Commissioners.

On the site of the present sheep market, and only a short distance from the church and vicarage, stood the Tithe Barn, a sketch of which appeared in "The

Mirror" of Saturday, December 13th, 1834, and of which our engraving is a
fac-simile, accompanied by the following remarks :—

"I send you a sketch of the Tithe Barn, now standing in the fields at the
extremity of Holy Lane, in the parish of Bromsgrove, Worcestershire ; in which the
celebrated Mrs. Siddons, when Miss Kemble, and a member of her father's company
of comedians, formerly performed. I am informed by a gentleman, a native and
resident of Bromsgrove, that he witnessed her appearance in the above barn, about
the year 1765 or 6, in a play entitled 'Charles the First,' in which she represented
the character of a young princess ; and my informant also witnessed there her
performance of *Ariel*, in 'The Tempest,' and her singing between the acts of
the play.

"From the circumstance of its being well known by many of the inhabitants
of the town of Bromsgrove, that the barn was formerly made use of by the Kemble
family for the above-named purpose, I am induced to send you this sketch. The
barn is now in so dilapidated a condition, that the proprietor will shortly take
it down.   "JOHN F. BOWDEN.

["We thank our Correspondent for this humble, yet interesting, memorial of
genius, as well as for his congratulations and good wishes. The date, supplied by his
informant, of Miss Kemble's performance in this barn, must be that of one of her
earliest appearances, if not her first appearance, on the stage. We regret that
Mr. Campbell, in his 'Life of Mrs. Siddons,' lately published, does not enable us to
settle the point, but rather adds to our doubt by a kind of information which is
characteristic of his work, and which is little better than no information at all. Such
as it is, we quote all that the poetical biographer supplies :]

"I am unable to state the exact date of Mrs. Siddons's first appearance on
the stage, but it must have been very early ; for the company was offended at
her appearance of childhood, and was for some time shaken with uproar. The timid

debutante was about to retire, when her mother, with characteristic decision, led her to the front of the stage, and made her repeat the fable of the 'Boys and the Frogs,' which not only appeased the audience, but produced thunders of applause. At thirteen, she was the heroine in several English operas, and sang very tolerably. In the 'History of Worcester,' there is found the copy of a play-bill, dated February 12th, 1767, in which Mr. Roger Kemble announces his company of comedians, as playing at the King's Head, in that city; with a concert of music. The play was 'Charles the First,' by an actor named Havard, indifferently written, and from its subject ill calculated for the universal sympathy of a British audience. The characters were thus cast: *James, Duke of Richmond*, by Mr. Siddons, who was now an actor in Kemble's company; *James, Duke of York*, by Master John Kemble, who was then about twelve years old. *The Young Princess*, by Miss Kemble, then approaching to fourteen; *Lady Fairfax*, by Mrs. Kemble. Singing between the acts, by Mr. Fowler and Miss Kemble. In the April following, Master John Kemble is announced as *Philidel*, in 'King Arthur,' and Miss Kemble as *Ariel*, in 'The Tempest.'"

The barn was sold by public auction, on May 7th, 1844, for £29 10s. 6d., and was shortly afterwards pulled down and cleared away.

"In an original valor of this diocese, at the First Fruits Office, dated 26 Henry VIII., signed by Bishop Latimer, we read: 'Cantaria beatae Marine in Bromsgrove, valet per annum £6 6s. 8d.'"—*Nash.*

The living of Christ Church, Catshill, valued at £300 per annum, with residence, is in the gift of the Vicar of Bromsgrove. The church, which consists of nave, chancel, and north and south aisles, and tower at the west end, was erected in 1838, at a cost of £1500. The present vicar is Rev. James Kidd, A.K.C., instituted in 1868.

The living of Holy Trinity Church, The Lickey, is also in the gift of the vicar of Bromsgrove. It is valued at £300 a year, with residence. Rev. John Goodwin, M.A., formerly curate of Bromsgrove, is incumbent. The church is built of stone, in the Early English style, having a chancel, nave, aisles, and bell cot with two bells; it was consecrated on June 5th, 1856, and cost about £2500.

The living of the new church of All Saints, valued at £300 per annum, with residence, is in the presentation of the Vicar of Bromsgrove. This church, built from designs of Mr. John Cotton, architect, of Temple Row, Birmingham, was opened August 6th, 1874. The present vicar is the Hon. and Rev. A. H. T. Massey, M.A.

In December, 1879, the livings of these churches were each raised to £300 per year by the Ecclesiastical Commissioners. At the same time an additional £120 per annum was granted to All Saints for curate's stipend.

There were formerly five other chapels dependent on the church of Bromsgrove, to each of which a curate was appointed by the vicar.

The living of King's Norton was in the gift of the Vicar of Bromsgrove till 1846, when it was made a separate incumbency on the death of the late Bishop of Rochester, who was Dean of Worcester and Vicar of Bromsgrove. The stipend was then increased, and the Dean and Chapter of Worcester retained the disposal of it themselves. The church, dedicated to St. Nicholas, is a large and handsome structure, with chancel, nave, aisles, and western tower and spire.

Moseley was a chapelry to King's Norton till 1853, when it had a district assigned to it. The church is a commodious structure, of stone and brick, with a square tower and three bells. It was repaired and enlarged in 1823, at a cost of nearly £2000. It has 557 sittings, of which 169 are free and unappropriated. The living is a vicarage, value £229, with residence, in the patronage of the Vicar of Bromsgrove, and held by the Rev. W. H. Colmore, M.A., formerly senior curate of Bromsgrove.

Withall, formerly a chapel to King's Norton, was formed into an ecclesiastical district in 1853. It is now an independent vicarage, for which a new church, designed by Mr. Preedy, and superseding a small brick structure erected in the last century, was erected in 1861 ; it includes the outlying portions of King's Norton, Alvechurch, and Solihull parishes. The church is built of brick, with bands of Bromsgrove stone. Bath stone is also used, for dressings and carved work, of which there is a considerable quantity, by Earp. It has north and south aisles, tower, forming the ritual chancel, with a sanctuary projecting about 20 feet beyond, and 352 sittings. The east window is of stained glass, representing the Virgin Mary, and presented by Mrs. Mynors and Robert Mynors, Esq. Two stained glass windows have been recently added ; one by Mr. Richard Burman, of Houndsfield, and the other by the children of the late James Johnstone, Esq., M.D. The living is in the diocese and archdeaconry of Worcester, and rural deanery of Northfield ; value, £150, with residence, and 35 acres of glebe ; patron, the Vicar of King's Norton.

The chapel at Chadwich, dedicated to St. Chad, is destroyed, and no trace of it is now left. The site is believed to have been on the north side of the Manor House, in a small pleck, now planted as an orchard, in a manor belonging to the Dean and Canons of Christ Church, Oxford, but now leased to Mr. Francis Tongue Rufford. It is said that they ought to keep the chapel in repair, and find a minister to officiate in it, but of this there is no evidence. Dr. Nash says : "Service has not been performed in this chapel, nor has it been fit for service, within memory." About 1410, the Master of St. Wulstan's Hospital, Worcester, disputed with the Prior and Convent, at Worcester, "as to the duty of finding a priest to officiate in the chapel of Chaddeswick, where the hospital held lands belonging to the Prior and Convent. The right of the hospital to nominate was allowed, but the incumbent was to be presented to the Prior and Convent, and a certain arrangement made as to his pay. This controversy lasted a long time." Lacy, referring to Chadwich yield, says : " Here is also a chapel-of-ease belonging to Bromsgrove church, but it is very ruinous ; it is about five miles to the north of Bromsgrove. Chadwich is parcel of the Rectory Manor, it paying a chief rent to it." And in another place the same writer says : "At Chadwich, or Chadisick, is a chapel-of-ease, belonging to Bromsgrove church (said to be dedicated to St. Chad) ; it is now in a ruinous condition, and used by the tenant of the farm on which it stands as a lumber room ; it is close to the mansion house at Chadwich."

The inhabitants of Chadwich have the right of burial at Bromsgrove.

There is no church at Grafton Manor, but there is a chapel adjoining the manor house, used, until a few years ago, as a Roman Catholic place of worship. The Rev. Henry Campbell, who died February 25th, 1874, at the age of 91 years, was the last resident priest, having lived at Grafton upwards of 60 years. In the reign of Edward I., a dispute arose between John de Grafton and the Prior of Worcester, relating to the advowson of the chapel of Grafton, when the former resigned his claim upon the payment of 35 marks by the priory of Worcester.* John de Grafton gave to God, the Blessed Virgin, and the chapel of St. Michael de Grafton, a messuage and lands near the king's highway, between the house of Robert Broke and the house of John Sirloc, which lands were 120 feet in length and 76 feet in breadth. The manor of Grafton was formerly a chapelry belonging to Bromsgrove, till the reign of Henry III., when an arrangement was made between the Prior and Convent of Worcester and Bishop William de Bloys, by which it was made over to the former, and has since become independent of Bromsgrove. There is a small burial ground adjoining the chapel, but no service is now held.

The inhabitants of Grafton bury at Bromsgrove, Upton Warren, and Stoke Prior.

---

* John of Grafton brought a suit, at the last presentation in the county, before four appointed officers, against William de Furnell, in the matter of the chapel of Grafton ; and William, in replying, states that he is a clergyman at Bromsgrove, and that the said chapel belongs to his church of Bromsgrove, and has been in seizin 40 years elapsed ; and he furthermore states that there was an agreement entered into formerly between himself and John, who has lately died, a farmer ; in consequence of which he had regained possession of the chapel, as belonging to his church at Bromsgrove, and that afterwards he let it to him as a farm for half a mark and one load of corn. And he also affirms that the said John died a farmer, not a clergyman ; and after the death of the said John he took the chapel into his own possession, and that, as such, he held his claim to it. And John, being asked what action he had taken during the continuance of the agreement, answered —Nothing. And seeing that the said William has been thence in seizin for so long a time, on account of his church at Bromsgrove, which he holds as a gift from the King, it is henceforth to remain in his seizin ; and John may make appeal to the King if he will. And the Bishop of Worcester is also charged to allow the said William de Furnell to hold in peaceful possession the said chapel, in face of all claims of the said John.

In Dr. Thomas's "Antiquities of Worcester" is the following : " On the 2nd of the Nones of June, Godfrey Gifford, ordained at Bromsgrove, and, as the Worcester annals say, forgetful of the Peace made between Him and his Convent, he would not suffer the Chantor to execute his office. And say further, That on the 3rd of the Nones of August, he extorted from them the Chapel of Grafton, and appropriated it to the use of the Sacrist, without making them any allowance for the Expense they had been at in recovering the same in the King's Courts, which amounted to no less than £200, having been seven years in law."

The chapel was nearly destroyed by fire in 1710, and it lay in ruins till 1809, when it was restored at the expense of the Earl of Shrewsbury. For several years, between 1740 and 1750, the Roman Catholics of the town and neighbourhood met in secresy in the attic of the old farm house at Whitford, to celebrate divine worship according to the rites of their own Church. In 1796, Andrew Robinson, clerk, of Grafton Manor, set apart a room for Roman Catholic worship, and Charles Weetman, born in Staffordshire in 1781, took upon himself the *Grafton* mission, and, dying in Worcester in 1813, was buried at St. Oswald's, in that city.

There was an agreement entered into between the Prior of Dodford and the Vicar of Bromsgrove, in respect of burials at Dodford, as follows :—

" To all good true Christians to whom this present indenture may come, brother Gwido, Prior of the Monastery of Dodford of the order of St. Augustine, and of the convent of that place, greeting in the name of the Lord. By the present we make it known to all of you that our monastery aforesaid being within the limits of the Parish Church of Bromsgrove situate and founded in the diocese of Worcester, each and every one of our lay servants who has not taken the vow aforementioned and all others in attendance or service upon us, now dwelling, or such as in future may dwell ; within the confines of our monastery, aforesaid, and in all other places belonging to us within the limits of the parish of the abovementioned church ; are fully entitled with other parishioners of the Parish Church of Bromsgrove while living ; to enjoy the benefit of all religious rites of the Church ; and when dead to be buried there with all due rites and solemnities, We the abovementioned Prior and Monks of the aforesaid places do hereby declare for ourselves and our successors who shall come hereafter, that we have never exacted, claimed, held or limited, in any way, nor on the other hand do we wish to exact, claim, hold or limit, anything affecting the rites and ceremonies of the aforementioned church in any way to the prejudice of Master Robert de la Felde vicar of the aforesaid parish church, of his successors vicars of the said church or of the church itself or of its vicarage, or of the rights and appurtenances of the above whatsoever, upon any occasion either by power or privilege obtained ; or hereafter to be obtained by us. Save and except to ourselves the burial of such as freely and willingly in their last will may have bequeathed, and of such as in future shall bequeath their bodies to be buried in the monastery in canonical form. Save and except to the aforesaid parish church all privileges in the matter of rites and ceremonies appertaining to the same."—Translated from *Nash*.

The patronage of the living of Bromsgrove is vested in the Dean and Chapter of Worcester. In the taxation of 1291, the church and its two chapels (Grafton and King's Norton), are together valued at £33 6s. 8d. yearly. Fifty years later (1341), they are set down at £41 6s. 8d. In 1536, the valuation of the mother church and its chapels are kept separate. The smaller tithes, &c., belonging to the vicarage are returned at £21 8s., as against £20 at King's Norton. In 1695, Bromsgrove, with the chapel of King's Norton, is returned at £41 8s. The tithes were commuted at £1100 15s., to which may be added an excellent vicarage house, fees, and a small allotment of land. In the "Worcester Diocesan Church Calendar" (1879), the nett value* of the living is returned at £800.

Bromsgrove is in the diocese and archdeaconry of Worcester, and rural deanery of Wych.

The Vicars of Bromsgrove.

NASH, in his history of the county, gives the following list of the Patrons and Vicars of Bromsgrove, with the dates at which they were admitted to the living, from 1309 to 1778 :—

PATRON.		ADMITTED.
Prior and Convent of Worcester.	Henry de la Lee	March 19th, 1309.
	Robert de la Felde, Presbyter	Sept. 9th, 1316.
	Richard de Kingswood, Presbyter	April 8th, 1320.
	John de Battisford, Chapter ...	August 2nd, 1321.
	William de Hampton, Presbyter ...	May 22nd, 1335.
	Phillip le Younge ...	——— 1340.
	Edward Brugge	Oct. 6th, 1357.

* The nett value shows the amount received by the incumbent after deduction of poor rates, land tax, tenths, and synodals. The incumbent must pay out of nett value all other charges, such as expenses of collections, curates' stipends, payment on account of mortgage to Queen Anne's Bounty, &c. The Vicar of Bromsgrove has to contribute £75 per annum to the living of Catshill, and £50 to the Lickey.

PATRON.		ADMITTED.
Prior and Convent of Worcester.	John de Oxon* ...	Oct. 8th, 1357.
	John de Merston	Oct. 21st, 1361.
	Richard atte Lake de Tewe	March 3rd, 1370.
	Richard Green, Presbyter	Sept. 19th, 1391.
	Nicholas Hambury, Presbyter	Oct. 13th, 1406.
	William Spooner, Presbyter ...	May 31st, 1408.
	John Potter, Chapter	Dec. 16th, 1409.
	Thomas Chase, Professor of Divinity ...	March 11th, 1421.
	John Grene, Chapter	Sept. 15th, 1424.
	Thomas Feysy	Nov. 4th, 1445.
	Richard Manning	Sept. 28th, 1446.
	Reginald Newton	Feb. 4th, 1446.
	Christopher Goldsmith, Chapter	July 31st, 1475.
	Peter Wever, Presbyter, A.M. ...	April 10th, 1557.
Dean and Chapter of Worcester.	Robert Notingham, A.M. ...	Oct. 13th, 1561.
	Thomas Hearle, A.M.	Sept. 23rd, 1581.
	Gervase Carrington, LL.B.	April 4th, 1590.
	John Archbould, Professor of Divinity	May 4th, 1613.
	John Hall, A.M.	June 6th, 1624.
Charles II.	John Wolley, Clerk	August 20th, 1660.
Dean and Chapter of Worcester. }	Thomas Warmstry, Professor of Divinity	Sept. 20th, 1662.
Bishop of Worcester.	George Glen, Clerk, A.M.	Oct. 26th, 1666.
Dean and Chapter of Worcester.	Thomas Wilmott,† Clerk, A.M. ...	Nov. 22nd, 1669.
	Thomas Wilmott, Clerk, A.M. ...	Jan. 26th, 1699.
	William Phillips, B.A.	Nov. 27th, 1741.
	John Waugh, B.A. ...	June 9th, 1754.
	Thomas Evans, D.D.‡	Jan. 6th, 1778.

* Both Brugge and Oxon claimed the vicarage : and in the meantime, Henry de Raggele, by the power of the Apostolic See, obtained possession of it ; but afterwards John de Oxon was admitted, May 23rd, 1359.

† In the year 1669, Thomas Wilmott, Vicar of Bromsgrove, laid an information at the sessions to the effect that, "being ready to attend his duty at the funeral of Jane, the wife of John Eckols, was by a tumult of Anti-Baptists affronted and disturbed whilst I was reading the service. They no sooner came to the grave but irreverently threw the corpse thereinto, and, having their hats on their heads, immediately, contrary to the orders of the Church, without the least respect to the service of the same, and without either clerk or sexton, with their feete easie in the mold and covered the corpse. Amongst which tumult there was one Henry Waldron, who, entring into the belman's house, without his leave, took away his spade, wherewith John Price, contrary to all civility and decency, notwithstanding he was checked by the minister, with his head covered, persisted to throwe the mold in the aforesaid grave."—*Noake.*

The Author is indebted to John H. Hooper, Esq., M.A., one of the secretaries to the Bishop of Worcester, for the completion of the list to the present time, as follows :—

PATRON.		ADMITTED.
Dean and Chapter of Worcester.	The Hon. St. Andrew St. John, D.D.§...	May 5th, 1786.
	Thomas Fountaine, M.A.	October 2nd, 1788.
	John Wingfield, D.D.	Oct. 31st, 1815.
	James Hook, LL.D.‡	June 1st, 1826.
	George Murray, Bishop of Rochester‡...	April 26th, 1827.
	William Villers, M.A.	July 20th, 1846.
	George William Murray, M.A.	April 3rd, 1861.

Mr. Villers preached his first sermon in Bromsgrove church August 9th, 1846.— "Bromsgrove Almanack."

For more than 70 years Bromsgrove was without a resident vicar, during which time various curates in charge were appointed, and amongst others—Rev. Mr. Cottam, Rev. Mr. Winpenny, Rev. J. N. Harward, and Rev. T. B. G. Moore, M.A., to whom a testimonial was presented in 1846 by the inhabitants ; a massive service of plate was also presented to Mr. Harward when he resigned his curacy in 1838, for a living in Kent. The children and teachers belonging to the Sunday Schools also presented the rev. gentleman with a costly pocket communion service.

On July 27th, 1681, John Bowater was committed to Worcester gaol, at the suit of Thomas Wilmot, priest, of Bromsgrove, for non-payment of small tithes, and removed to the Fleet Prison, and while there a heifer worth £1 10s., belonging to him, was taken.

The *Vicar's Fees*, as taken from an old MS., were—

	£	s.	d.
Christening			
Churching	0	0	4
Wedding by Banns	0	3	6
Wedding by Licence			
Burials			
Easter "Dews" for single persons ...	0	0	6
For the "Garding"	0	0	1

Clerk's Fees.

	£	s.	d.
Registering Christenings ...	0	0	2
For examining the Register ...	0	0	4
Weddings by Licence			
do. by Banns ...	0	1	6

‡ Deans of Worcester.   § Archdeacon of Worcester.

For Burials			
Easter " Dews " for House Dwellers ...	0	0	4
Sexton's Fees.			
For Making a grave (churchyard) ...	0	0	6
For Ringing the Bell	0	0	6
For Burying a still Born Child	0	0	4
For " Briering " a Grave	0	0	4
For Moving a stone in the Churchyard	0	1	0
„ „ Church or Chancel ...	0	4	0
For Making a grave in the Church or Chancel	0	2	0
Ringing the Bell twelve hours	0	6	8
Ringing the four and Eight o'clock Bell per year ...			

The Author has met with the following printed copies of sermons preached in Bromsgrove church :—

TALBOT's (W., Dean of Worcester) Sermon, Preach'd in the Parish-Church of Bromsgrove in Worcestershire, May 1st, 1695, upon occasion of a Charity given to that Place, by Sir Thomas Cookes of Bentley, Kt. Bar.

J. PORTER, of Aulcester. A Caution against Youthful Lusts, in two discourses, occasion'd by the Death of Mr. Thomas Webb, who departed this life July 18th, 1708, and requested upon his death bed that Youth might be warn'd to avoid those Lusts that he had found more bitter than Death. Preached at Bromsgrove in Worcestershire, and published at the Desire of the Youth that heard it.*

TYNDAL's Funeral Sermon at Broomsgrove, on Mr. John Spilsbury, 1769. Birmingham : Baskerville.

HUMPHREYS, J.—Sermon at Bromsgrove, on the death of Mr. Benj. Humphreys. April 19th, 1789.

HOOPER, Rev. FRANCIS J. B., Rector of Upton Warren.—Sermon, preached at Bromsgrove, May 22nd, 1844, on "The Old and New Dispensations, contrasted."

---

* The preacher was a native of Bromsgrove, but there is nothing in the book to prove that the sermon was actually preached in the *church*. It was sold by John Halford, at the *Hand and Pen*, in Bromsgrove. Halford appears to have been a schoolmaster, for at the end of the book this curious "advertisement" appears :—

WRITING, in all the Hands of *Great Britain* ; *Arithmetick*, Vulgar and Decimal, by Logarithms, and Algebraical ; also Instrumental, *i.e.*, by *Gunter's* Line with Compasses, or by Sliding-Rules ; with their Uses in *Book-keeping*, after the most plain, practical, and *Italian* manner. Measuring of Board, Glass, Tiling, Paving, Timber, Stone, and irregular Solids.

As also Geometry, Planometry, Stereometry, Gauging, Trigonometry, Dialing, Navigation, and other useful parts of the *Mathematicks*. Together with the Art of Writing most sorts of Characters, or Shorthand.

Likewise the art of *Spelling* and *Reading True English*, &c. ;

Are all Taught by JOHN HALFORD, at the *Hand and Pen*, in *Bromsgrove*, and YOUTH Boarded.

JACOB, Rev. G. A., D.D.—Sermon on Thursday, March 31st, 1853, being the Tercentenary of the Foundation of the Grammar School of King Edward Sixth. "Connection between True Religion and Sound Learning."

COLLIS, Rev. J. D. (Bromsgrove).—Sermon preached on Sunday, January 30th, 1859, being the first Sunday after the reopening of the church.

MURRAY, Rev. G. W., Vicar of Bromsgrove.—Sermon on Sunday, July 4th, 1869. "Changes in the Services of the Church," &c.

MURRAY, Rev. G. W., Vicar of Bromsgrove.—Sermon on Sunday, January 16th, 1870, on "Almsgiving: Its Mode, Motive, and Measure."

BLORE, Rev. G. J.—A Sermon preached in the Parish Church of St. John the Baptist, Bromsgrove, on Sunday, July 6th, 1873. "Prosperity to Bromsgrove."

The Clerks and Sextons.

 T appears impossible to trace the various holders of the offices of clerk and sexton to any considerable period. The first notice found in the books of the parish is in 1684, when it was "Agreed that the Minister's Clerk and belman," who, according to ancient custom, was sexton, was to "walk the church and dig the graves and ring the bells, and to have 2ˢ 2ᵈ for the Burial and Registering of any one that has pay from the parish." At this time Edward Carter was clerk. In 1703, Thomas Hemming was sexton.

On May 6th, 1753, "It is agreed that John Hill shall come into the house (? what house), and that he shall walk the church and wind up the church clock and chimes as *sexton*."

On August 2nd, 1772, at a vestry meeting, it was agreed to appoint William Rose sexton of the parish, in the room of William Southall, deceased.

Judging from these dates, it would appear that William was the *first* of the Rose family who have, in unbroken succession, supplied the parish with sextons ever since, and with clerk's latterly. The Author has thought well to give all the information in his possession with reference to the connection of this family with the duties of sexton and clerk, as there is something pleasing in the succession of attachments to offices of the church.

William Rose held the office of sexton for 18 years. He died July 14th, 1789, at the age of 75, and was succeeded by his son Thomas, who was sexton for 35 years. The appointment of the latter took place July 19th, 1789, according to the following extracts :—

"At a vestry meeting this day held we the undersigned inhabitants of this parish do appoint Thomas Rose in the Room of his Father, William Rose, deceased. And it is ordered and agreed that from and after the death of the parish clerk of this parish, or his quitting such office, the perquisites of Ringing the Bells for funerals shall belong to the sexton.

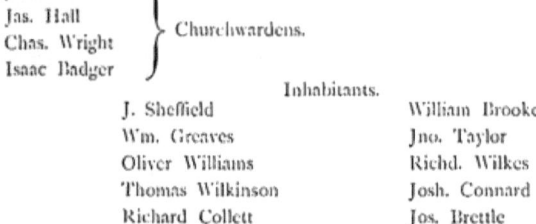

John Ashmore
Jas. Hall
Chas. Wright
Isaac Badger
      } Churchwardens.

Inhabitants.

J. Sheffield	William Brooke
Wm. Greaves	Jno. Taylor
Oliver Williams	Richd. Wilkes
Thomas Wilkinson	Josh. Connard
Richard Collett	Jos. Brettle

"If the Church Wardens of the Parish, with the Consent of the Majority of the Inhabitants paying Scot and Lot, have appointed Thomas Rose Sexton of this Parish, his office or employment then is, to look after the Body of the Church, *i.e.*, to keep the seats, &c., clean, to ring the 5 and 8 o'clock Bell, to look after the Bell Ropes, to dig the Graves, and ring the funeral Bell, as also to take care that the sacramental wine is always ready and suff!

"The Churchwardens pay him for ringing the 8 and 5 o'clock Bell, as also Parishioners pay for digging the graves and ringing the funeral Bell or Bells.

"Bromsgrove, 18th Aug't 1789."   "Chas. Harris.

There is in the possession of the family the following account of the duties and remuneration of the office, as held by Thomas Rose :—

"To Wind up the Church Clock and Chimes I have 5 Locks to unlock and lock every morning, which makes 1825 times in the year ; I have 47 Stairs to walk up, which makes 17155 Stairs in the year ; I have 7 cwt. to wind up every morning, which makes 2555 cwt., or 127 tons 15 cwt.

"The number of Yards I have to wind the weights up every morning is 30, and that total is 10950 or 6 miles and 390 yards ; my Salary for that is £3 12s. 0d., and divide that into 365 parts makes $2\frac{1}{4}^{d.}$ and $\frac{1}{3}^{rd}$ of a farthing each time.

"I have 625 different times to Ring a Bell in the year, and to walk up 28 Stairs each time, which makes 17500 yearly ; for that I receive £2 16s. 0d., and divide that into 625 parts, it makes $1^{d.}\frac{1}{12}^{th}$ each time.

"Then to add 365 times to the 625 for the Morning Bell, would make 990 times yearly. I should then have to walk up 28 Stairs each time, which would make 27720 stairs yearly, and would reduce the £2 16s. 0d. in proportion to ¼d. and ¾ths of a farthing nearly for each time.

"Sweeping the Steps £1 6s. 0d.

"Winding the Town Hall Clock up £1 6s. 0d. On Sundays for attending the services of the Church £2 0s. 0d. There is 104 services, and 4¾d. for each service would be 1s. 2d. in the year more than my salary; and then

"I don't take into account Christmas day, Good Friday, Wit Monday and Thursday, and May day.

"Five Stoves, Gas, Cleaning Glasses.

"June 6th, 1842, Reference to the Churchwardens' order book.

"Mending Ropes.

"Thomas Rose Elected Sexton, July 19th, 1789."

The latter part of this account cannot refer to Thomas Rose, who died January 11th, 1824, aged 73 years.

Shortly after his death the following notice was issued :—

"The Churchwardens request the inhabitants whom it concerns to give them the meeting in the vestry, on Thursday next, at two o'clock in the afternoon, to appoint a Sexton to succeed the late Thomas Rose, deceased.

"Sunday ye 18 January 1824."

There being more than one candidate for the office, the election took place by poll—

For John White,	For Joseph Rose,
149.	152.

Joseph Rose was accordingly elected.

White was town bellman, and was succeeded in that office by Thomas Edwards.

On June 25th, 1842, "The Sexton's Salary was made £11 11s., because 10s. 6d. was taken from him for attending Parish Meetings."

During his term of office, an adjourned vestry meeting was held July 17th, 1846, at which it was moved by Mr. Day, and seconded by Mr. Wildsmith, and resolved unanimously, "That the following shall be the duties of the Sexton of Bromsgrove Church :—

"To keep the church and pews cleanly swept and dusted.

"To attend the church during divine worship, in order to open the pew doors for the parishioners, and to prevent disturbance, &c.

"To ring the bell every night at 8 o'clock.

"To ring on every Sunday 2 bells at 7 and 1 bell at 8 in the morning, and 2 bells at one and one bell at ½ past one in the afternoon.

" To wind up and regularly attend to the church clock and chimes and Town Hall clock.

" To light a fire in the vestry when necessary, and keep the same clean.

" Regularly to remove the nuisance behind the stones in the churchyard, and to sweep the churchyard walks, the churchyard steps, and other approaches to the church."

Resolved (on the motion of Mr. Day, seconded by Mr. Watton), " That the Salary for the above duties shall be £13 a year from the 24th June last, to be paid quarterly by the Churchwardens, and that if the duties of the Sexton are not properly and satisfactorily performed, the Churchwardens are authorised (after due notice) to employ any other person or persons, and to deduct the remuneration paid to them from the Sexton's Salary."

A copy of these resolutions is framed, and hangs up in the vestry.

Joseph held the office of sexton nearly 45 years, and was deputy clerk for about 18 years. He died 27th December, 1868, aged 74 years.

The following report appeared in the *Bromsgrove Messenger* of January 2nd, 1869 :—

" DEATH OF MR. JOSEPH ROSE, PARISH CLERK AND SEXTON.

" On Sunday evening last, Joseph Rose, who had been for nearly 45 years sexton, and for 18 years clerk and sexton, of Bromsgrove, died peacefully at his residence, the Cemetery Lodge. For some months previously he had been missing from his accustomed seat in the parish church, his failing health, and the increased infirmities of age, having prevented his fulfilling the duties he had assiduously performed for so many years, and which, in his absence, were efficiently carried out by his son John. Since May last, deceased has been almost entirely confined to his house, and his death was, therefore, not unexpected.

"The deceased was a member of a family who had filled office in this parish for nearly a century. His grandfather was sexton for 18 years ; his father held the same office for 35 years ; and his brother William (whom he succeeded in the office) was parish clerk for 30 years. Deceased was an officer of the Court Leet for 50 years ; he was for many years an active change ringer, and one of the old society ; and, being possessed of a remarkably fine bass voice, and considerable musical talent, he was for many years a prominent and useful member of the church choir, in which his abilities were used with considerable advantage and effect. He will, doubtless, long be remembered by the inhabitants of Bromsgrove.

" The burial of deceased took place on Thursday last, his remains being interred in the cemetery. The funeral was attended by many of the parishioners, the pall bearers being Mr. W. Holyoake, Mr. A. Bennett, and Mr. George Kings, church-wardens ; Mr. T. White, Mr. G. Dipple, and Mr. W. F. Wilmshurst. The mourners were the sons and other relatives of deceased. The service in the church was choral, nearly every member of the choir being present to take part, and Mr. J. B. Tirbutt presided at the organ. The Rev. A. Waller was the officiating minister in the church, the service at the grave being read by the Rev. Ll. Jones. There was a very large attendance of spectators, in the church and at the grave. At the conclusion of the beautiful service, the members of the society of change ringers showed their respect for the departed ringer by giving a touch of change ringing, with the hand bells, over his grave. They also rang peals upon the church bells (which were muffled) before and after the interment."

And in the January number of the " Parish Magazine," we read—

" DEATH OF THE PARISH CLERK.

" The last funeral in the dying year, 1868, is an event which we cannot pass over without a brief notice in the 'Parish Magazine.' It is that of one who was for more than 40 years officially connected with the parish church.

" Joseph Rose, son of Thomas Rose, formerly sexton of Bromsgrove, was born on the 5th July, 1794. In 1824 he was elected sexton, by a general poll of the parishioners. Possessed of a fine bass voice, he was for many years a prominent member of the church choir. In 1850 he was appointed clerk, and the duties of this office, together with those of sexton, he continued assiduously to perform until compelled to desist by failing health and the increasing infirmities of age. Since May last he has been entirely confined to his house.

" A few days ago he was seen to be sinking, and on Sunday last (December 27th), as the bells were calling us to the evening service, he passed away, apparently in sleep, in the 75th year of his age. The familiar form and features of 'Sexton Rose' will not soon be forgotten in Bromsgrove."

With the death of Joseph Rose, the long white rod formerly carried about the church by the sexton also disappeared.

On January 9th, the following advertisements appeared in the local paper : —

PARISH OF BROMSGROVE.
NOTICE.

A VESTRY MEETING of the inhabitants will be held in the VESTRY of the PARISH CHURCH, on MONDAY NEXT, the 11th day of JANUARY, 1869, at Twelve o'clock noon, to ELECT a SEXTON, in the place of Joseph Rose, deceased.

The Churchwardens desire to inform the Ratepayers that as soon as a meeting is made, it is their intention to move an ADJOURNMENT, at the TOWN HALL, and they suggest that the Parishioners should give their attendance there instead of at the Vestry.

TO THE RATEPAYERS OF THE PARISH OF BROMSGROVE.

My Lords, Ladies, and Gentlemen,—

By the lamented death of my Father, the office of Sexton of your parish (which he held for 45 years) has become vacant; and Monday next, the 11th instant, at Twelve o'clock, at the Vestry of the Parish Church, is fixed for the Election of his successor.

I beg respectfully to acquaint you that I am a Candidate for the situation, and to state that for upwards of five years I have assisted in the performance of the duties, and during the last *eight months* I have done the whole of the work attached to the office, in consequence of my Father's illness preventing him leaving his room; and I hope I may be pardoned in venturing to refer you to the manner in which such duties have been performed as the *best* testimonial in my favour.

The facts that this office has been held by members of the family, uninterruptedly, for the last 100 years; and that (should I be honoured with your choice), I shall have the valuable assistance of my widowed Mother in carrying out the various duties appertaining to it, will, I trust, be received by you as favourable to my candidature.

I propose doing myself the pleasure of personally calling upon as many of the Ratepayers as I possibly can before the day of the Election; but, as the time is so short, and the parish so extensive, I fear I shall not be able to call upon all of them.

I shall feel very grateful to those Ratepayers who are in my favour, if they will *endeavour to make it convenient to attend* at the above time and place, for the purpose of recording their votes in my favour.

I have the honour to remain,

My Lords, Ladies, and Gentlemen,

Your most obedient Servant,

Cemetery Lodge, Bromsgrove,   John Rose.
    January 7th, 1869.

The meeting was held as advertised, and, as there was no other candidate proposed, John Rose was declared duly elected.

At the quarterly meeting of the Burial Board, held on January 13th, 1869, Mrs. Rose was elected lodge keeper, and John Rose elected registrar and grave digger, in the place of Joseph Rose, deceased.

In July, 1870, the sexton's salary was increased from £16 to £20 per annum.

John Rose held office till March 22nd, 1879, when he met with a shocking death, by falling from the bellringers' floor to the floor of the church beneath. An account of the inquest, and other particulars, as it appeared in the *Messenger* of March 29th, is here reproduced :—

SHOCKING FATALITY AT THE PARISH CHURCH.

—o—

On Saturday night (March 22nd), a thrill of deep feeling was sent through the town at the news that Mr. John Rose, sexton, &c., of the Parish Church, and keeper of the Cemetery, had met with a sudden and terrible death, through falling from the belfry to the floor of the church beneath, a distance of over 40 feet. It appeared that Rose was busy in his usual avocations preparing for the Sabbath services at the church, and among other duties he had to wind up the clock, for which purpose he had to ascend above the belfry. This he seems to have done between seven and eight o'clock. In the centre of the belfry floor is a large square opening, to admit of the hoisting or lowering of the bells to or from their position. This is closed by two folding trap doors, raised several inches above the floor level ; and it seems that it was the custom, on the appearance of smoke in the body of the church from the warming apparatus, to raise these trap doors for the smoke to pass out by the windows placed north and south in the belfry. Such, apparently, was the case on Saturday, when one half of the trap door was opened, and it is conjectured that the deceased, who had already wound up the clock and fastened the windows, was turning from the north window, when, not observing it in the darkness, he fell through the open portion as stated. The rope of the small bell, or "ting-tang," as it is familiarly called, led through and across the trap opening, and this bell was heard to give four or five strokes in an unusual manner about the time the accident occurred, and it is supposed that deceased must have fallen across, or, in his descent, clutched this rope, which was found broken in two. A nephew of the deceased, Joseph William Rose, who resided with his uncle, and used generally to perform the duties in question, but who was otherwise engaged on this particular day, suddenly remembering the trap door, ran up to the church to warn his uncle, but he had scarcely opened the door when he heard a groan, somewhere on the floor of the church, but could see nothing in the darkness. The deceased, however, was sensible, knew his nephew, and addressed him by name, and the latter lifted and assisted his uncle to a seat, and remained with him several minutes, when, as he said, he appeared to die. The nephew then ran for a surgeon, and found Dr. Wood, who returned with him to the church, where they found poor Rose still alive. Dr. Wood wished him to take a draught, but after drinking a portion he refused to take more, and wished to be raised up. This was done, when the poor fellow almost immediately expired. The police were communicated with, and the body was at once removed to the deceased's residence, the cemetery lodge.

As may be expected, the dreadful event formed a topic of conversation of deep interest in the town and district throughout Sunday, and the Vicar (the Rev. G. W. Murray), feelingly alluded to it at the morning service at the parish church; and Mr. Titbutt, the organist, played the "Dead March" as the concluding voluntary.

The inquest on the body was held at the Horn and Trumpet Inn, Kidderminster-road, on Tuesday, before W. S. P. Hughes, Esq., coroner, acting as deputy for R. Docker, Esq., and a respectable jury, of whom Mr. T. Billingham was the foreman.

Joseph William Rose, nephew of the deceased, who was the only witness called, said his uncle was 38 years of age, and was clerk and sexton at the parish church, and cemetery keeper. Witness lived with him, and was 20 years old within a month. On Saturdays he generally assisted his uncle by performing several duties for him at the church, such as winding up the clock, lighting the stove warming apparatus, and cleaning the vestry ready for the services the following day. But on this occasion (on Saturday last) he did not do so, for, being a pupil teacher at the National Schools, and preparing for examination, he was studying for that purpose. About six o'clock in the evening, through the Board-room window, he saw the deceased coming as from town. His uncle knew he was studying, and though he didn't speak with him he presumed he went to the church for the purpose of doing the work he (witness) was accustomed to do; there could be no doubt about it. Witness afterwards learnt from his aunt that his uncle had gone to the church. After a while he recollected that he had left open the trap door, and he immediately ran up to the church for the purpose either of preventing his uncle going into the belfry or warning him that the trap lid was open. This was about twenty minutes to eight, as nearly as he could judge. On opening the west door of the church he heard a groan from the floor, directly under the trap door. It was quite dark, and witness could not see anyone, but he felt his uncle, who was conscious, and knew him, calling him by name. Witness lit the gas. His uncle did not tell him what had happened, and he saw no signs but the open lid above. Deceased complained of his hips, and asked witness to raise him, and he did so, putting him, with some difficulty, on to one of the nearest seats, and having to support him with his arm. He asked him if he had been upstairs, and he told him in reply once, twice (and he would not say whether it was not thrice), that he had not; but a few minutes later he said that he had been up. Some three or four minutes elapsed before witness went for a doctor, and when his uncle appeared to have died in his arms. Witness then laid him down in the aisle of the church. Being questioned more particularly as to what actual evidence he had that the deceased had been in the belfry, witness said the ting-tang rope was broken in two, and he himself had opened the belfry windows at twenty minutes to five o'clock, but when he and

Superintendent Tyler, who was sent for, went up subsequently, the windows were found to be closed and fastened, and the clock was wound up. No one but the deceased could have done these things. The keys of the church were kept at the cemetery lodge, and the keys of the tower at the church. The deceased's right arm was completely shattered, there was a wound over his right eye, and a small one on the head. The height from the trap door to the floor of the church had been measured, and was found to be a few inches over 40 feet. Dr. Wood tried to administer a draught to the deceased, who lived for some five minutes after he came. That would be about a minute or a minute and a half after he arrived. Deceased swallowed part of the draught, but refused to take the remainder. He said— "I shan't; never mind what the doctor says; heave me up; I shan't take it." Witness accordingly lifted the deceased, and he died immediately.

To the Foreman of the Jury: His uncle was already dead when the Vicar arrived.

To the Coroner: There could not be the slightest doubt that death was caused by the deceased falling through the trap door.

Henry Rose, brother of the deceased, who was present at the inquiry, but who was not sworn, said that his wife heard the ting-tang at an unusual hour, and on looking up at the clock she found that it was just twenty minutes to eight. He suggested that the deceased must have closed the south window and gone across to the north window, which he also closed, and then, on stepping off the "tenor block," on which he stood to fasten the window last named, fell through the half-open trap door.

This was the whole of the evidence, and the jury, without any consideration, at once returned a verdict of "Accidental death," appending a recommendation to the Vicar and Churchwardens either that the trap door should be permanently closed, or a grating fixed over it for ventilating purposes, if that were considered absolutely necessary. (This recommendation was immediately afterwards carried out, and an iron grating was put over one half of the aperture, and so arranged that the other door could not be opened without the removal of the iron bolts of the grating. The work was done by Mr. William Ledbury, at a cost of 25s.)

We understand (although the fact was not brought out in evidence) that Dr. Wood, who was the first to arrive at the church when fetched—Mr. Joseph Rose having waited for the draught in question—found the deceased quite sensible, and he expressed a wish to "walk home."

The deceased and his ancestors had filled the offices of parish clerks and sextons of Bromsgrove for considerably over 100 years, and the poor fellow who has just now met with such a sad end, was generally respected as a worthy representative of his line. He was intelligent, of a cheerful temperament, ever possessing a kindly and good-natured word for everybody with whom he was brought into contact, and his pleasant and genial manners will be missed by many of his fellows in the rank of life in which he moved. Much sympathy is expressed in all quarters, not only at his untimely death, but with the sorrowing widow, relatives, and children, of whom there are four, the youngest only about a fortnight old.

The funeral took place on Thursday afternoon, with choral service, rendered by the combined choirs of St. John's and All Saints' churches. A large congregation assembled, both at the church and at the grave side. The churchwardens, Messrs. W. Holyoake, J. R. Horton, T. Billingham, and W. Corbett, acted as pall-bearers, and large deputations from the local lodges of Odd-fellows, the " British Queen," and the " Loyal Queen's Own," the latter of which the deceased was a member—were in attendance. A beautiful wreath and cross of exotic flowers was placed on the coffin. The ceremony was conducted by the Rev. P. Ellis and the Rev. Garnons-Williams, curates. Psalm xc. was chanted, and after the lesson, hymn 142 was sung. As the procession left the church, Mr. Tirbutt played the " Dead March ;" hymn 163 was sung on the way to the grave, and hymn 117 on returning.

The untoward circumstances of the death of the deceased, and the solemn occasion drew tears from many eyes independent of those immediately concerned. Muffled peals were rung on the church bells at intervals during the day.

In the *Messenger* of April 5th, the following advertisements appeared :—

PARISH OF BROMSGROVE.

A MEETING of the INHABITANTS of the PARISH of BROMSGROVE will be held in the VESTRY of the PARISH CHURCH, on THURSDAY NEXT, the 10th day of APRIL instant, at Ten o'clock a.m., for the purpose of APPOINTING a PARISH SEXTON in the place of Mr. John Rose, deceased.   G. W. MURRAY, Vicar.

Wm. Holyoake,
Jno. R. Horton,
Thos. Billingham,   } Churchwardens.
W. Corbett,

TO THE RATEPAYERS OF THE PARISH OF BROMSGROVE.

LADIES AND GENTLEMEN,—

By the lamented death of my late Uncle, JOHN ROSE, the OFFICE OF SEXTON of your Parish (which he held for a number of years), has become VACANT ; and Thursday next, the 10th instant, at Ten a.m., at the Vestry of the Parish Church, is fixed for the Election of his successor.

I beg respectfully to acquaint you that I am a CANDIDATE for the SITUATION, and to state that for the past three or four years I have assisted in the performance of the duties, especially at times of my late uncle's temporary absence from illness or otherwise; and I hope I may be pardoned in venturing to refer you to the manner in which such duties have been performed, as a good testimonial in my favour.

I have also excellent testimonials from the Vicar, Churchwardens, and my late Schoolmaster, Mr. William Dodd; together with the support of a large majority of the Gentry and Inhabitants of the Parish of Bromsgrove.

The fact that this office has been held uninterruptedly by members of the family for the last 150 years, and that (should I be honoured with your choice), it is my intention to assist in the maintenance of my widowed aunt—Mrs. John Rose —will, I trust, be received by you as favourable to my candidature.

I shall feel very grateful to those Ratepayers who are in my favour, if they will *endeavour to make it convenient to attend* at the above-named time and place, for the purpose of recording their votes in my favour. But as the time is short and the parish so extensive, I fear I shall not be able to call upon them all.

I have the honour to remain,

Ladies and Gentlemen,

Your most obedient Servant,

JOSEPH WILLIAM ROSE.

Cemetery Lodge, Bromsgrove,
April 3rd, 1879.

A meeting of the inhabitants of the parish was held in the Vestry of the Parish Church of St. John, on Thursday morning, April 10th, for the purpose of appointing a sexton, in the place of Mr. J. Rose, deceased. The Vicar (the Rev. G. W. Murray) presided, and the attendance, at a tolerably full meeting, included—Messrs. W. Holyoake, J. R. Horton, W. Corbett (churchwardens), W. Llewellin, T. White, W. Jefferies, E. Ward, C. B. Steedman, H. Parry, W. Bolding, C. Field, T. Grove, H. W. Lewis, R. Cook, and others.

The Chairman opened the business by reading the notice convening the meeting, and regretting the cause for it. He remarked that although ordinarily the appointment rested with the incumbent, he found that at the last election the very useful custom had been followed of election by the ratepayers, which he did not wish to upset on the present occasion.

Mr. Holyoake proposed the election of Joseph William Rose, nephew of the deceased sexton, remarking that he was an intelligent youth, and had been fully accustomed to perform the duties in his uncle's lifetime.

Mr. J. R. Horton seconded the nomination, which was further supported by Mr. W. Jefferies.

After a pause the Chairman asked if there was any other nomination, when Mr. W. Wildsmith proposed Mr. Frederick Bellamy for the office. The latter, however, who was present, said he did not wish to oppose Mr. Rose, but simply to have his own name before the ratepayers if any legal difficulty should arise on the score of Mr. Rose's age. Mr. Horton and the Chairman both said there was no difficulty of the kind. Mr. Bellamy accordingly withdrew his name, and there being none other before the meeting, Mr. Rose was unanimously elected, and thanked the meeting, assuring it of his earnestness of purpose in respect to his aunt and family.

A suggestion by Mr. T. White that the appointment should be for twelve months only, the permanent appointment to follow, was not entertained.

Before the meeting dispersed, Mr. Holyoake introduced the subject of raising a subscription for the widow of the late sexton, and proposed that a committee be formed for that purpose. Mr. White seconded the proposition, which was supported by Mr. Jefferies and Mr. Corbett, and carried, the Vicar and Churchwardens being appointed a committee for carrying out the object.

A vote of thanks to the chairman brought the proceedings to a close.

William Rose, son of Thomas Rose, previously mentioned, and brother to Joseph Rose, was appointed clerk in 1819, on the death of William Brooke. He died April 6th, 1850, having held the office for 31 years. Returning from a wedding, he fell, going down the church steps, and broke his leg, from the effects of which he never recovered. From this time the offices of clerk and sexton have been combined, Joseph Rose being the first member of the family holding both appointments.

Joseph William Rose is the present clerk and sexton.

In the churchyard are gravestones to the memory of several members of this family.

The Registers.

THE first parish register* commences in March, 1590, and continues till 1650, the early part of it being written in Latin. In this, and the three succeeding books, the christenings, marriages, and deaths are entered indiscriminately. The most curious remarks made in the first of these books are as follows :—

"The 29th day of January, 1604, was buried John, the son of Thomas Wyllar, of this town : vide infra :

"The 9th day of February, 1604, was buried William, the son of Thomas Wyllar, of this town. The plague was at this time in this town, and in this family. Vide infra : "

During the first 20 years of the register there were married, christened, and buried 2940 persons.

The next volume contains three distinct register books bound together. On the front leaf of the first—

"William Suthwell, of the Parish of Bromsgrove, in the County of Worcester, make cause before me (being one of the Justices assigned for the keeping of the peace for the County of Worcester aforesaid)† this . . third day of October, 1653, and desire to be admitted to take the oath of Parish Register of the Parish of Bromsgrove, being thereunto duly elected according to the . . of an Act of

---

* In the 30th Henry VIII., Sep. 1538, Cromwell, the King's vicegerent in ecclesiastical affairs, issued the following injunction :—

"*Item.*—That you and every parson, vicar, or curate within the diocese, for every Church keep one Book or Register, wherein he shall write the day and year of every Wedding, Christening, and Burial made within your parish for your time, and so every man succeeding you likewise, and also there insert every person's name that shall be so wedded, christened, and buried. And for the safe keeping of the same Book, the parish shall be bound to provide of their common charges one sure coffer, with two locks and keys, whereof the one to remain with you, and the other with the Wardens of every parish wherein the said Book shall be laid up, which Book ye shall every Sunday take forth, and in the presence of the said Wardens, or one of them, write and record in the same all the Weddings, Christenings, and Burials made the whole week afore, and that done, to lay up the book in the said coffer as afore ; and for every time that the same shall be omitted, the party that shall be in the fault thereof shall forfeit to the said Church iij⁵ iiij⁴ (3s. 4d.), to be employed on the reparation of the said Church.

† Under the administration of the Protectorate, the Parliament, about the year 1653, directed registrars to be chosen by every parish, to be approved of and sworn by a Justice of the Peace, for the registering of births and burials.

Parliam! bearing date the four and twentieth day of August, 1653, intituled an Act
touching Marriages and the registering thereof, and also touching Births and Burialls,
the truth of which election appeared unto me by certificate, under the hand and
seale of Humphrey Lowe, gent., and divers others of the Inhabitants of the Parish of
Bromsgrove. And, giving due audit to the same certificate, I have administered our
oath to the said William Suthwell for the true and fast keeping of this Register Book
according to the forementioned Act of Parliament, having placed his name in this
booke and . . . . . . And hereby publish, order, and ordain him Parish
Register of Bromsgrove aforesaid. Witness my hand, the day and year above
written.   "William Suthwell.   "George Milward."

On March 17th, 1657, this entry occurs : " Published the 3ᵈ time in yᵉ market
an intended marriage between Ambrose Crowley of Oldswinford, Nayler, and Mary
Hall of this parish, spinster, without contradiction. Married April 2ⁿᵈ by the
Justices of Kidᵈ" (Kidderminster.) There are numerous similar entries.

On August 24th, 1653, an Act of Parliament was passed—" That whosoever
should agree to be married within the Commonwealth of England, after the 29ᵗʰ
September, 1653, should (21 days before such intended marriage), deliver in writing
unto the Register (thereinafter appointed) for the respective parish, where each party
to be married lived, the names, surnames, additions, and places of abode of the
parties so to be married, and of their parents, guardians, or overseers, all which said
Register should publish three Lord's-days then next following, at the close of the
morning exercise, in the public meeting-place, commonly called the church or chapel,
or (if the parties desired it) in the market-place next to the said church or chapel, on
three market-days, in three several weeks next following, between the hours of 11
and 2; which done, the Register should make a certificate thereof, without which
the persons thereinafter authorised, should not proceed in such marriage. That
such persons intending to be married, should come before some Justice of the Peace
of the same county, city, or town, with such certificate, and if no impediment, the
marriage was to proceed," &c.

The second part of this book is entitled, "The Register Booke for the Towne
and Parish of Bromsgrove in the County of Worcester, since the 29ᵗʰ of November,
1671." Tho. Wilmott, Vicar.

The third part, "A Register of the names of all that were born, marryed, and
buried in the parish of Bromsgrove since the Act for the Births, Marriages, and
Burialls tooke date, being May the 1ˢᵗ 1695."   Thomas Wilmott, Vi :

The Act just mentioned ordered that the parents of every child thereafter born,
shall, within five days after the birth, give notice to the vicar, &c., of the parish, of
the day of the *birth* of the child, under a penalty of 40ˢ ; which vicar, &c., were,

under a like penalty, to take an exact and true account of, and keep a distinct register of such so born, and not christened, for doing which the parents were to pay to the vicar 6^{d}

These registers of births are occasionally found entered in the registers, but not in a separate book.

The following are a few extracts from this volume :—

July 18th, 1659.—Bu : Darby serv^{t} to Mr Williamson.

„ 27th, „ Born Samuel son of William Sheldon, gent :

Mar. 19th, 1660.—Memorandum that upon a Licence granted to Mr Abigail Tayler of Barn Green in the Parish of Bromsgrove being sick on the 12th of this instant . . to eat flesh-meates for seven days according to ye statute, If her sickness continues so long. Her weakness and Indisposition yet enduring I do further license her as much as in me lies to eat flesh-meates for seven days more from ye date hereof. And have accordingly entered ye same into ye church Register of Bromsgrove aforesaid according to ye statute before one of ye churchwardens.

Witness my hand ye day and year above written in the presence of

George Parteing   J. Woolley vic. of
his mark ×   Bromsgrove.

March 26th.

The Indisposition of Mrs Abigail Tayler continuing Her license to eat flesh-meats was renewed according to ye statute for seven days longer by me

Jos. Woolley vic. of Bromsgrove.

Renewed again April 3rd
Renewed again April 10th
Renewed again — 17th
By me J. Woolley Vic.

Sept. 6th, 1661.—Antony Cole of Chawich was buried twice, first by the Quakers and after in the Churchyard.

Jan. 1st, 1696.—Interred a child of Matthew Spurston unbaptised.

Feb. 1st, 1699.—Bur. A Stranger.

Dec. — 1704.—Born a child of Onionss (?) at ye Rose and Crown.

Oct. 16th, 1719.—Bur. Mr. Edward Mitten of ye Parish of Colmington, and sojourner with one Mr. Henry Hayns att Sparckfield in Cornedale In Shropshire.

Elizabeth D. of Thomas Cookes was bap. Feb. 1st. 1705. when about 8 years old.

The third book contains the entries from 1719 to 1733.

This Booke bought by us undernamed

> John Bidford,
> John Cartwrit,
> Nicholas Spriggs,
> Nicholas Hill.

It contains these entries—

April 1st, 1721.—Bur. A child of a Vagrant.

May 31st, 1727.—Bur. Humfrey Lowe, Esq. Affidavit made

> In the year 1729 55 M. B. and christenings.

July 7th, 1727.—Bur. Mr. John Smith, Dadford.

In Jan. 1733, a list of the children of Thom. Willkes, maker of linen cloth, is inserted.

The fourth book commences April, 1734, and continues till 1754.

> Be noticed that on January 28th, 1743, Francis Son of John and Sarah Spilsbury was baptised. (see page 60.)

The title page of the fifth book is—

> "The Register Book of the Christenings, Marriages, and Burials in the Parish of Bromsgrove.

> "Be it Remembered that the Revᵈ Mr. John Waugh was Instituted to the Vicarage of Bromsgrove the . . day of . . 1754. Inducted the . . day of . . following."

The christenings, deaths, and marriages are kept separate in this and the remaining books, and appear to have been entered periodically from other books. At this time the entries are written in a very good hand, and the register well and carefully kept.

The book contains the following entries :—

Aug. 9th, 1754.—Christ. Benjamin Son of Sarah Badley, of Bromsgrove, a Bastard.

Nov. 8th, 1754.— ,, Elizabeth Daughter of Joshua and Ann Bourne, sojourner.

April 26th, 1755.— ,, Nancy Daughter of John and Hannah Giles of the Lickey, Nailer } Twins.

,, Hannah Daughter of John and Hannah Giles of the Lickey, Nailer }

April 26th, 1755.— ,, Ann Daughter of John and Mary Broomfield of Wildmoor, Nailer } Twins.

Hannah Daughter of John and Mary Broomfield of Wildmoor, Nailer }

May 6th, 1755.—Christ. Betty Daughter of William and Mary Croley, a Soldier.

Dec. 28th, 1755.— ,, Sarah.

April 28th, 1756.— ,, Elizabeth Lewis Daughter of Mary Strange, Pauper, a Bastard.

Dec. 6th, 1769.— ,, Frances Daughter of John and Ann Bing Sidemoor, Nailer, 3 months old.

,, 19th, 1769.— ,, George Son of Elizabeth Woolmere of Bromsgrove, Illegit.

Nov. 6th, 1753.—Buried Rev. Mr. Wm. Philips, A.B., late Vicar of this Parish.

Feb. 15th, 1754.— ,, The Rev. Mr. George Wilmott, A.M., late Fellow of Balliol College, Oxford.

Sept. 29th, 1750.— ,, Samuel, a Foundling.

,, 13th, 1762.— ,, A Stranger.

Mar. 16th, 1771.— ,, Rich. Walker Fellow of Worcester College in Oxford, Clerk.

There are numerous entries of the burials of "paupers"—sometimes as many as four or five in a month—and "strangers." The trades of the respective persons are given in this register, forcibly calling to mind the time when Bromsgrove was in a much more flourishing and prosperous condition than at present. We give a few of the trades mentioned—

Brush maker	Hatcheller	Sawyer
Breeches maker	Heel maker	Swingler
Chandler	Higgler	Tanner
Clog maker	Maltster	Turner
Currier	Needle maker	Whitster
Dyer	Patten wood maker	Whitener
Flax dresser	Rope maker	Wool comber
Hatter		

Amongst the Christian names found are—

Ambrose	Cuthbert	Hezekiah	Phelis
Arabella	Dorothy	Joan	Priscilla
Aquilla	Deborah	Joannah	Rephael
Bridget	Drauahy (?)	Judith	Sabina
Bety	Dennis	Justinian	Temperance
Bartholomew	Emblem	Lilyan	Ursula
Abigail	Fortune	Nathan	Winifred
Baldwin	Gregory	Oswald	Zechariah
Cyril	Gleodosia	Obadiah	

From March, 1755, to March, 1775, there were married, christened, and buried, as under, viz.:—

	Marriages.		Christenings.	Burials.
1755	24	...	164	80
1756	31	...	100	108
1757	27	...	137	148
1758	29	...	111	107
1759	21	...	139	112
1760	39	...	144	96
1761	34	...	141	100
1762	35	...	141	128
1763	35	...	132	147
1764	43	...	145	127
1765	44	...	143	153
1766	39	...	115	130
1767	40	...	158	127
1768	50	...	150	107
1769	58	...	152	123
1770	49	...	158	158
1771	38	...	158	129
1772	35	...	151	105
1773	38	...	141	128
1774	50	...	137	119
Total ...	759		2817 ...	2432

Until the year 1754, and between the years 1784 and 1813, there are no entries of places of residence; after that date such entries were compulsory by Act of Parliament.

On November 17th, 1824, a meeting of the churchwardens was held at the Vicarage to inspect the registers, and " it was found necessary to order the repair of the bindings of several volumes which were defective; also that some of them (the leaves being loose), should be resewed." Mr. Maund was instructed to do the work.

At the same meeting it was ordered that a parish meeting be called, " for the purpose of laying before them the Act of Parliament requiring that the Parish Register be kept in an iron Chest, and, there being no such chest, to make an order for procuring one."

A meeting was accordingly held on February 23rd, 1825, and an iron safe ordered. This safe is at the Vicarage, and the registers and communion plate are kept in it. There is also the old oak parish chest, about 3ft. 6in. long, having three trunk locks, with iron ties at the corners; together with a large box, at the Vicarage. The latter is full of papers and books relating to parish matters, but the dampness of the situation is doing much damage to them.

The Vicarage.

THE present Vicarage House was built in 1848, by Mr. Robinson, of Redditch, from designs prepared by Mr. Henry Day, and cost about £1800. Of this sum about £1200 was obtained from Queen Anne's Bounty, and was repayable by the several vicars in annual payments extending over a period of 30 years. The last payment was made in 1878. The remainder of the contract sum was made up by the sale of the materials in the old vicarage, which was in a very dilapidated state, and other items. The building is of brick, with stone dressings, and occupies a site near to the former vicarage house, which covered a considerable area, owing to additions, of an irregular character, being made to it from time to time. A part of the cellaring of the previous building still remains intact, and may be entered from the garden of the present vicarage.

The Sunday School.

IN connection with the church is a Sunday School,* attended by about 800 scholars. It was till recently supported by subscription and part of the proceeds of a collection in the church on one Sunday in the year, the other part going to the day schools. Every year £10 is allowed by the school managers for the support of the Sunday school, in lieu of the old arrangement.

The Church Sunday School in Bromsgrove was originated by a Mr. William Brooke, about 1788, in a house in St. John Street, opposite the church steps, and consisted of two boys and seven girls. The premises belonged to a Mr. Bell, and he and Mr. Brettell, who lived at The Steps, took great interest in the welfare of

---

* A searching enquiry has recently been made on the subject of the origin of Sunday Schools, with the following historical result :—Cardinal Borromeo (Roman Catholic), of Milan, sowed the first seed in 1580, which was followed by Rev. Joseph Alleine (Nonconformist), Bath, 1650; then by Mrs. C. Bevey (a lady of the Church of England), Flaxley, in 1717 ; Rev. Theophilus Lindsey and Miss Catherine Cappe (Unitarians), in 1764-65 ; Miss Hannah Ball (Methodist), High Wycombe, 1769 ; Mr. William King (Whitfieldite), Dursley, 1774 : James Heyes (Presbyterian), Little Leven, 1775 ; Rev. Thomas Kennedy (Episcopalian), Downpatrick, 1776 ; Rev. Thomas Stock and Mr. Robert Raikes (Church of England), Gloucester. Thus it appears that this philanthropic work was not chiseled out by any one sectarian instrument.

R

the scholars. The school increasing, the Quakers' meeting house was used as a girls' school, the boys retaining the old quarters until they removed to the old Town Hall, but that building becoming unsafe, the school was again removed, and held for a time in the old cotton factory. On November 17th, 1830, at a meeting for the purpose of electing a Committee of Management, it was represented that the number of children in the Sunday Schools had greatly increased, and that the accommodation was insufficient, and it was resolved that suitable accommodation should be obtained as soon as possible, and that the committee be empowered to prepare some plan to submit to a future meeting. At the following meeting, held on November 30th, it was thought that the wants of the parish in other respects should be considered, and it was deemed expedient to erect such a building as would combine the wants of a schoolroom and Town Hall. It was the opinion of the meeting that the best situation for the building was on the north-west side of High Street, on some land belonging to Mr. Tidmas. It was decided that a plan and estimate should be prepared by Mr. Woodhouse, under Mr. Adams' inspection, for a building two stories high, 60 feet long and 24 feet wide—inside measure, or such larger dimensions as shall be found necessary to accommodate 500 children at least in each room. It was further decided that the plan be made with the utmost regard to economy, "the building to be as plain as possible, and no allowance to be made in the estimate for ground to build upon." At the next meeting, held on November 26th, Mr. Adams produced the plan and estimate, from which it appeared "that, to accommodate 500 children in each room, the rooms must contain an area of 1295 feet, and that the expense of building such rooms in the plainest manner will be £700." Mr. Adams had also made a calculation that a suitable Town Hall and Market Place might be attached to, or united with, this building, at an additional cost of £300. It was then resolved, "That the Churchwardens do wait on Mr. Wm. Robeson, as agent of the Earl of Plymouth, and lay before him such parts of the old Churchwardens' books, and a certain lease granted by the Churchwardens in 1777, as tend to establish the property of the Parish in the Town Hall, and request him to communicate with the Earl of Plymouth on the subject, and report to next meeting."

On February 10th, 1831, it was decided to call a public meeting on the reply of the Earl of Plymouth, but at a meeting of the committee, held in the Vestry November 30th, it was deemed expedient to relinquish the idea of building a Town Hall in combination with schools; and as a means to raise funds for building schools, it was resolved to hold a concert and ball, and apply the proceeds or profits. Mr. Simms, the organist, was made a member of the committee, and requested to preside as leader of the band. The total receipts were £78 9s. 6d., and the expenses £30 9s. 6d.; the net profit of £48 was handed over to a building fund.

At a committee meeting, held in February, 1832, it was stated "that the Rev. the Vicar having expressed his desire that an accommodation of land should be given by the Dean and Chapter of Worcester, on which Sunday Schools may be erected," it was resolved—" That as the Town Hall will be taken down next month, and as no other room can be obtained, permanently, for the schools, it is become indispensably necessary that new schoolrooms should be erected with all possible despatch."

At the annual meeting, held July 23rd, 1832, it was thought that, owing to correspondence with the Dean and Chapter and the Earl of Plymouth, a lease of 21 years, renewable every term at a peppercorn rent, might be obtained, and it was decided by a majority of five "that it is expedient to build on such a tenure." Mr. Maund was then instructed to make application for "that portion of the garden immediately adjoining the churchyard, which lies between the Crown Close and Sidemoor Lane," and supposed to contain about a quarter of an acre. This land was formerly the bowling green belonging to the Crown Hotel, the present Institute.

At a committee meeting, held on December 8th, it was stated that the consent of the Earl of Plymouth and the Dean and Chapter of Worcester had been obtained for the grant of land above recommended for the site of the Sunday Schools, and that all was ready (except the nomination of trustees), for the conveyance of the land, and it was decided to call a public meeting to sanction the proceedings ; however, at the public meeting, held on January 4th, 1833, an adjournment was moved, in order to afford time to find a freehold site, if possible ; but at the adjourned meeting it was resolved, " That if the money required could be obtained, the proposed site near the churchyard should be adopted." It was further resolved, " That the most advantageous plan of accommodating 500 children in each room appears to this meeting to be that the rooms should be 86ft. long, 32ft. wide, and each room 14ft. high—inside measure. The Chairman was instructed to communicate with Messrs. Woodhouse, Skidmore, Wm. Hill, Wm. Kings, Joseph Brooke, John Robinson (of Redditch), and Thos. Edwards, desiring them to send in to him, on or before Monday, the 21st instant, sealed tenders for completion of the above rooms, upon an elevation to be proposed by the several builders. Woodhouse's plan was " assumed as the general basis of the building."

On January 28th, at an adjourned meeting, the Chairman stated "that the Earl of Plymouth had munificently expressed his intention (£700 having been raised from the weighing machine and funds of the school) of supplying gratuitously any deficiency which may arise in the funds for the completion of the proposed building, provided the same do not exceed £300, and provided the work be executed under the direction of Mr. Lee, of Beoley, as surveyor." The best thanks of the meeting were then accorded to the Earl for his noble donation.

On May 9th, 1833, the following tenders for the erection of the schools were
opened :—

		£
John Barnett, 20, George Street, St. Paul's, Birmingham	...	1091
William Woodhouse, Bromsgrove		990
Thomas Holland		960
John Robinson, Redditch		950
Samuel Hartle, Birmingham		857

Hartle's tender was accepted, and it was agreed to give the contractor £50
extra if his contract was completed by 21st November, but not otherwise.

The building was opened as a Sunday School for the first time on Christmas
Day, in 1833. The Rev. J. N. Harward, Curate-in-charge, was the prime mover in
the erection of the schools.

On January 31st, 1834, it was decided to make application to the National
Society to receive the schools into union, and to afford them assistance towards the
completion of the building to the extent of £200, which the society did.

At a meeting, held on February 19th, 1834, it was represented that in
consequence of an unforseen expense of £77 8s., in securing a solid foundation
for the schoolrooms, the building fund was exhausted, and the sum of £75 remained
due to Mr. Hartle, the builder. It was therefore decided to draw to that extent on
Messrs. Rufford and Co., the bankers. The total cost of the schools was £1244 6s.

At a meeting of the Committee of Management, held on April 1st, 1835, in
conformity with a resolution passed at a meeting held on December 8th, 1834, it was
resolved, "That an Infant School be forthwith established in the lower Sunday
School." This resolution was confirmed at a public meeting held on the 16th of
April following.

The minute book, from which many of the foregoing notes were extracted,
abruptly terminates here, and no further minutes are recorded till October 7th, 1846,
when, at a meeting of the committee of the Sunday and of the National Schools,
" it was considered expedient that for the future these schools be united ; that they
be supported by a common fund, managed by the same committee, and be in
all respects considered as one institution." At this meeting it was resolved, " That
an application be made to the Dean and Chapter of Worcester for the purpose
of getting the buildings conveyed to trustees in perpetuity for the use of the
schools ;" and, "That after the buildings are so conveyed, an application be made to
the Committee of Privy Council for a grant in aid of any fund already raised, or to
be raised, for the payment of any debt which may have been contracted for the
repair of the schools, and also for any alteration of the present buildings, or the
erection of any additional ones which may be found necessary." These resolutions
were confirmed on October 14th, 1846.

The plan of union was decided as follows :—

1. The two schools to be supported by a common fund, managed by the same committee, and to be considered in all respects as the same institution.

2. The buildings and premises to be conveyed to the vicar of the parish and the churchwardens for the time being, in trust for the purpose of educating the children of the poor of the parish of Bromsgrove in the principles of the Established Church.

3. The vicar of the parish to have the sole order and direction of the religious instruction ; direction and government of the schools to be vested in, and exercised by, a committee.

4. Such committee to consist of the vicar of the parish, his curate (if any), the Curate of Catshill, and 14 other persons, chosen annually by the subscribers, and that five be empowered to act.

5. No person to be qualified to vote for the committee who is not an annual subscriber of five shillings at least to the schools.

6. The vicar, if present, to be chairman of the committee. If the vicar be not present, the chairman to be chosen by the members present. The chairman to have a casting vote in case of an equality of vote.

A portion of the profits derived from the town weighing machine were, from its erection in 1795, applied to the support of the Sunday School, and at a meeting of the trustees, held December 6th, 1833, it was resolved to mortgage the machine, &c., for £300, to Mr. John Holyoake, the proceeds to go towards the erection of the present National Schools. The principal and interest (five per cent.) were paid off August 27th, 1841. The schools were considerably damaged by a fire which occurred on January 5th, 1857. They were enlarged in 1871, at a cost of £410 ; and a schoolmaster's house built, at a cost of £270. In connection with the weighing machine trust, a deed was executed August 15th, 1805, in which it was declared "that £20 of the profits should annually be applied (as heretofore) towards the maintenance and support of the Protestant Sunday School in Bromsgrove, for the better instruction and education of the poor of the parish, in the principles and duties of the Christian religion, according to the Church of England." In 1812, the amounts received at the machine appear to have been paid monthly by the man in charge, to Mr. John Taylor, the acting trustee, and expended yearly about July 20th, by £20 per year " for a salary to the organist, and the remainder, be what it may, to the Sunday School." In 1868, the Local Board purchased the machine and building of the trustees, for the sum of £35, and a meeting of the latter body was held on November 12th, 1868, for the purpose of finally closing the accounts connected therewith. After discharging all liabilities, there remained a surplus of £25 10s., which they resolved to apportion as follows :—To the Bromsgrove Town Schools,

£10; to the Catshill Schools, £10; and to the Lickey Schools, £5 10s. The sundry liabilities amounted to £9 10s., making up the total paid to the trustees by the Local Board. A vote of thanks was accorded to Mr. A. Palmer, for his gratuitous services for many years as honorary secretary and treasurer. It was somewhat a curious coincidence that Mr. Walter Brooke should have been chairman at this meeting, and that his grandfather, Mr. William Brooke, was present at the first meeting, and chiefly instrumental in establishing the machine, in November, 1794, and also the Sunday School. The income derived from the machine prior to the existence of the railway was very considerable, and the trustees, during a period of upwards of 70 years, contributed largely to the support of the schools, and other deserving objects of the parish. In 1831, £40 was paid to the schools; in 1832, £50; in 1833, £50; and in 1842, £30; but now that coal, &c., is chiefly brought by rail, the present site of the machine is inconvenient, consequently its income has lessened of late years. The last trustees were Mr. Walter Brooke (chairman), Messrs. Richard Dunn, Alfred Palmer, and George Dipple.

We are informed by one who attended the school when held at the Town Hall, that it was no uncommon thing to see boys driven by one of their parents with a stout stick to school, or brought by the father by the collar of the coat. Discipline was maintained by the use of "the logger"—a long, round piece of wood, attached to a chain, the one end of the chain being locked round the leg of the refractory boy, who was obliged to hold up the wood in his right hand. Any boy punished with the logger had to walk to church with it fastened on his leg, his coat being turned inside out; and in this manner he stood during service in front of the pulpit. This instrument of punishment is now in the possession of Mr. William Ledbury. The birch rod was also used and stoutly administered by the vicar or curate-in-charge in deserving cases, on the bare back of the boy whilst he was being carried on the back of another up and down the schoolroom. A youth named Riley was the last who was flogged in this manner. The punishment was inflicted by the Rev. J. N. Harward, in 1836, in the boys' schoolroom, after the afternoon service in church. The lad was then expelled the school, and was some time afterwards transported beyond the seas. At a meeting of the School Management Committee, held on November 26th, 1830, it was resolved, "That two or more of the committee do always attend at the Sunday School during the whole time of instruction, morning and afternoon, to see that the business of the school is regularly and efficiently conducted." In February, 1831, it was resolved to make a trial of 24 boys on the "National system" in the Sunday Schools. The children attended church every Sunday morning and afternoon, and were mostly stowed away under the tower on a series of graduated seats, where probably they could hear very little and see less. In front of these seats, which were called the "dog kennel," sat for many years, during service, one John Price, with cane in hand, ready—and always willing—to administer justice to offenders. The seats were placed here in 1824, and completely blocked up the western entrance, and converted it into a receptacle for rubbish. Other boys sat in the chancel on forms and on the steps below the communion rail. For many years Mr. J. Richardson was superintendent of the Sunday Schools, but he retired from the post in 1831, and received the best thanks of the committee. He was succeeded by Thomas Banner. Mary Price was superintendent of the girls' school for many years, and in the cemetery is a gravestone—

In Loving Memory
OF
M A R Y   P R I C E ,
FOR NEARLY 50 YEARS
SUPERINTENDANT
OF THE GIRLS
CHURCH SUNDAY SCHOOL,
WHO DIED JUNE 5TH, 1872,
AGED 79 YEARS,

"TASTE AND SEE THAT THE LORD IS GOOD
BLESSED IS THE MAN THAT TRUSTETH
IN HIM."
Fear Him, ye saints, and you will then
Have nothing else to fear.
Make you His service your delight,
Your wants shall be His care.

Before schools were erected at Catshill and the Lickey the children from these districts attended the Bromsgrove schools. As the morning school began at half-past eight in the summer, and half-past one in the afternoon, the children brought their dinners with them in bags slung over their shoulders. Then, as now, all boys were not honest, and occasionally a dinner was stolen and consumed by another; but as experience begets wisdom, those who had been once robbed followed the example shewn by the bride with the water of the well of St. Keyne. "They took their dinners to church," and during a long service it was not uncommon to see them having a bite at an apple dumpling or piece of cake. Boys were rewarded by cards, having a text of scripture on the one side, each card representing one penny in value; but it was found that at the end of the year the boy who had the most money standing to his credit in the books, had, perhaps, no cards, and *vice versa*; and, upon enquiry, it was ascertained that the boys amused themselves in church by tossing up for their cards, accordingly they were discontinued. During the time the school was held at the old Town Hall it was visited, about 1820, by the then Bishop of Worcester, who singled out 10 of the most promising boys and heard them read. One, if not more, of the bishop's old pupils, is still living.

At a school committee meeting, held at the Town Hall, on October 20th, (?) 1832, "a communication was made from the Earl of Plymouth, of his lordship's munificent intention of giving the children of the Sunday School a dinner of roast beef and plum pudding, on the occasion of the arrival at Hewell of their Royal Highnesses the Duchess of Kent and the Princess Victoria, and of his wish that the children should be so disposed in some suitable place as that the Princess may have a distinct view of them in passing." The old worsted factory was utilized to dine the children, and a committee appointed to carry out the details. The children were ranged on the right side of the Worcester Road, beginning at Dyer's Bridge.

Much of the time spent in school was devoted to teaching the children their letters, and to write. Mr. Brettell had a class of the most orderly of the elder boys, who were taught by him writing, &c., on Sunday and other evenings. Of course, education was not so general as now, and Sunday was to a great extent devoted to the teaching of those subjects which a child now learns at the National or Board School.

It was the custom in the school to provide entertainments on fair days for the girls attending the school. In the minute book of the school is this resolution, on July 23rd, 1832, "That it is expedient that the entertainment given to the girls at the schools, for the purpose of keeping them out of the fair on the fair days, be continued, and that the treasurer do pay £3 out of the funds of the school annually for that purpose." The entertainments consisted of a good tea, with games afterwards, at Break-back Hill, or other suitable place. Children who went to the fair, after attending the "treat," forfeited the tickets standing to their credit in the superintendent's book.

The centenary of Sunday Schools was celebrated in Bromsgrove by a tea meeting, held under the auspices of the congregation of the parish church, at the Corn Exchange and in the Assembly Room adjoining, on Wednesday evening, June 30th, 1880. Upwards of 300 sat down. The Vicar (the Rev. Canon Murray, M.A.) presided at a well attended public meeting which followed. The Rev. C. A. Dickins delivered a lengthy and interesting address on the subject of the Sunday Schools generally, being followed by Mr. W. A. Cotton, with a paper on the origin of the movement in Bromsgrove. Mr. Ledbury also gave a very interesting address, during which he exhibited, amidst no small curiosity, the identical "logger," or block of wood, which in the "good old days" was used as mentioned. The proceedings were interspersed with some capital singing by the choir, and altogether a very agreeable evening was spent.

White metal Sunday School Centenary Commemoration Medals were afterwards given to all the teachers.

The rules for the Sunday School scholars are as follows :—

1. The school will commence punctually at half-past nine in the morning, and at half-past two in the afternoon.

2. That no scholar be admitted to the school under the age of six years, except to the infant school, when they may be admitted at the age of four years.

3. All scholars will be admitted to the class-room after confirmation, and not before.

4. That any scholar staying away from school *one* Sunday without giving a satisfactory explanation to the teacher, forfeit a day's marks ; and any scholar staying away from school for four Sundays in succession, without giving a satisfactory explanation to the superintendent, forfeit all marks.

5. Marks will be given morning and afternoon, according to behaviour, attendance, and diligence in learning the lessons during the week.

6. Marks will be forfeited, at the discretion of the superintendent, for ill behaviour either in church or school.

7. No scholar will be admitted to the annual treat, whose conduct has been unsatisfactory, or who has been irregular in attendance during the year.

8. The prizes will be given at a public meeting, soon after Christmas. *Three* will be given to each class, and they will consist of Bibles, Prayer Books, and Hymn Books, unless the successful candidates can prove to the superintendent that they already possess those books.

No scholar's name will be placed on the books before being baptized.

And for the teachers—

1. That no person be admitted to the school as teacher without the sanction of the vicar.

2. That teachers be careful to set a good example of punctuality to the scholars by being *in their places in school* five minutes before the time appointed for commencement (9.30 a.m. and 2.30 p.m.)

3. All teachers unable to attend school, are expected to give timely notice to their superintendent.

4. In case of the absence of any scholars, the teachers of the classes to which they belong are requested to enquire, in the course of the week, the reason for such absence ; or, if unable to do this, to give the name and address of the absentee to the superintendent, which will be forwarded on Monday morning to the clergyman of the school.

5. That all teachers attend the preparation class on Friday evenings, at eight o'clock, when the lesson for the following Sunday afternoon will be given by one of the clergy.

6. That there be catechising in church on the third Sunday in the month, and on the fifth Sunday, when there happens to be five Sundays in the month. That teachers always attend church on these occasions, and that on other Sundays they arrange to be present *alternately*.

7. That all teachers walk with their respective classes to church.

8. That supernumeraries be appointed to act in the place of absent teachers.

9. That each class shall consist of not more than twelve, and not less than eight scholars.

All teachers are expected to be regular communicants.

The present superintendents are—

Boys' school : Mr. George Nicholls and Mr. W. H. Lewis.
Girls' school : Miss Dunn and Miss E. Scott.

The following is a copy of the trust deed : —

WE, THE VERY REVEREND THE DEAN AND CHAPTER of the Cathedral Church of Christ and the Blessed Mary, the Virgin, of Worcester, Appropriators of (amongst other hereditaments) the Rectory or Parsonage and Glebe Lands of the Parish of Bromsgrove, in the County of Worcester ; and We, the Right Honorable William Pitt Earl Amherst and John Drummond, Esquire (Devisees in trust of a Lease granted by the said Dean and Chapter to us of the said Rectory or Parsonage and Glebe Lands, bearing date on or about the twenty-third day of June, one thousand eight hundred and thirty-seven, named in the last will and testament of The Right Honorable Other Archer, late Earl of Plymouth, deceased, for the benefit of The Honorable Robert Henry Clive, of Hewell Grange, in the Counties of Worcester and Warwick, and Lady Harriet Clive, his wife) ; and We, the said Robert Henry Clive and Lady Harriet Clive, under the authority of an Act passed in the fifth year of the Reign of Her Majesty Queen Victoria, intitled "An Act for affording further facilities for the Conveyance and Endowment of Sites for Schools," and of another Act made and passed in the eighth year of the Reign of Her said Majesty, intitled "An Act to secure the terms on which Grants are made by Her Majesty out of the Parliamentary Grant for the Education of the Poor, and to explain the Act of the fifth year of the Reign of Her present Majesty for the Conveyance of Sites for Schools," Do hereby freely and voluntarily, and without any valuable consideration, grant and convey to the Vicar of the Parish of Bromsgrove for the time being and the Churchwardens of the same Parish for the time being, All that piece or parcel of Land as the same is now staked and marked out, and shewn with the abuttals and boundaries thereof in the Plan drawn on the margin of these Presents, containing two roods and nineteen perches or thereabouts, adjoining to Bromsgrove Church Yard, in the Parish of Bromsgrove, part of which said Land,

containing one rood and nineteen perches, was given by the said Late Earl of
Plymouth in his lifetime, for the purpose of erecting a School thereon, and the said
Dean and Chapter consented to such Gift, and upon part of which said Land a
school has several years since been erected, but no Grant or Conveyance thereof has
ever been executed, and all our and each of our right, title, and interest to and
in the same Land and premises and every part thereof, To hold the same unto and
to the use of the said Vicar of Bromsgrove and his successors, and the Churchwardens of the said Parish and their successors for the time being, for the purposes
of the said Acts; AND UPON TRUST to permit the said premises and all Buildings
thereon erected, or to be erected, to be for ever hereafter appropriated and used as
and for a School for the education of Children and Adults, or Children only of the
laboring, manufacturing, and other poorer classes of and in the Parish of Bromsgrove
aforesaid, and for the erection of a Dwellinghouse for the Teacher or Teachers
of the said School, and for no other purpose, and which said School shall always be
in unison with and conducted upon the principles and in furtherance of the ends
and designs of the incorporated National Society for promoting the education of the
Poor in the principles of the Established Church; and subject to and in conformity
with the declaration aforesaid, the said School and premises shall be directed,
controlled, governed, and managed in manner hereafter specified, that is to say: the
Minister for the time being of the said Parish of Bromsgrove shall have the sole
care, order, and direction of the moral and religious Instruction of the Scholars
attending the said School, but in all other respects the general management, direction,
and government of the said School and Premises shall be vested in and exercised by
a Committee, consisting of the Minister of the said Parish for the time being,
his Curate or Curates (if the Minister shall appoint him or them upon the said
Committee), and also of the Minister of Catshill Chapel, the Churchwardens of the
said Parish of Bromsgrove for the time being (if Members of the Church of
England), and of Fourteen other Persons, Members of the Church of England,
Residents, or having a beneficial interest to the extent of a life estate at the least,
in real property situated in the said Parish, and Subscribers in the current year
to the amount of ten shillings at the least to the said School: the said last mentioned
fourteen persons to be elected annually in the month of December or January
by Subscribers to the said School to the amount of ten shillings per annum at
least, and qualified in other respects as the Persons to be elected: So, however, that
no default of election or vacancy during any current year shall prevent the other
Members of the Committee from acting until the next annual election, or until
the vacancies shall be otherwise supplied. AND WE DO DECLARE that no person
shall be appointed, or shall act as a Master or Mistress of the said School, who shall
not be a Member of the Church of England. The Vicar for the time being shall be

Chairman (if present), and when not present, any other Member of the Committee selected by the members present shall preside, and in case of an equality of votes the Chairman for the time being shall have a second and casting vote. AND WE DO FURTHER DECLARE that the said School shall be at all times open to the inspection of the Inspector or Inspectors for the time being appointed or to be appointed in conformity with the Order in Council bearing date the tenth day of August, one thousand eight hundred and forty. AND we do hereby for ourselves, our heirs, executors, and administrators, covenant with the said Vicar and Churchwardens and their successors, that notwithstanding any act or default of ours, or any of our Ancestors, We have good right to assure the said premises to the said Vicar and Churchwardens and their Successors in manner aforesaid. And that the said premises shall at all times hereafter be held and enjoyed upon the trusts and in manner aforesaid without interruption from and free from all encumbrances by us or our heirs, or any person lawfully claiming under or in trust for us or them or any of our Ancestors. And that We and our heirs, and all persons claiming under or in trust for us or them or any of our Ancestors, shall upon every request, and at the expense of the said Vicar and Churchwardens and their Successors, make and perfect all such further assurances of the said premises as may be required by them for conveying the same to the use of the said Vicar and Churchwardens and their Successors in manner aforesaid. IN WITNESS whereof the said Dean and Chapter have hereunto caused their corporate Seal to be affixed, and the said other conveying parties have hereunto set their hands and seals this twelfth day of April, one thousand eight hundred and forty-seven.

> AMHERST. (L.S.)   JOHN (L.S.) DRUMMOND.
> (L.S.)   R. H. CLIVE.   HARRIET (L.S.) CLIVE.

> Signed, Sealed, and Delivered by the within-named Earl Amherst, in the presence of *James Swift*, Groom of the Chamber to Earl Amherst.
> Signed, Sealed, and Delivered by the within-named John Drummond, in the presence of William Weight, Thomas Tovey, Clerks to Messrs. Oddie and Co., Solicitors, 18, Carey Street, London.
> Signed, Sealed, and Delivered by the within-named Robert Henry Clive and Lady Harriet Clive, in the presence of James Tomson, of Alvechurch, Worcestershire.

The deed is endorsed on the back as follows :—

WHEREAS, since the execution of the within Deed, the Committee of Council on Education has, upon the application of the Managers of the within School, agreed to authorize the payment of a sum of money out of the fund voted by Parliament for Public Education in Great Britain, to be expended in and about the enlargement of the said School, upon the condition of receiving such a declaration as hereinafter set forth ; Now THEREFORE it is declared and agreed by the persons undersigned, being a Majority of the Committee of Managers of the said School for the time being, that notwithstanding anything contained in the within Deed, so soon as any such money shall have been paid to the said Managers for the purpose aforesaid, all the provisions of the Elementary Education Act, 1870, which constitute a Public Elementary School, shall apply to the School constituted under this Deed and be in force therein, and shall continue to be so applied thereto until the Committee of Management of the said School pass a Resolution at a meeting composed of a majority of the Managers for the time being to repay the grant so made as aforesaid, and until the said Committee shall accordingly repay that amount to the Lords Commissioners of the Treasury for the time being, and that thenceforth the aforesaid declaration whereby this School shall be constituted a Public Elementary School within the meaning of the Elementary Education Act, 1870, shall forthwith cease to be of any effect so far as regards the Committee of Council on Education or the Education Department.

As Witness our hands and seals, this   .   .   .   day of   .   one thousand eight hundred and seventy-two.

GEORGE W. MURRAY, (L.S.) Vicar.

WM. HOLYOAKE,	(L.S.)	
ALFRED BENNETT,	(L.S.)	
JNO. R. HORTON,	(L.S.)	Churchwardens.
SAMUEL SAYWELL,	(L.S.)	
WALTER BROOKE,	(L.S.)	
ROBERT CORDELL,	(L.S.)	
JOSEPH AMPHLETT,	(L.S.)	
RICHARD DUNN,	(L.S.)	
G. W. GIBSON.	(L.S.)	

Signed, Sealed, and Delivered by the said George W. Murray, William Holyoake, Alfred Bennett, John Robeson Horton, Samuel Saywell, Walter Brooke, Robert Cordell, Joseph Amphlett, Richard Dunn, and George William Gibson, in the presence of

HENRY WRIGHT,

Clerk to Messrs. Scott and Horton.

Solicitors,

Bromsgrove.

The Cemetery.

Y an Order in Council, dated June 25th, 1856, burials were ordered to be discontinued from and after January 1st, 1857, in the parish church and churchyard of Bromsgrove, and in the Baptists', Wesleyans', and Independent burial grounds, with certain exceptions. On November 24th, 1855, the following notice was issued :—"We hereby convene a meeting of the Vestry of this Parish, to be held at the Town Hall, within the said Parish, at eleven o'clock in the morning of Monday, the third day of December next, for the purpose of determining whether a Burial Ground shall be provided for the said Parish, under the provisions of the Acts 15 and 16 Vict. c. 85, 16 and 17 Vict. c. 134, and 18 and 19 Vict. c. 128. And if it be resolved by the Vestry that such Burial Ground shall be provided, to appoint not less than three, or more than nine persons, being rate-payers of the Parish, to be the Burial Board of such Parish."

T. D. THOMAS,
ALFRED PALMER, } Churchwardens.
HUGH PHILLIPS,

BENJ. JOHNSON, } Overseers.
WALTER BROOKE,

The meeting was accordingly held, the Rev. Mr. Villers in the chair. It was proposed by Mr. George Dipple, and seconded by Mr. A. Huxley, "That a New Burial Ground be provided by this parish, under the provisions of the Acts relating thereto, as referred to in the foregoing notice." It was further resolved that "nine ratepayers be appointed the Burial Board for this parish."

The first meeting of the Board was held in the Town Hall, on December 21st, 1855.

At a meeting held January 11th, 1856, directions were given to the clerk to apply for terms and price of part of the present cemetery, which had an area of 6a. or. 37p, and on May 21st, it was agreed to purchase the land, at a cost of £904 8s., including £587 1s. 6d. received by the Dean and Chapter of Worcester, and £274 2s. 6d. paid to the Baroness Windsor for her interest, the land being glebe land, and leased by the Ecclesiastical Commissioners to her ladyship.

The entrance lodge, lich gates, &c., cost £985 13s. 5d. ; laying out the ground, and planting shrubs, &c., £378 10s. ; architect's commission and law charges, £235 14s. 7d., or a total of £2504 6s., to pay which sum a loan of £2500 was obtained.

In "*The Civil Engineer and Architects' Journal*," for 1858, we find the following account of the " New Cemetery, Bromsgrove, Worcestershire " :—

For the last few years, the attention of architects has been much devoted to the arrangement of cemeteries. This has been principally caused by the prohibition of intramural interment ; and in consequence, a gradual improvement has taken place in the laying out of cemeteries. But, notwithstanding, there are many which present such injudicious features, that there is ample room for improvement in the designs, both with regard to the economising of the ground, and the rendering them more appropriate for their purpose.

We think a great error has been committed in the almost universal endeavour to give to a cemetery the appearance of a highly ornamental garden ; it should have an unmistakeable resemblance to the end for which it is contrived. By our assertion we do not mean to infer that it should be like a field, having a path skirting along its sides, but that it ought to have a utilitarian character given to it that should at once betoken the sacredness attached to its purpose. Therefore the paths should not, as a principle, be of a curvilinear or circular figure, but formed in such squares or parallelograms as would sufficiently subdivide and diversify the appearance of the ground. This judicious arrangement would allow nearly the entirely allotted space to be serviceably employed ; and not, as is frequently the case now, where such repeated serpentine meanderings are employed, cause one-third of a limited space of ground to be rendered unserviceable by the improper figures into which it has been inconsiderately divided.

It is thought by many, that the more curvature the walks possess, the greater is the effect and variety given to ornamental grounds, and in some cases it may be so ; but when the ground is sufficiently undulating, an equal picturesqueness may be obtained, and a result far superior, when the paths are straight : for it should be remembered that the undulation alone will give a curved appearance to the paths, and anything like monotony may be destroyed by skilful and judicious planting.

We have been led to make these remarks, from observing that the ground of the New Cemetery, at Bromsgrove, presents a successful adaptation of the style we have pointed out. The plan of the plot of ground, containing about six acres, has been so designed, with its roads and paths running at right angles : the only exception to the rule being a partly circular road from the lich gate to the centre compartment at a junction of the road from the entrance lodge. The fine old church at Bromsgrove, now under restoration by Mr. G. G. Scott, is situated on the top of a hill, overlooking an extensive tract of country, at the foot of which lays the cemetery. A view of the entire ground may be commanded from the fine avenue of lime trees that surround the church.

The lich gate and entrance lodge (represented in Plate X.) of this place of burial are extremely striking features ; and as they present variety, both in design, treatment, and construction, to the lodge and chapels belonging to another cemetery figured in our present journal, we have thought them worthy of being laid at the same time before those of our readers who may be occupied in cemetery arrangement.

The lodge, through the gate of which an entrance is obtained from the churchyard to the cemetery, is built with red brick, having Bath stone dressings ; the roof is covered with blue and red tiles in bands. It contains a waiting or Board-room, with an open roof, wrought and stained, living room, kitchen, scullery, pantry, &c., and three bed-rooms, with a lean-to or porch attached to the tower entrance.

The lich gate, which is seen from one part of the High Street, is built in a cutting, the level of the cemetery being about nine feet above the road at that corner, the banks of which are sloped down on each side. The entrance gate is of English oak throughout, and it is covered with similar tiles to the lodge, having an ornamental cresting at the top.

The Burial Board of the parish is deserving of much commendation for causing so efficient a work as the cemetery to be provided, which is in every respect appropriately and substantially carried out, and will long remain an ornament to the town. No less praise ought to be given to the architect, Mr. C. H. Cooke, of John Street, Bedford Row.

The entrance lodge and lich gate have been built by Mr. Walker, of Evesham. Messrs. Cole and Sharpe were the contractors for the ground work.

On May 1st, 1872, it was decided to enlarge the cemetery, by the purchase of 4a. 2r. 36p. of land in the rear, at a cost of £952 9s. 10d. To this sum £306 must be added for laying out the ground, shrubs, &c.; £53 9s. 3d. for fencing, £111 6s. 2d. for solicitor's charges, £11 1s. 6d. for surveyor's charges, and £58 6s. 6d. for incidental expenses; total, £1492 13s. 3d. To meet these payments, loans to the extent of £1500 were borrowed. The first loan is entirely paid off, and at the time this work was published £200 was also paid towards the second sum, leaving £1300 still owing by the ratepayers on account of the cemetery.

ENTRANCE LODGE OF BROMSGROVE CEMETERY

The present Board consists of nine members, three retiring yearly by rotation, but being eligible for re-election. A meeting is held about the 25th of March annually to fill up vacancies.

In 1858 there were buried			182	persons.
1859	,,	,,	249	,,
1860	,,	,,	155	
1861	,,	,,	193	,,
1862	,,	,,	183	,,
1863	,,	,,	174	,,
1864	,,	,,	171	,,
1865	,,	,,	189	,,
1866	,,	,,	167	,,
1867	,,	,,	195	,,
1868	,,	,,	165	,,
1869	,,	,,	190	
1870	,,	,,	216	,,
1871	,,	,,	183	,,
1872	,,	,,	142	,,
1873	,,	,,	196	
1874	,,	,,	214	
1875	,,	,,	219	
1876	,,	,,	170	
1877	,,	,,	161	
1878	,,	,,	252	,,
1879	,,	,,	216	,,
1880	,,	,,	131	
		Total	 4313	

From a return sent to the Home Office, March 8th, 1876, the total number buried in the cemetery since its opening, to 31st December, 1875 (18 years), was as under :—

In consecrated ground...............	2529	140·9
In unconsecrated ground...........	854	17·8
Total	3383	187·17

Population of the Burial Board district, 11,791.

Amongst the entries in the registers occur the following notable instances of
longevity, &c. :—

Aug. 26th, 1858.—Hannah Phillips......... aged 91, Widow, Lickey End.

Dec. 9th, 1862.— William Sanders......... „ 90, Needle maker, New Buildings.

Oct. 31st, 1864.- Elizabeth Clewell ...... „ 90, Widow, Cemetery Lodge.

June 25th, 1865.—Hannah Phillips......... „ 93, Dodford.

Sep. 19th, 1865.—Mary Barber .... „ 93, Widow, Alms Houses.

Jan. 31st, 1867.—Elizabeth Wright ...... „ 93, Widow, Station Street.

Nov. 21st, 1869.—Alice Johnson............ „ 90, Widow, Strand.

  „ 29th, 1869.—Elizabeth Morgan ...... „ 90, Widow, Woodcote.

Mar. 27th, 1870.—Christiana Cotrill ...... „ 93, Bewell Head.

Jan. 18th, 1871. Charles Brooke .... 90, Brazier, High Street.

  „ 19th, 1872.- Joseph Lacy .... „ 99, Butcher, Union House.

  „ 1st, 1875.—Thomas Munn .... „ 94, Nailer, High Street.

  „ 6th, 1875.—Elizabeth Chesterton ... „ 92, Sidemoor.

May 10th, 1875.- James Mason .... „ 101, Union House.

  „ 22nd, 1875.—Ann Rea................. „ 100, Alms Houses.

April 25th, 1877.—George Clements ...... „ 91, Gardener, Station Street.

Dec. 4th, 1867.—Lousia King, found dead in a field at Park Gate, November
24th, 1867.

July 1st, 1872.—A man, unknown, found dead (hung) at the Lickey.

Mar. 23rd, 1878.—A man, unknown, who died suddenly in the Strand. (See order
book).

In the order book is this note : " May 31st, 1878. This body was exhumed (for
the purpose of identification), in the presence of Superintendent Tyler, W. S. Batten,
M.D., Mrs. Merry (the supposed widow). &c. : but the result was not satisfactory,
the body not being clearly identified."

On January 6th, 1858, the cemetery was consecrated, and on the day following
the first interment took place Constance Voila Sanders, aged 1 year, daughter of
F. H. Sanders, The Mount, Bromsgrove : Rev. W. Villers clergyman, and Joseph
Rose sexton—and on the 10th, Sarah Hedges, aged 2 years ; and on the 14th, John
Adams, of Perry Hall, one of the oldest and most influential inhabitants of the
parish. Mr. Adams died on the 7th of January, at the advanced age of 91. To
his memory the Cemetery Cross was erected, by the Rev. Thomas Housman,
Incumbent of Catshill, one of his executors, and Dr. Collis, who contributed one-
third of the expense. The design was furnished by Mr. W. Prosser, the clerk of the
works during the church restoration.

At the base of the column are the four symbols mentioned in Ezekiel i. 10, and
Rev. iv. 7, the name and death-date of Mr. Adams, the date of the consecration of

the cemetery, and the text, 1 Cor. xv. 55, "O death, where is thy sting? O grave, where is thy victory?" on alternate faces.

The inscriptions and emblems on the pediments are as follows:—On the south side, a small Latin cross, with the motto of the Emperor Constantine beneath it, "In hoc signo vinces."—In this sign shalt thou conquer.

On the east side, the Alpha and Omega, interlaced: beneath, "Ego Resurrectio et Vita."—I am the Resurrection and the Life.

On the north side, the I.H.S., or the first three letters of the Greek word for Jesus; beneath, "Beati Mortui in Domino."—Blessed are the dead who die in the Lord.

On the west side, XP, the two first letters of the Greek name of Christ: beneath, "Ego Via, Veritas, Vita."—I am the Way, the Truth, the Life."

The following are the rules and regulations of the cemetery:—

1.—The registrar's or coroner's certificate must be given up before interment. In cases of children still-born, a certificate from a surgeon, midwife, or some other responsible person will be required.

2.—The excavation, removal of surplus soil, masonry and smith's work, for bricked graves and vaults, to be borne by the parties requiring the same, and all cramps used for putting together stone-work above ground, to be of copper.

3.—The mound over any grave not to be left more than six inches high immediately after interment.

4.—The Board reserve the right of allotting the spaces on each side of the pathway leading from the lodge to the circular mound, the same being intended for vaults and bricked graves only.

5.—Coffins of wood only shall be used in unpurchased graves, no plank or any other description of covering except earth permitted, and only one body shall be buried in each of such graves at one time, unless the bodies be those of members of the same family, and every such grave for the first interment shall not be less than seven feet deep for a child under 12 years.

6.—No body shall be buried in any vault or walled grave unless the coffin be separately entombed in an air-tight manner; that is by properly cemented stone or brick-work, which shall never be disturbed.

7.—No unwalled grave shall be re-opened within fourteen years after the burial of a person above 12 years of age, unless to bury another member of the same family, in which case a layer of earth not less than one foot thick shall be left undisturbed above the previously buried coffin. No coffin shall be buried in any unwalled grave within four feet of the ordinary level of the ground, unless it contains the body of a child under 12 years of age, when it shall not be less than three feet below that level.

8.—Before the erection of any gravestone, monument, or memorial, a drawing thereof and a copy of the proposed inscription must be submitted to the Board for their approval. After erection they must be kept in order by the owner. The number of the grave space must be legibly fixed on every memorial.

9.—No brick or stone-work nor any memorial or monument, other than a head-stone, will be allowed in or over any grave the exclusive right of burial in which has not been purchased, and any head-stone erected over any such grave may be removed by direction of the Board after it has been up 14 years.

10.—The cemetery, by permission of the Board, is open to the public from 7.0 a.m. until 9.0 p.m. from Lady-day to Michaelmas-day ; and from 8.0 a.m. until 5.0 p.m. from Michaelmas-day to Lady-day. Children under 12 years of age will not be admitted, unless under the care of some responsible person ; and all persons are required to keep on the walks, unless visiting a friend's grave, and to refrain from touching the shrubs and flowers.

11.—Small shrubs, plants, or flowers may, subject to the approval of the Board, be placed over any grave, but must not be cut or carried away without the consent of the Board, and the Board reserves the right to prune, cut down, or dig up and remove any of the shrubs, plants, or flowers at any time when in their opinion the same have become unsightly or overgrown, or when necessary for the purpose of allowing the grave to be again used.

12.—No carriages drawn by horses, and no dogs or other animals will be allowed to enter the cemetery, and no person will be permitted to smoke therein.

13.—Every person who shall wilfully destroy or damage any of the fences, shrubs, or trees, or injure any gravestone, monument, or memorial, or unlawfully disturb any persons assembled there for the purpose of burying any body therein, or be guilty of any disorderly conduct, will be proceeded against.

Mr. H. Barrett is clerk to the Board, at a salary of £15 per annum.

BROMSGROVE CEMETERY.—REVISED TABLE OF FEES.

	For the Board	Vicar in Consecrated Ground	Officiating Minister in unconsecrated Ground	Clerk in Consecrated Ground	Sexton in Consecrated Ground
On every Interment in the order allotted by the Board in Sections A, B, C, &c. D, E, H, &c. I, K, L, M, Q, S, and T (except in the borders), on plan — Adults	4 4 0	1 6	1 6	1 0	1 6
— Children under Twelve	3 0 0	1 0	1 0	1 0	1 0
On every Interment in Ground selected by the friends of the deceased — Adults	2 0 0	6 0	6 0	0 0	6 0
— Children under Twelve	8 0 0	2 0	2 0	1 0	1 0
On Interment of a Still-born Child	4 0 0				
Grant of Grave space, Nine Feet by Four Feet, for unbricked Graves, in perpetuity	1 10 0	10 0			
Grant of Grave space, Nine Feet by Four Feet, for bricked Graves, in perpetuity	2 0 0	10 0			
VAULTS — Nine Feet by Eight Feet	4 0 0	3 0 0			
Nine Feet by Twelve Feet	6 0 0				
Re-opening a Vault	15 0	10 0			

FOR PERMISSION TO ERECT, &C.

	For the Board	Vicar in Consecrated Ground	Officiating Minister in unconsecrated Ground	Clerk in Consecrated Ground	Sexton in Consecrated Ground
A Head or Foot Stone, not exceeding One Foot at base and Five Feet high, with one Inscription	1 0 0	13 0			
A Head and Foot Stone, erected at the same time, not exceeding One Foot at base and Five Feet high, with one Inscription					
A Head or Foot Stone, exceeding One and not exceeding Two Feet at base, with one Inscription	1 10 0	1 0 0			
Every additional Inscription on the above, or any Inscription on the border found any Grave space where there is a Head or Foot Stone	5 0	10 0			
A raised Body or Flat Stone, not exceeding Twelve Inches high, with one Inscription	2 0 0	3 0 0			
Every additional Inscription	7 0 0				
A Monument with the Railing fixed at the time of erection, with one Inscription	4 0 0	10 0			
Every additional Inscription	10 0 0				
Railing subsequently fixed	10 0 0				
Palisading or Railing to any Grave space or Vault in perpetuity					
A Grave Marker, not exceeding Twelve Inches high, or of Wood, not exceeding Thirty Inches high, with one Inscription	6 0				
Every additional Inscription	1 0				

Note.—Double the above Fees will be charged in all cases for Persons brought from other Parishes for Interment.

	For the Board
For Entry in Register of grant of vault or grave space	2 6
For a Certificate of such grant, including stamp	5 6
For Searching the Register of Burials, for one year	6 6
For Searching the Register of Burials, for each additional year	0 6
For each certified Copy of Entry	1 0
For Excavating Graves, Seven Feet deep from surface, and making good, for Adults	
For Excavating Graves, Six Feet deep from Surface, and making good, for Children under Twelve	
For Excavating Graves, Three Feet deep from surface, for Still-born Children	
For Excavating Graves, every extra foot in depth, above Seven Feet	
For Bricked Graves and Vaults, per cubic yard	

This Revised Table of Fees has been sanctioned by the Right Honourable H. A. Bruce, one of Her Majesty's principal Secretaries of State, and approved of by the Lord Bishop of the Diocese, and by the Parishioners in Vestry assembled.

BROMSGROVE:
PRINTED AT THE "MESSENGER" OFFICE,
HIGH STREET.